Journey

of Love and Betrayal

"Love and Betrayal" Series

Book 1

Gillian Du Caurroy

Acknowledgments

Special thanks go to Mark, Cameron and Jeremy
for supporting me and helping me to materialize this dream.
Also, huge thanks to Mum and Dad, for their continued support
in many, many ways.

To my friends and mentors over the years who have helped me,
whether they know it or not, your support has meant so much:
Dayna, Nantah, Keith, Patrick, Anja, Ed.

To everyone who has supported me, and listened to me
talking about 'one day publishing a book',
I thank you for your patience.

I cannot leave out my furry family:
my precious Piccolo, for his love and cuddles always,
especially when I was writing, right to the very end.
Misty – well, for being Misty,
and to my beautiful Cleo, who always ends up very close to me,
enjoying my kisses and pats in between writing.

I can't go without acknowledging the expertise of
my editor, Angelica Bentley. Her professionalism and
dedication to help me with this process, and to go above and beyond
the realms of 'just editing', are truly appreciated.

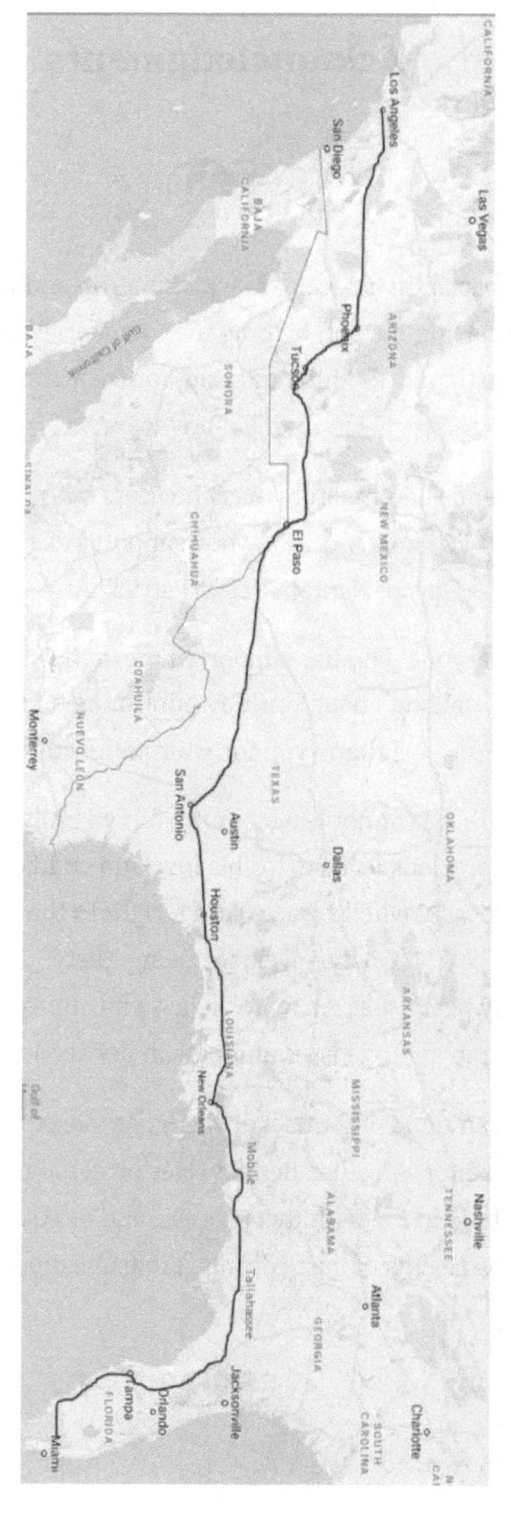

Table of Contents

Chapter 1

Caught in the Act

"Good evening, Sir, Madam," the maître d' welcomed them to the intimate French restaurant.

It had been a long day, in fact, a long week. Friday nights were always busier, but Phillipe would go out of his way to locate a private table for his favorite regulars.

"How are you, Phillipe?" inquired Hamish, gently placing his hand on Monique's bare back.

"Very well, thank you," said Phillipe as he promptly guided the couple to a private table for two.

Monique followed closely as Phillipe led the way, walking through the clear path between other tables. Her smooth saunter, along with the air of a certain *je ne sais quoi,* attracted attention to her.

"I love how he gives us special attention," gushed Monique, tilting her head in a seductive way, yet maintaining a sense of sophistication.

Other patrons in the restaurant continued to look at the striking couple as they sashayed confidently to their private table.

The restaurant was a short stroll from the hotel they were staying at. It didn't take long for the staff to get to know them. In fact, since they started seeing each other, they had visited the restaurant on many occasions, hence the special attention. It was discreet, intimate, and a haven for them to relax without worrying about who was around the corner.

"A bottle of the Silver Oak Cabernet Sauvignon 2001, please," said Hamish, knowing the wine list by heart.

Hamish enjoyed treating Monique to fine dining. In fact he enjoyed sharing most things with her, so indulging in one of the ritziest restaurants in town became a pleasure.

Since their relationship had begun, they had been very careful to choose restaurants and bars that were out of the immediate vicinity of their office and homes. Meeting at particular places at odd times became increasingly difficult, so after two months of sneaking around late at night, they decided to hire a hotel room on a regular basis. Being an attorney-at-law, Hamish had certain privileges that included accommodation in a city hotel or apartment. This was meant for when there was a long court case that required early starts and late finishes.

"Guess what I'm having tonight," said Monique as she seductively stroked her shoulder-length auburn hair which had been straightened to look like liquid silk.

"Hmmm, let me think. Snails?" joked Hamish, knowing quite well that Monique detested them. Hamish's boyish good looks were very attractive to Monique, who flirted continuously. His relaxed state of mind showed in his eyes, which crinkled in the corners giving him an edge of maturity.

"No! You always say that. I'm going to have oysters," she said with a sexy smirk, batting her false eyelashes at him.

"Oh, I see. Well, maybe I'd better have some too. I wouldn't want only one of us feeling amorous tonight, would I?"

They played to each other's heart strings. The age difference didn't seem to alter their tastes at all. Monique, at twenty-five was a junior in the law firm. Hamish, thirty-seven, was a partner. Their paths met when working together on a high-profile case. The many late nights spent at the office led to many shared takeout meals, and one thing led to another.

"No, definitely not. I've got some work to do on you tonight," she teased, as she freed her foot from the stiletto and slowly caressed Hamish's inner leg.

Their fingers found each other between the wine glasses and decorative candle that sat in the middle of the cozy table. The dimly lit restaurant was perfect for flirting. Work was the last thing on their minds now as they drank each other up.

Just as their entrée arrived, they saw quite a few people were gathering outside the restaurant. Torn between his desire to start eating and his curiosity about what was happening, Hamish stood up to see what all the commotion was about. At first he couldn't see much, since dusk was falling and the lighting was quite muted. Then, in an instant, the blood drained from his face as he saw that it was his wife, Virginia, on the ground with several people trying to help her. It appeared she had fainted. "What the hell!"

"What is it?" asked Monique, her oyster fork poised and ready to start on her entrée.

"It's Virginia. She's outside." His face told the story as Monique put her fork down, pushed her chair back and strained her neck to peer over the other people who had gathered at the window.

"Gosh! She must have been spying on us. Looks like she's fainted or something because she's on the ground," stated Monique.

"What should I do?" Hamish panicked.

"Well, you can't go out there. Just wait and see if she's all right."

A few moments later, the fallen woman was helped to her feet by a few bystanders, and the commotion soon died down in the restaurant as she was helped to her car.

"Luckily she didn't turn around!" Hamish cursed, settling back at the table.

The mood throughout dinner was tense as Hamish repeatedly thought to himself that he had been caught in the act, and his recent rendezvous with Monique would come to a grinding halt.

"Look, you saw her getting into her car, so she must be okay. Stop overthinking things. As far as she knows, *if* she saw us, we were just having a bite to eat after work. Anyway, you'll be seeing her tomorrow, won't you?" stated Monique, her tone derogatory.

The next morning...

At eight o'clock, the sounds of Marvin Gaye crooning "Got To Give It Up" on Hamish's iPod woke them. The curtains of the luxury suite in the Four Seasons Hotel, situated in the heart of Miami, were left open last night, and now the sun shone brightly across Biscayne Bay and into their room.

Hamish turned over with a groan, glanced at Monique still asleep, then stretched over to turn the music down. The events of the previous evening were put aside for now.

"Hey, you," he purred, cuddling in behind her, kissing her hair, and she stirred herself into the warmth of his chest. He traced his nose along her jaw and kissed her neck, then trailed his mouth over her ear and up to her forehead. Her eyes were still closed, but her body warmed to his touch.

It wasn't every Saturday morning that they woke up together, so when it did happen it was a delight. They savored every minute in the luxurious surroundings.

Hamish had to be at the office at midday to meet a high-profile client before the court case on Monday, but he did have to go home first. This meant they had roughly an hour before he had to leave. Not wasting any time, he slowly pulled the sheets off Monique and wrapped himself around her until she gave in to his unbridled passion...

As far as Hamish was concerned, life at home was dull with Virginia. It had become a chore to go home to her with the constant talking about the IVF treatment and her constant chatter of what color to paint the nursery. His heart just wasn't in it anymore, and Virginia had changed. The dream of having a baby took over their lives. In fact, his every wish to begin with was for them to have a baby, but much to his dismay, it turned Virginia into an oversensitive, obsessive person. All she could think of was falling pregnant, and each time she found out that she wasn't pregnant, he would have to bear the brunt of all the tears and emotions. Being her rock was hard on him as he too was upset, but he knew that to have any chance, they would both have to relax for the magic to happen. He became more and more distant as a mechanism for coping.

That's when Monique started working at the law firm. She provided some light relief among the chaos at work and the disarray at home. With her quick wit, her generous attitude, and her oh so sexy, flirtatious behavior, Hamish was a much more tolerant and loving person at home, which Virginia sensed and loved. In fact, Virginia fell pregnant soon after and was over the moon, which alleviated Hamish's anxiety somewhat about going home each night, yet now he had 'built' this way of life and was actually enjoying it.

Work became busier, and Hamish spent countless hours working late. Virginia's job as a features writer for a newspaper meant that she could keep fairly normal working hours. Her evenings were spent planning for the baby and searching through numerous mother-and-baby magazines. The list grew daily of things she wanted to buy.

Hamish began to feel caged in on his return home from work each day, as every single thing they did or looked at had something to do with having the baby. He no longer knew exactly what he wanted, but he did realize something had changed. There wasn't the spark that they once had together. In fact, he couldn't remember the last time they had made love. Gone were the spontaneous nights out, the picnics under the stars, and the relaxing beach escapes they once would enjoy.

He wished in some ways that he had not been given the opportunity of a partnership in Miami because it was this promotion that gave them the stability and money, which allowed them to go on the IVF program. Months of treatment had cost a small fortune and caused an agonizing wait each time, hoping she would be pregnant. He felt the pressure of supporting Virginia, and his increasing workload became more and more stressful.

"Damn it! I can't believe the time! I'm going to be late."

Hamish was frantically looking for his socks and shoes which were kicked off in a hurry the previous evening. The luxury hotel had become his second home in recent times.

"Don't worry, babe, you've got plenty of time. The appointment isn't until midday," gushed Monique as she stretched out on the king-size bed.

"True," replied Hamish, busying himself with gathering his belongings.

"Don't forget your cell phone," she reminded as she gestured toward the small kitchen where it sat plugged into a charger.

"I hope Virginia didn't see us last night. She was right outside the restaurant, for God's sake! We've got to be more careful from now on."

"She wouldn't have seen us, we weren't exactly right near the window or anything." Monique was getting sick of this subject now.

"Still, that was too close for comfort. Mind you, I don't know how she would have known to come to *our* restaurant. I'm going to go home first, then I'll meet you at the office, okay?"

Hamish was businesslike now. The smooth, carefree lover of the previous night and this morning had vanished since reality reared its ugly head.

"Sure, babe, but why are you going home? Won't that just make matters look even more suspicious?"

"No, Virginia knows that even if I'm tied up all night with work, I usually make an effort to go home, have a shower, and then head back out again."

"Okay then." Monique had resigned herself to the fact that she was dealing with a married man who had obligations. Also, being an attorney made him even more pedantic.

Putting up with his baggage was nothing, considering the perks she got from their relationship. The luxury suite was one of them.

Checking himself in the mirror above the dressing table, Hamish smoothed out his clothes, put his tie loosely around his neck, tucked his shirt into his pants, and decided it was time to leave.

Chapter 2

Breaking the News

"How dare he come here and act as if everything is normal!" she bellowed to the empty house.

Virginia's constant sobbing had been replaced by anger. The rage she felt toward her husband was intense. The impeccably dressed, intelligent, and beautiful journalist, who had everything she could possibly want in life now that she was finally pregnant, had been dealt a totally unpredictable ending to the fairy tale.

Since she had seen Hamish with the other woman, her life had turned upside down. The vision had stamped an imprint on Virginia, and she barely got that image out of her mind.

It wasn't about being strong anymore. The shock, grief, sorrow and coming out the other end of this was all well and good to hope for, but nothing could erase what she saw that day and the heartache that it had caused.

"Oh...why? Why?" she wailed, while looking at her reddened face in the mirror. Replaying the scene over and over in her mind was like reconstructing a murder scene where each step was played out, each sound was heard, and then time would stand still when the image of Hamish with that other woman would come to the forefront of her thoughts. It seemed the intrusion of images plagued her no matter what she did.

The torture was relentless. Her mind would picture the two of them in the restaurant, and then she would imagine what they were doing at any given time. At nighttime, she would picture them cuddling on the sofa, then going to bed together. In the morning, she would picture them waking up in each other's arms, having breakfast together, showering, offering each other endearing words of love as they each left for work. There was no relief, no single second that she would not have him or *them* out of her thoughts.

Her life had spun around on its axis. Virginia showered, ate, dressed, drove, worked, cooked – all to the thoughts that would be on a constant rotation in her mind. It was tiring, stressful, and not in the least bit helpful to her situation.

One morning, it dawned on her. She opened her swollen eyes after the nightly sobs had become part of her bedtime ritual, along with the tossing and turning, thinking about the position she was now faced with, and as she lifted her heavy body out of bed, she decided that she would let the people closest to her know. She couldn't hold on to this burden any longer.

The sorrow continued, day in, day out, and it made no difference what day of the week it was or at what time. It was a relief when she didn't have to put on a brave face and head off to work on a weekend.

The emptiness seemed to affect everything in her life. In the bed she had shared with her husband, she felt its spaciousness. The bathroom seemed empty without his toothbrush, razor, and cologne. The closet showed gaps where his shirts once hanged. In every room and in every part of her life, she felt a hollow feeling.

Feeling so vulnerable was not something that Virginia had ever experienced before. The attractive, confident brunette, who was always so perfectly groomed, was usually ready for what came her way in life. That was before this horrible situation. In the fast-paced business of professional journalism, she was always prepared. That's just the way journalists are ready for action and waiting on the next big headline.

For the best part of three months, Virginia kept her secret. The thought of telling anyone made it all the more real. It wasn't until it dawned on her that the situation couldn't be hidden anymore...people would notice.

On the other side of the country, in Los Angeles, Gabby was soaking up her favorite day of the week. Saturdays were spent sleeping in, going on leisurely walks, taking yoga classes and, on occasion, attending yoga retreats. Today, she was attending a special double session of yoga with like-minded people that she had met through the Lotus Yoga Center.

Having plenty of time before she had to leave, she made herself a cup of chamomile tea while methodically packing her backpack with all the essentials for the class. Her cell phone rang, which startled her out of her thoughts, and she didn't notice the caller ID.

"Hello," answered Gabby in her usual cheerful way.

"Hi...Gabby."

"Is that you, Virginia?"

"Yes, it is, Gab. How are *you*?" inquired Virginia in an almost too enthusiastic tone. She nervously looked at the piece of paper with everything she wanted to say written down, so she wouldn't stumble.

"I'm great, thanks, Gin. Just getting ready to go to a double session of hatha yoga...but more to the point, how are you? You sound...different."

"Oh, do I?" Realizing her friend had picked up on something, Virginia felt a little guilty for putting on a brave act.

"I just felt like calling you for a chat. But I guess I called at a bad time." She became despondent in an instant at the thought of disturbing her friend.

"Don't be silly. I'm a bit early actually. I'm eager to get out of the house," declared Gabby.

"Oh, I just remembered...it's midday there, isn't it?"

With all the preparation to actually make the call, Virginia had forgotten the time difference and was now annoyed with herself.

"Yes, it is. You always forget we are behind you folk on the East Coast. But for you, my dear friend, I always have time...I'll just grab my cup of tea and head to the lounge."

Gabby sat comfortably now, stretching out her shapely legs. Sweeping her long, brown hair to one side, she checked the time and relaxed back into the overstuffed cushions, ready for a nice chat with her oldest and dearest school friend. "So what's been happening?"

"Oh, you know, just the usual," lied Virginia.

"You sound different, Gin, are you okay?" hinted Gabby again, as she detected sadness in Virginia's tone and thought it was unusual for her to sound so vague, given that she had called for a chat. Having a journalistic background, Virginia would usually be so colorful with her speech, even when she was describing the dullest of things. "It's just that..."

Virginia couldn't be strong any longer. The list she held in her hand was now a crumpled mess. The floodgates had broken. This was her best friend, and her emotions got the better of her. The barrage of tears broke free.

"Virginia, tell me, what's wrong? You said the babies were fine, is this really true? Are you okay?"

After a long pause, Virginia willed herself to say one word at a time. She felt as though she was in a time warp as her mind visualized *that* day. Her heart began to thump, remembering how her knees went weak as she collapsed on the sidewalk in front of everyone.

"It's Hamish. He's, he's..." sobbed Virginia.

Gabby put her cup of tea down onto the coffee table in front of her. Sitting upright now, she gave her full attention to her devastated friend on the other side of the country.

"Is he all right?"

Looking absently across the road through the sheer curtains, Gabby noticed her neighbors were out and about chatting to each other, probably about their gardens and families.

Through muted sobs, Virginia managed to blurt out, "Yes, yes, he's all right."

"Then tell me, what is it?"

Taking a deep breath now, she managed to say, "Hamish is having...an affair."

Somehow, saying the words out loud seemed to make it even more real. She sobbed and sobbed. Gabby waited patiently while her best friend took time to let go, comforting her the best way she could over the telephone.

"Ginny, tell me how you know this. Are you sure?"

Gabby had a very calming nature. In school she was always the peacemaker. "Yes, I'm sure. I know because I caught him out, and he admitted to it. It's awful, Gab – I'm finally pregnant after all we've been through with the miscarriages and the IVF program, and now look what he's done. It's just not fair!" She wept uncontrollably, while the crumpled paper lay in shreds by her feet. Her eyes wandered around the lonely house as her stricken voice seemed to echo in its spaciousness.

Shocked and worried by her best friend's predicament, Gabby did what she did best. She listened, and she comforted Virginia.

"Now, listen to me...I want you to calm yourself down. First and foremost, you need to think of the babies' well-being. They need you to be calm."

"Okay...I'm sorry..."

"Don't be sorry. I just want you to relax." Gabby took on an authoritative tone, but still remained calm.

"Yes, okay, I'm fine now..."

"Good. Now...are you sure?"

Her strength didn't hold out. Tissue after tissue, Virginia's sobs did not let up. The barrage of anger had burst, and now it was letting her escape the imprisonment of keeping such a secret.

"Yes, I caught him out nearly three months ago. He's disgusting...he moved out of our house shortly after I found them out," blurted Virginia.

"Three months ago! Oh Gin, I feel terrible for you. Why didn't you tell me earlier? Have you told anyone? Oh Ginny..." Gabby's heart poured out for her friend. She felt the angst and sadness in her own heart as a reflection.

"I couldn't bring myself to tell anyone. I thought it would all go away...but it didn't, it won't, and now I have to look after the babies..."

The sobbing started again. This time, she was almost heaving with sorrow. The pain that Gabby could empathically feel was horrendous.

"Shush now. It's all right," comforted Gabby, tears streaming down her own face.

"I'm sorry. I thought I could keep it together, but it's too much..."

"You don't have to keep it together, Gin, let it all out. It's okay."

Gabby's calming voice and tender words soothed Virginia. She slowly stopped sobbing.

"Sorry. I'm fine now."

"Gin, are you positive? I mean, are you really sure?"

"Yes, I know for sure. I had the ghastly honor of seeing the two of them with my own eyes. And I know who she is. She works with him, and her name is Monique. She worked on a case with him not so long ago." Virginia wiped her eyes as she blankly stared into the kitchen.

Gabby took all this information in, calming her own emotions to help her think rationally. It looked like her neighbors were all inside now; no one was to be seen apart from a couple of birds sunning themselves on the porch railing.

They spent the next forty-five minutes on the telephone before Gabby realized what time it was. She would be late for her class, but it didn't matter. Virginia was more important.

"Oh, Gabby, I'm keeping you, aren't I? I'm so sorry." Virginia realized that she had kept Gabby on the phone for almost an hour.

"No, no. Honestly, it's fine. You are much more important. I'm happy to stay at home and be here for you to talk to.

Virginia had regained some composure. With the phone tucked between her ear and shoulder, she placed the used tissues in the waste bin. It was as if the explosion of tears had freed her and released an inner self-assurance now.

"Gab, I couldn't do that to you. I know how you look forward to these things. I'll be all right, promise. I'm going to go and see Mom and Dad, and maybe I'll stay over there for the weekend. I'm sorry I called you, I forgot about the time difference; I really didn't want to upset your plans. I just thought it was time I told people."

"Are you sure? It's not like I *have* to go. You are much more important," said Gabby who couldn't be more sure about canceling her yoga. This was her best friend from school.

"Yes, I'm sure. I would feel so bad if you missed out on my account. Plus, I really need to tell Mom and Dad today too..."

"Well, okay, if you're sure. I'm glad you have told me. Just remember you've always got my support, no matter what happens."

"I haven't mentioned anything to Dianne yet."

"I know she will want to support you more than ever. Remember, Gin, the three of us can get through anything together. We'll always support you. But you do what you have to do, and let her know in your own time, if you want to."

"Thanks, Gabby, I don't know what I would do without you and Dianne. I am going to call her, but I feel so emotionally drained. If you are speaking to her, I don't mind if you tell her. Just let her know I'll give her a call over the weekend...if that's all right with you."

Sensing that Virginia had released some of the burden by sharing it, she did a swift 360 degree turn to lighten the mood of the conversation.

"I can do that. Now, go and grab a cup of chamomile tea, sit down, and breathe through your *chakras*!"

"Oh, Gabby, you are so funny! I don't even know where my chakras are, let alone how to breathe through them!"

"Well, I'm going to have to teach you, aren't I?"

With that said, both women were feeling better in their own way, and they said their goodbyes and promised to call each other.

Chapter 3
Details, Details, Details

"Oh. My. Gosh!" exclaimed Dianne, who always spoke in staccato whenever she was in shock and lost for words – which was quite rare. Her long, blond hair was pulled into a low ponytail as she stretched her calf muscles in readiness for a jog to the beach.

"I've only just told Mom and Dad. This morning I called Gabby and told her," added Virginia, hoping to keep her composure.

"Ginny, I am so sorry. How could Hamish do this? You guys had...have...everything – together!" blurted Dianne, stretching her hamstrings. She then felt like kicking herself for being so insensitive.

"I'm okay, Di. I've been looking after myself. If it wasn't for these babies, I'd have given up a long time ago."

"Well, I'm glad to hear that. Have you thought about what you're going to do?"

"At this stage, I'm just taking one day at a time. I've got a doctor's appointment soon, and I'm busy at work. I haven't spoken to Hamish for a while," conceded Virginia.

Dianne, feeling helpless, paced the length of her apartment. Gazing out in the direction of the ocean, she was inspired by an idea.

"Ginny, maybe Gab and I should come over and help you out," reflected Dianne as she gazed out toward the ocean, twirling her hair between her fingers in a contemplative mode.

"Don't be silly, Di, I'll be fine. Besides, what are you two going to do? I'll be fine, I'll work it out," said Virginia, not really believing a word of what she was saying.

Inspired by her idea, there was no stopping Dianne now. She didn't hear a word of Virginia's.

Fixated on tidying the cushions on her white leather couch, she pondered the situation. From the lounge she walked out onto her balcony, which overlooked the beautiful ocean. It wasn't directly facing it, but one street back. Never one to sit still, she hopped on her exercise bike and gazed into the horizon.

The idea was growing...

With Gabby's dislike of plane travel, a road trip would be the answer! Her mind was so active; she quickly put together a plan of how she was going to convince Gabby that going to see Virginia was a good idea.

This was positive. Dianne liked positivity – in fact she thrived on it. She was very motivated, and with all the excess energy that she had generated from the excitement of her idea, it didn't take much for her to decide on a quick jog to the promenade and back. Her jogging provided much time for thinking.

Reaching the promenade in record time, she decided to call Gabby and put forth her idea. It was disappointing when she was told by Gabby's husband that she wasn't due back until about 4 p.m.

Checking the time constantly throughout the day, she must have done at least two hundred sit-ups, fifty bicep curls, several planks, and twenty or so boot camp star jumps, not to mention riding her stationary bike. It was now 4 p.m., and hoping that Gabby would be home from her yoga class, she dialed her number.

"That's a three-thousand mile road trip, Di", exclaimed Gabby as she unpacked her backpack with the phone wedged between her shoulder and her ear.

"I know it's not a short trip, but won't it be fun!"

"Well, yes, and I'd love to go...but..."

"Come on, as well as it being fun, we'll be helping Virginia out."

"I know your intention is good..." said Gabby, knowing Dianne had a tendency to get overexcited.

"Even if we aren't there for the birth, at least her knowing we're coming over would bring some hope," persisted Dianne.

"I guess it should be okay. I am due for holiday leave, I suppose, having been at the bank for twelve years and never really taken much time off. On Monday, I'll check with my manager. Those two have always been inseparable. I am sure they'll work it out."

"I hope you're right. You and your 'feelings' are usually spot-on. So what do you think then?"

"We're no Thelma and Louise, Di. We could just fly there... but then, I really don't think I could go through the panic attacks again."

"I hadn't forgotten your fear of flying, that's why I thought a road trip would be perfect. Don't worry, I have no intention of driving off a cliff or any such thing. It will be something that I'm sure she will look forward to," beamed Dianne.

"I'm sure she would appreciate our support, plus it's a great excuse to get away. I would really love to do it, so I'll check it out with Ken and then think of a way to tell Anthony. He'll come around." Gabby said with a sly smile. "Besides, even if he doesn't, I'll still go."

"Tell me, you two aren't having problems as well?" said Dianne half-jokingly.

"Okay, I won't."

Gabby desperately wanted to share her frustration, so she eventually confided in Dianne. "I don't know, Di...we don't have anything in common anymore. He irritates me. Plus, I'm so bored with our routine, and to top it off my work is so monotonous...Maybe I just need a holiday..."

Picking up the remote control, she turned on the television. It was no surprise that it automatically switched on to the sports channel, Anthony's favorite. Gabby didn't watch much television at all, preferring to play guitar or read.

"Sounds like it to me. A holiday usually freshens up everything. Old things become new again, you know?" Dianne had her positive cheerleading voice on now. Twirling her chain once more, she contemplated her idea coming to fruition.

"Hmmm. Don't get me wrong, I would love to go. Just leave it with me. I'll sound things out and let you know, okay?"

"Okey dokey," gushed Dianne, happy that she had convinced Gabby to even want to go. She was certain all would turn out as she wanted.

"Oh, before I go, how is Dan? How are you two getting on, and when do I get to meet this 'wonder boy'?"

The media had tagged Dan as the Dodgers' latest 'wonder boy'. Gabby knew that Dianne liked to stay away from the hype of media frenzy, but decided to throw that one in for a bit of a dig.

This wasn't the first time Dianne had dated a well-known sporting figure. Gabby was used to her friend being seen in the social pages.

"Dan's great! We get on well together. It's been fun going out for dinner, exercising together, and just simple things like cooking dinner together, watching movies, and just chilling out." Dianne was distracted by her thoughts and tugged at her dangly earrings, gazing over toward the ocean view.

"Correct me if I'm wrong, but since when do you like just 'chilling out'? You usually can't sit still for two minutes."

"Yes, but Dan's pretty nice to chill out with."

"Oh, I see. Sounds like you enjoy each other's company. Just promise me one thing, you won't get into a boring routine and always, always, always have your own interests."

"Whoa! You are in a bad place, aren't you? Okay, I promise. As for your 'other' problem, why don't you do an aromatherapy course? Or a natural therapies course...or what about taking on a yoga group of your own? Or maybe ask at the yoga center if they need any help or have any suggestions. Just ask around. You have a lot of interests, and I'm sure someone in those areas can either suggest or help you find something."

Dianne was surprised by her own advice and secretly smiled to herself, pleased with the ideas she came up with. Her fingers were now twirling and twisting the long chain again.

"Thanks, Di, you are so full of ideas. Who would have known," teased Gabby.

"Gee, thanks, your positivity must have rubbed off onto me. You need to remember your own advice."

"Yes, I probably do, don't I?"

"I think I'm getting used to portraying a positive attitude from coaching my ever-wavering teenage cheerleaders and keeping my older girls in line. I always have to think ahead to get them motivated and staying healthy."

"I can imagine how hard that must be...I will ask around. At least that will be a start, won't it?" Sounding hopeful, Gabby made a mental note on the subject.

"That's the spirit! Glad I can be of some assistance. That will be $150 consultation fee, thanks."

"Ha ha. So when do I get to meet Dan?"

"How about Saturday night? By that time, hopefully, we will have sorted a few things out."

"Okay then. Sounds like a plan. Thanks, Di, talk to you soon."

"Bye, Gab."

After the phone call, Gabby sat down on the couch and thought about their conversation. Dianne had made her think about a few things that she herself had been thinking of but was not sure what to do about them.

Meanwhile, Dan had just returned home after baseball practice. He lived quite close to Dianne. His coach, Dean Fraser had given him a contract to read over. Dan was in two minds about this. As he contemplated the thick pile of papers, he wondered if he should sign the contract. Procrastinating, he decided to call Dianne instead.

"Hey, babe, how are you?" Dan yawned into the phone.

"Not too bad now that you've called! You sound really tired. How was practice?"

"Hard. Coach Dean had us pitching at a maximum ninety-mile force for twenty-minute intervals from the mound. My shoulder feels like a lead weight."

"Poor baby. I could come over and give you a massage..." suggested Dianne.

"Mmm, that sounds tempting, but I think I might fall asleep and not be much company, babe."

Dan would have loved Dianne to come over, but he needed to read through the contract and didn't want her snooping around. This was confidential business between himself and his coach.

"Okay, I get the hint. I guess I can sleep all alone tonight. Actually, I've got some planning to do," she added, quite pleased with herself.

"What are you planning, babe?"

"Oh...just a trip to Miami..."

"What!" Suddenly the sleepiness Dan had felt was gone. He sat upright, hardly believing the coincidence.

Besides the fact that he was genuinely surprised about Dianne's news, he couldn't believe that she was going to Miami of all places.

"I was talking to Gabby, and we decided...well, actually, I came up with an idea that we should go and see Virginia, a friend of ours who is having a hard time at the moment."

"That's no good," said Dan, wanting to know more about the Miami part of the trip.

"Gabby has this terrible fear of flying, so we will have to drive over."

"That's a huge drive, babe. Are you both up to it?" Dan put the thick contract down on the coffee table and gave Dianne his full attention.

"Yeah, I think so. We're just seeing if it's possible at the moment...which reminds me of something. I asked Gabby and Anthony if they'd like to have dinner with us on Saturday night. It shouldn't be a very late night. I know you've got the game during the day, so even if you could just come for a little while, it would be great," chirped Dianne while she twirled her chain around her index finger.

"Yeah, that should be fine, babe."

Dianne happily chatted about her thoughts on where they could possibly stay along the way. She asked Dan what he thought Dean Fraser would say when she asked him for time off.

"I think he'll be cool with it. As long as you've got everything covered, he should be fine."

Dan knew that Dean would be fine, more than fine actually. Normally, taking time off during the season would be sacrilege, but on this occasion Dan knew she would get Dean's blessing. This could lead to a further bonus if he played his cards right. He thought about the contract, and a pang of guilt swept over him until he thought of the money offered to him. That's what inspired him now.

"Anyway, babe, I think I better grab some dinner and hit the sack. I'm so tired. I'll see you tomorrow night?"

"Yep, can't wait. Nighty night, hon."

Happy with all the plans made so far, Dianne lay in bed thinking of the trip ahead and satisfied that she could convince the Dodgers' management that her two main assistants were capable of taking over the reins for a short period. The finals season wasn't for some time, so routines would still remain roughly the same until the pace picked up later on. She turned her bedside light off and drifted peacefully to sleep.

The day's events had taken their toll, and Virginia, now having confided in her closest family and friends, found herself very weary.

Being at her parents' home was comforting, even at thirty-five, and she realized that parents didn't stop supporting their children even when they were adults.

"Don't you worry, my gorgeous babies, Mummy will always love you and support you, no matter what." She spoke to her rounded belly as she rubbed her hands over it.

Making herself comfortable in the bed she used to sleep in many years before when visiting in the holidays, covered in a pale blue and white floral-patterned duvet cover with matching European pillows, she stared at the familiar walls, still covered in the printed wallpaper and border chosen when she was in a Laura Ashley phase of her life. The pictures of the 'three musketeers', Virginia, Gabby and Dianne, still hung on the wall above her bed, and many framed certificates, awards, and trophies still adorned her room. *This place feels like a time warp,* she thought to herself. It's no wonder she always felt so comfortable whenever she stayed over. Her mom had gone to great lengths to make the room like her old room, when they lived in Brentwood, Los Angeles. Strangely at thirty-five the familiarity of the room was so comforting, though at the same time, she felt somewhat removed from it. A sad feeling swept over her again, and she muffled her sobs into the soft down of the pillows for what seemed like an eternity...

Chapter 4

Dropping the Bombshell

The next morning...

On a roll and motivated to get the road trip organized, having made an appointment, Dianne drove to the Dodgers' head office at the stadium in the Elysian Park neighborhood of Los Angeles. Her phone call with Craig Mendez, the Dodgers' Manager, was a tense call, and he was not willing to commit to giving his approval until Dean Fraser had approved. Now for Dean Fraser, Head Coach. Parking her car, she began to feel less than confident. This panicked her, and she didn't enter the building with the gusto that she had felt earlier in the morning.

"Good morning. Dianne Grayson to see Dean Fraser," she informed the overly made-up receptionist with red hair that seemed to have been plastered with hair spray.

"Please have a seat, Ms Grayson. Mr Fraser will be out in a moment," said the receptionist.

Sitting in the lounge area and viewing all the trophies, awards, and signed jerseys, she really hoped and prayed that this meeting would be a positive one. Her palms began to sweat from nerves.

"Hi there, Dianne," boomed Dean.

He had his arms outstretched ready to give Dianne a hug.

"Hello..." she blurted as he gestured toward her. The vision of a fairly short, round man, receding hairline, light gray checked pants, and a pale pink open-neck shirt with gold chain glistening was not how she had pictured him. His demeanor was enough to make her forget the nervousness felt just a few minutes earlier.

"Hi, Dean, thanks for seeing me on such short notice." Dianne felt awkward that Dean hugged her, but at the same time she felt relieved that he was so accommodating.

"Not a problem – let's go into my office," he said as he began to walk in that direction.

Dean took his chance to eye his perfectly groomed and beautiful visitor walk into his office as he let her enter the room first. Her sexy, tight, white dress jeans and a silky white top, which draped slightly off one shoulder exposing her tanned skin, took his attention. Her dangle earrings and long chain shimmered as she walked, the enticing scent of her perfume trailing behind her.

Turning into the large, airy corner office, sporting more team paraphernalia, he motioned to her to take a seat. Dean was 62, and his balding forehead shone under the light above his desk. A ruddy, tanned appearance, coupled with that gold chain, gave him a shifty look. Or was that just because she had heard some rather suspicious stories about him?

"How have you been?" he inquired, leaning back into his luxuriously appointed leather chair.

"Good, thank you. How have you been?" she replied self-consciously, smoothing out some imaginary creases as Dean appeared to be eyeing her in great detail.

"Fine, thanks. How's that fella of yours been treating you?"

"Oh, he's great, thanks – he trains more than anything these days, but I guess you know all about that!" added Dianne, knowing that Dean would know exactly what she was talking about.

"Well, if you're going to be the star pitcher for your team, that's got to be your focus, hasn't it?"

"Yes – he is definitely focused!"

"So, to what do I owe this pleasure?" He almost seemed distracted by the pile of open files on his desk. Dianne could tell that they were printouts of the statistics from the games as she had seen Dan's stats on a sheet of paper just like that.

"Well...I have a situation that I would like to run by you, and hopefully we can come to a positive outcome," suggested Dianne rather boldly now that she had relaxed.

"Sounds serious – what is it?" He was still distracted by the paperwork on his desk, and Dianne's sexiness was not helping his thoughts. Her fragrance wafted in the small office, doubling her sex appeal.

"Well, you see, I have a friend who is in a horrible situation, and I would dearly love to go and see her. She lives in Miami, Florida, and I was hoping that I could take some time off to do that."

"During the season? How much time are we talking here?" Dean's ears pricked up at the mention of Miami. He settled back in his chair and watched Dianne's perfect lips intently as she spoke.

"Well, to tell you the truth, it really depends on you. If I organized everything to run here at the team, and of course with your blessing, I would love to make it a sort of road trip with my good friend, so at most it would be three weeks..."

"Three weeks to drive to Florida and back? Why don't you just fly?"

"My friend has a terrible fear of flying."

"Hmmm," is all Dean could manage at this point. His mind was racing ahead and to the possibilities that could emerge from this situation. Under normal circumstances, taking time off during the season would be out of the question. This, however, wasn't a 'normal' situation. He realized that the phone call from Dan this morning, that he abruptly hung up on, must have been to tell him about this.

"I have already asked Kristin and Renee, my assistant coaches, if they are comfortable with the arrangement, and I have shown them the plan, routines, and dress schedules for the next eight weeks, not that I'll be away for that long. They have been my right-hand assistants for the last two years now." She shifted in her seat, crossing her lithe legs and straightening her back.

Dean found it hard to shift his gaze from her legs that seemed to go for miles. "What about the cheerleaders themselves? Would a change of leadership shift that dedication? We do need consistency, you know, and even though some people may just see it as cheerleading, it is a huge part of the game. The look, the feel, the vibes that the girls provide at the game is really important. Positions like yours don't come around too often...there'll be another coach waiting to pounce on your position."

"Oh, uh..." Dianne was getting really worried now. Usually nerves never bothered her, but this meant so much. Little did she know that Dean had already made up his mind, he was just making her sweat it out.

"Yes, I know. I haven't mentioned it to them, of course, because I wanted to clear it with Kristin, Renee, and you. I am 100% confident that they will be fine. They are all mature girls, and as I've said, they are dedicated to the team. They aren't doing this because their parents are pushing them to – they really want to be a part of the whole Dodgers team. If you would prefer, I can put it to them tonight at practice and gauge the response," offered Dianne in the most encouraging tone she could muster. "That way, we will be in a better position to make the decision."

Dean thought to himself that the reason was all about him wanting a job done. A very important job done... "That would be a good plan," he said.

He became quite distant as his mind wondered to thoughts of the connections he had and how he saw this as a great opportunity to 'help' the upcoming job that would bring him copious amounts of money.

"Thank you, Dean. I can certainly do that. Friday night practice is usually really pumped, so all the girls will be eager to do well, and I'm sure they will be fine about it. Did you want me to let you know after the game tomorrow afternoon? The assistant coaches are genuinely on my side, and I really wouldn't expect either of them to jump into my position."

"That would be terrific. As you say, I'm sure they'll be fine, but we'll just wait and see. I'll wait for your update and talk to Skip, Corey and the other coaches to let them know.." He was being much more positive at this stage which eased Dianne's nerves. "I would also like to see your schedule of plans, etc., okay?"

"Sure, that's fine with me, Dean. Thank you so much for your time. I really appreciate it."

"Not a problem, Dianne. I'll see you after the game tomorrow. We're at Dodgers Stadium, so I'll be around the pits and up in the boxes with the other coaches. Oh, by the way, have you planned your route to Florida at all?"

"Not yet, but now with your blessing, we can go ahead and plan, plan, plan!" she enthused prematurely. "Oh, I mean after you give me the A-okay, of course!"

"I'd be interested to know where you are stopping. I may have some recommendations for hotels and stops along the way, if you're interested."

"Okay. That'd be great! Thanks again!" said Dianne excitedly. Her nerves had turned to positive energy because she knew the girls would be fine, her assistant coaches were in agreement, and she practically had Dean's blessing. "Yes! I'm going on a road trip!" she smiled to herself as she walked through reception and to her car.

The drive back to her home was a delightful one. The Pacific Ocean on one side, the open highway ahead of her, and the crisp wind blowing her long, blond hair as the Black Eyed Peas sang 'I Gotta Feeling'. Tonight's practice was going to be a good one. As Dianne drove home, she mentally prepared how she would tell the girls.

The next day...

Gabby had showered and dressed, and was eating her breakfast when Anthony walked into the kitchen. Still not fully awake, he opened the fridge to get some orange juice and caught sight of Gabby sitting at the breakfast bar, looking like she had been up for some time.

"Good morning!" Her tone was bright and chirpy.

"Morning," mumbled Anthony, "why are you up early and so chirpy?"

"It's a beautiful day. I thought I'd go for a walk. Did you want to join me?"

Gabby knew that it would be the last thing Anthony would want to do.

"No, thanks. I'm still waking up."

Preferring a simple life, Anthony moved sloth-like around the kitchen. His large-framed body couldn't manage anything faster than a shuffling speed in the morning, especially on a Saturday.

Gabby, on the other hand, was ever ready to grab a sunrise walk, or do some morning yoga moves to get her body going. She allowed enough time for Anthony to pour his orange juice, empty cereal into his bowl, cut up a banana, and put the kettle on. "I've been thinking about a change of career lately," she said cautiously, still watching his every move.

"Oh?" he managed in between chewing cereal and glancing at some brochures left on the kitchen bench.

"Yes. I've been thinking about it for some time, and yesterday afternoon it dawned on me what I really want to do."

Realizing Gabby was being serious, he put his spoon down and looked at her. "Whoa! Where did all this come from? I thought you were happy at the bank."

"I haven't been happy there for ages. I've had some ideas, though. You know the place where I do yoga? Well, there was talk of hiring a person to help out one of the teachers as the classes are getting quite large. I might give them a call," she spoke the words as if emphasizing to herself that this was exactly what she was going to do.

Anthony listened while eating his cereal. A drop of milk stayed on the outer edge of his mouth, which he didn't feel, nor wipe away. Gabby found this unsightly.

"I don't know, Gabby, you don't know anything about those places. Do they have a secure business structure? Will you get the regulation employment benefits? How secure would those types of jobs be? How do you know there will be something available anyway?"

There goes his negativity again, thought Gabby.

"Look, it's just an idea. Besides, it doesn't hurt to ask. I know the owner, and I'm sure she can steer me in the right direction. And stop referring to it as '*those types of jobs*'. You sound like a snob!" Her disgust for him grew by the second.

"What about salary? How will that type of job match your salary at the bank?"

"There you go again, 'that type of job'. Well, that's the only part I am unsure about. Though, in saying that, I can always do courses to assist in teaching and learn new skills. I can eventually teach a class myself! Wouldn't that be good?" she chirped. Her enthusiasm was one-sided.

"Are you sure this isn't one of those phases that you go through? I just think it sounds unstable. Besides, how would we cope? We've got the mortgage, you know. Also, let's not forget we were thinking of buying that investment property," he added as he stood up from the kitchen stool to put his dish in the sink.

"You know very well that my salary is mostly saved, Anthony. We are well ahead of the mortgage. In fact, last time I checked the bank statements, we probably only have about a year of payments left, and the mortgage will be paid off! I know that people our age are usually up to their ears in debt." The conversation was really testing Gabby's calm personality now. She could feel her heart start to race.

This topic was one that could be stretched into discussing why they hadn't had children yet. Something Gabby had wanted so much.

"This would allow me to really focus on doing something I actually like doing..."

"It sounds too risky to me."

"Risky? Anthony, if you don't take some risks in life, you'll never get anywhere or do what you really want to do. You'll die wondering."

Anthony shuffled around the kitchen while contemplating Gabby's outburst. With his long torso stooped over the breakfast bar and his unruly dark hair, he looked like an old man. Gabby couldn't help feeling sorry for him now, in a pitiful way.

With the bombshell out of the way, Gabby decided to change the subject and tell Anthony about dinner next Saturday night with Dianne and Dan.

"I guess we can go.... I was going to watch the Yankees game, though." Cringing at his own words, he regretted what he said as the words came out and now waited for the slaughter from his wife.

"Anthony, you can watch it later on cable! You're such a stick in the mud – all you ever want to do is watch TV! Sport! Urgghhh!!"

"Repeats are not the same, Gabby, and it's never bothered you before. Why now all of a sudden?" Anthony spluttered.

"You're wrong, Anthony, it's bothered me for ages. I just haven't said anything about it. Maybe I should have..."

"Okay, okay dinner is fine with me."

"Good!"

Anthony knew he watched a lot of TV, but that was what they both used to love doing – at least he thought so. With a sniffle and a cough, he walked over to the lounge, sank his head into the back of the chair, and stared at the television.

Feeling inspired to make a positive effort, Gabby dialed the number of The Lotus Yoga Center and spoke to Kara, the owner. Gabby mentioned how she had loved coming to the center for the last five years and wondered if she knew of any job vacancies that would be suitable to apply for. The impeccable timing had Kara in a momentary state of silence, which Gabby felt very uncomfortable with now.

"I don't believe it. I don't think you will either, but we had just decided to advertise for someone to help out with the meditation/yoga workshops that Mick holds. You would be perfect! I'm sure Mick would think so too."

Gabby didn't need any time to think about this suggestion, and she felt guilty for knowing that they might be hiring, but she kept that to herself and told Kara she was interested straight away.

She sent a quick text message to Dianne, saying that they could come to dinner on Saturday night, and told her that her idea had sparked a possible job.

Dianne immediately texted back. "Really? So soon? Fantastic! Oh, dinner is booked at The Green Ivy, 7:30 p.m."

"Really? THE Green Ivy?"

"I have Dodger connections ☺"

"Perfect!"

Dianne couldn't keep texting. She wanted to find out more, so she called her good friend.

"Hi! Sorry, I just thought I'd call you instead," said Dianne.

"Hi."

"What did Anthony say about the road trip?"

"Um, well, actually I didn't mention it. Can you imagine him after breaking the change in career news to him, then a road trip! I think he would have had a heart attack...No, I'll approach that subject tomorrow, I think!"

"Okay, I'm sure you know what you're doing."

"Yes, we'll see you Saturday then?"

"Yeah, hope he takes it well."

"Okay then."

"Bye, Gab."

"Bye, Di."

Thursday afternoon came around fairly quickly, and Gabby was dreading going home. She was not going to the gym today as her teacher had phoned in sick, and there wasn't a fill-in teacher available. When Gabby arrived home, she noticed Anthony's car was in the driveway. *Hmmm, I wonder what's up*, she thought to herself. It was very unusual for Anthony to be home before her, let alone home before 7:30.

Walking in through the front door, she could hear the television on. Baseball, of course, it was the celebrity game. Celebrities would team up with the professional players, and usually it would be an entertaining game to watch. Each player would be fitted up with a microphone and commentate on the game as they saw it.

As Gabby saw Anthony lying on the couch watching TV, she felt disappointed she didn't have the house to herself before he got home. She usually liked to relax by either listening to her favorite music, or playing guitar, or simply doing the household chores in her own time. It was this feeling that she got which made her realize that Anthony arriving home late from work was actually allowing her to do things she loved doing. Taking in a breath, she approached the living room.

"Hi, what are you doing home so early?"

"I thought I'd leave the office early for a change and watch the game."

"Oh," is all Gabby could manage in reply. She walked straight into the kitchen and prepared a vegetable frittata to have with some salad and garlic bread for dinner.

Gabby thought to herself, *He could have at least thought of what they could have for dinner*. They sat on the couch and ate their dinner while watching the baseball game. *Boring, boring, boring*, she chanted to herself. While staring at the television screen, but distantly thinking of her possible new job and the road trip, the time seemed to fly by. Her thoughts switched to dinner on Saturday night, which reminded her she needed to tell Anthony about the trip before then!

Okay, here goes...she thought to herself.

"I called Virginia the other day to see how she was. She's having a really tough time, you know."

"I can imagine she must be very stressed out, not that she needs that with being pregnant and all."

"Yeah, she's really stressed, and Hamish is living in some hotel or apartment near his office. Poor Ginny, I really wish they could work things out."

"Poor gal."

Irritated by Anthony and the way he was talking, Gabby took a deep breath and eased into the news.

"I was talking to Dianne, and we both came to the decision that we should go over to be with Virginia while she is going through all of this."

As if waiting for a blow to come striking down on her head, she looked at Anthony and noticed he had a blank facial expression as if to say, "Well, of course you should go. What are you thinking?"

Quite simply, he said, "Maybe that's a good idea." His fair, pasty skin, moist with sweat, seemed to glisten in the light of the living room.

Gabby nearly fell over. Did he really say that? You mean there's no, 'What about your job' or anything? Stunned, she quickly kept the momentum going, not wanting to look or sound surprised.

"I think so. We were thinking of driving there and stopping a few nights on the way. You know, making it a bit of a fun road trip."

"Sounds like a good plan. When is she due? When did you think you would leave?" he said, still staring at the television.

"Well, we thought we would scope everything out with our jobs and then, if all is good, leave in about four weeks or so."

"Not wasting any time then. So, how long do you think you would be away for?"

"It depends. Dianne has more complications with regards to the Dodgers season and all that, so it really revolves around her. I've already asked Ken, and he has given the green light on a replacement for me for up to three months. Not that I'll be gone that long, but it's cleared anyway."

"Hmm. Looks like you two will have a good trip then. Did you want to take the Jeep? I'll get it serviced, and we needed to get new tires anyway, so if you like I'll get Mike to pick it up."

Gabby almost felt sorry for him at that point.

"The Jeep would be comfortable because Dianne still has the small sporty BMW. I am sure Dianne's boyfriend Dan gets a good deal with a mechanic associated with the team. So I might organize it through him. Thanks for the offer though. On Saturday night we can discuss a lot of the details."

"I'm sure you girls will have a lot to discuss."

For Gabby, the prospect of a new career, a road trip, and seeing her best friend soon - not to mention the possibility of working with Mick on the horizon - made for exciting days ahead.

Chapter 5

One Husband, One Lover

"That was really nice, wasn't it?" Gabby looked over at Anthony driving as she took off her slingbacks and delighted in the comfort of the soft carpet under her feet.

The famous Green Ivy's elegant surroundings provided a lovely backdrop to the evening. Gabby, Anthony, Dianne, and Dan enjoyed good food, good company, and the discussion of the road trip. Gabby was quite excited at the prospect of dining so close to so many celebrities, though she tried very hard not to show it.

Getting into the car felt like a world away from what they had just experienced.

"Yes, the food was great!" replied Anthony.

"There were so many celebrities there, I couldn't believe George Clooney was so close by! It was nice to finally meet Dan," gushed Gabby.

Reflecting on the evening for the rest of the trip home, Gabby glanced over at Anthony driving. He had been positive about her road trip with Dianne, as well as suggesting she take his car, but those nagging feelings came back to her. There were no sparks left, no light in the fire, no fireworks in their relationship. She thought how she wanted to go on courses to develop her interests, and he just did the same old, boring things. He had no passion, no interest, no anything! She became quite agitated within herself now and began to shift in her seat. Anthony noticed.

"What's up?" he asked. "Do you want me to change the radio station?"

"No! Just tired," Gabby sighed.

Anthony seemed oblivious to Gabby's troubled state. She put it down to a male trait, but somehow she thought other males were no way near as insensitive as Anthony.

The next morning...

Gabby decided to check her Facebook and emails. Catching her eye immediately was The Lotus Yoga Center advertising a one-day-only yoga and meditation with Mick Doherty. Gabby was thrilled! She accepted and replied straight away, thinking of the job opportunity and the prospect of changing careers.

A week had passed since Gabby had spoken to Kara, and there hadn't been any more discussions. So when her cell phone buzzed with the center's number, Gabby's heart did a dance in anticipation.

"I've been meaning to call you, Gabby. Mick and I were wondering if you could come in tomorrow for an informal meeting about the job."

"Oh, sure. Is the job going to be with Mick?"

"Yes, it is. I have to tell you, as soon as we heard you were interested, we thought you would be perfect for the position. We'll discuss the details at the meeting. I'm so happy you are interested, Gabby. Seriously, the applications I have received so far are so way off the mark."

Having the positive response from Kara was wonderful, but it also brought about a sense of whether she would live up to this praise.

"I'm worried that I don't have any qualifications in this area. As you know, I've worked in the banking industry, but my passion isn't there at all. My interest in yoga and meditation has opened up a side to me that I am very keen to explore and develop. All I can offer is that I am passionate about yoga and meditation, and I'm willing to do any courses that will help."

"Don't worry about all that now, Gabby. We'll discuss it later. We know that you are dedicated to yoga. You've been a loyal member of the center for so long now, and the fact that you are keen for a change is perfect!"

As Gabby put the phone down, she felt a surge of excitement run through her body. From the thrill of going on the trip and now this, she felt positive about the things that were changing for her. She couldn't believe that a career change could materialize so quickly. To top it off, she had a whole day of yoga with Mick coming up! What a weekend. A distant sound of sneezing interrupted her thoughts.

Walking upstairs to tell Anthony her news, she found the bedroom dim, with the curtains drawn still, and Anthony propped up on pillows with tissues strewn all over the carpet. She hadn't noticed this an hour before when she had got out of bed.

"You don't look very good."

"Gee, thanks. I feel terrible."

One week later...

There was so much activity in Gabby's life at the moment. She had tied up a lot of work projects, planned the road trip, and started writing lists of what to pack for the trip. A perfect, sunny morning saw her bouncing out of bed and getting ready with a spring in her step. Still sleeping in the spare bedroom because of Anthony's cold, she found herself thoroughly rested on waking, which was a real change. *I should have made this change a long time ago*, she thought with a sneaky smile on her face. Anthony was feeling much better by this stage. He was still moping around the house, but generally seemed to have improved.

"You finally look as though you're feeling better," Gabby remarked as she squeezed some oranges into the juicer.

"Yes, thank goodness. I hate being sick. Where are you going today?" Anthony asked, noticing Gabby was already dressed and very sprightly.

"Remember I told you about that one-day yoga workshop? Well, that's on today. I'll be there for the whole day."

Gabby never bothered mentioning anyone's names because Anthony would rarely remember or show any interest anyway.

"Oh, that's right. I forgot."

"Okay, well, I better head off. Did you need anything from the shops on my way back? I'll probably be fairly late, like about sevenish."

"Really? Why so late?"

"Actually, that's quite reasonable considering the program. Anyway, I'll have my phone on silent, so if you need something from the shops just send me a text message, okay?"

"Righteeo."

"Great! See you later. Have a good day," said Gabby, walking to the door. She still didn't want to be within even a small radius of Anthony for fear of catching his germs.

He felt a bit down and walked into the living room, turned on the television, and that's where he spent the whole day.

The workshop proved to be just as wonderful as Gabby had imagined. She took in everything Mick said and did. Throughout the day, he offered profound advice, not just to do with yoga practice, but for life in general. He came across as very worldly, wise, and genuinely interested in teaching his students.

Loving every minute of it, she gracefully worked into the asanas. Mick would walk around the room and help his students with the positioning of their bodies to gain the best advantage from the pose, stopping and adjusting a leg here or there, gently pulling back someone to reach their full potential. He adjusted Gabby's stance at one point, and she could feel a pounding sensation building in her chest as the warmth from his body radiated through to her core. Not wanting to lose balance, but keeping her gaze soft but focused, she calmly looked at Mick, whose face was now only inches away from hers. His eyes were soft and gentle, looking straight into Gabby's eyes. There seemed to be a current that ran straight through her every time she was near him or if he looked at her with those gorgeous eyes.

It was time for a ten-minute break for the class. Gabby was relieved she could regain her composure before starting back into some further poses. It was at this time that Mick could not keep himself away any longer. He walked over to where Gabby was kneeling down, having a drink from her water bottle. She nearly spluttered the water.

It wasn't until he started talking that Gabby had the strength to stand back up again and take in exactly what Mick was saying. Annoyed at her heart for thumping, her knees for shaking, and her palms for sweating, she calmly took a breath in and let it out slowly so all was somewhat restored, until... Mick asked her if she would like to have a coffee with him after the workshop.

"Oh, sure...umm, that would be great."

"Great. I was hoping you would say that. There's a coffee shop just down the road from here we could go to."

"Sounds good."

"Great. I'll let you have a break before the next session."

He was so friendly, so calm, so...sexy. Gabby practically skipped out of the room to breathe in some air, all the while thinking, *Why does he want to have a coffee with me?* The thought made her smile. How on earth was she going to calm herself down for the rest of the afternoon?

Mick Doherty was a gifted yoga teacher and clairvoyant medium. He combined the two so students would benefit not only from his yoga instruction, but also his insight.

When everyone returned to the room and sat around in a circle, ready for the kundalini yoga session, he asked if anyone would like a short reading before they started. Two people put their hands up. Gabby really wanted to put her hand up but was afraid at what he might reveal. Ignoring this thought, she gave in to the idea and put her hand up. Mick then started to read Ellen, the lady sitting on his left. It seemed Ellen was satisfied with the reading and explained to the group the significance of what Mick had just told her.

The next person was Kim. She too was taking in each and every word that Mick said. Nodding and smiling, acknowledging the truth in what he revealed about her and the position she was facing at the time.

When it came time for Gabby to have her reading, Mick took a long breath in and seemed to focus on an imaginary spot on the ground somewhere in the middle of the circle between himself and Gabby. He then took his time, looked at Gabby, and told her that she had reached a fork in the road. There were two ways presenting themselves to her. Both ways would be fine, but one would directly lead her to what she loved and wanted the most. The other would carry her on a roundabout journey and eventually lead her to where she was meant to be. He spoke about new ventures and letting go of the past, as well as massive transformation.

Gabby thanked Mick, and for the rest of the afternoon, she found it challenging to focus entirely on her breathing and postures. It was a very uplifting feeling by the end of the day, and everyone seemed to feel much better, physically and emotionally. You could see the gratitude when each and every student thanked Mick. Before all the mats were put away, Mick talked about the next workshop, which would be held at the end of next month, and invited everyone to join his yoga classes which were held at the Lotus Yoga Center as well as another venue nearer to the beach.

"You ready, Miss Gabby?" He seemed to be in a playful mood now.

Gathering up her backpack, she really didn't know what to expect or if she should even be feeling any expectation. In the back of her mind, she sensed that he was attracted to her, but she didn't want to admit it to herself.

"Yep. Ready, let's go."

They walked down the road to the coffee shop. It was obvious that Mick was a regular here, as the waitress knew exactly which coffee he preferred. Ordering a Soy Latte for Gabby and a Strong Cappuccino, they sat at a corner table. Mick seemed slightly nervous, which made Gabby slightly uneasy.

"I'm so glad you are contemplating the job. You'll be a great asset to the classes and, of course, to me."

He ran his hand across the fringe of his hair and across his forehead, possibly a nervous habit as he did this quite frequently. His dark brown hair seemed to fall at just the right place to make him look irresistible.

"To be honest, it's my dream job. I am so lucky to be in the right place at the right time. Really, considering I've only just begun making inquiries, it is amazing!"

"Yes, you're right. It's all about timing, isn't it..."

There was something on Mick's mind that Gabby couldn't quite figure out. He asked her out for coffee, and now he was being vague.

Seemingly more nervous now, Mick ran his hands through his hair again, from fringe to the back. Gabby didn't think of it as a nervous habit now, but it certainly made her want to touch his hair.

"Are you okay?" asked Gabby.

"Yes, thanks. I'm fine. I was a bit nervous asking you out for coffee, and now that I have, I guess I'm lost for words."

Mick had thought about this day for a long time. Earlier today, it felt that it was the right time to tell Gabby that he had seen and sensed her in meditations going back over a year ago. Right now though, he was sensing that he should wait.

Gabby felt more at ease now and relaxed into the conversation as they chatted for about an hour. Conversation flowed effortlessly because they had a lot in common, however, Mick still felt as though this wasn't the right time to tell Gabby that he had seen her in his meditations.

After finishing a second cup of coffee, Gabby and Mick walked slowly back to the parking lot. The evening air was fresh, the stars were out, and the moon was showing itself. Each step they took seemed to echo in the deep silence. The swishing of Mick's jacket and the sway of their bodies through the night air became a rhythmic beat. The silent walk back to the parking lot seemed to ignite the magnetism between them even more. On entering the parking lot, Mick took Gabby's hand in his as they walked together toward her car. The rhythmic pulse that now echoed in Gabby's heart was beating so fast she became slightly breathless. Reaching her car, she unlocked the door using her keyless remote. She opened the door of her Honda Euro, placed her handbag on the driver's seat, and turned ready to say goodbye.

Mick encircled her waist with his hands and drew her into him. Kissing her tenderly on the cheek, then her temple and forehead, he then bent down to kiss her neck. She felt a sense of breathlessness coming back and took a gasp of air, bending her neck and pushing her hair back to allow Mick easier access to her neck. Gabby stroked Mick's back and arms. With her face now inches away from his, she looked into his eyes and tenderly kissed him on his soft lips. They kissed gently at first, enjoying the sweet taste of each other. Then their tongues entwined, and passion grew stronger as Mick caressed the swell of her breasts. As Gabby arched her back, Mick began kissing down her neck, pulling her yoga top off her shoulder.

It took monumental effort, but Mick stopped before things got heavier.

"I'm sorry, Gabby." He pulled back, turning his gaze to the distance.

"Don't be sorry." She felt hot, frustrated, but composed herself as she smoothed back her hair.

"I was overwhelmed...with desire, and I'm sorry. This isn't how I wanted it to be..." said Mick, now helping Gabby with her top.

"I don't know what to say." Gabby's focus had completely turned as she sensed Mick regretting what had just happened.

It was her turn now to gaze into the distance, preferring the light of the moon to looking into Mick's eyes.

"I went about it all wrong. I'm so sorry. It's just that..."

She became pensive. "It's okay. I understand...I mean, I... well, I'm attracted to you. That's why I let you..." she persisted, not letting her emotions get in the way. "Why don't we get together before I go on my trip?"

She couldn't believe the words that were coming out of her mouth. Was this the new, improved, confident Gabby? She had experienced about ten different emotions in the last hour.

"I would love to and shall count every second until then!"

Like a breath of fresh air had just taken the awkwardness away, Gabby and Mick relaxed, as if given a second chance.

They kissed again; this time it was a gentle kiss on the cheek.

"I'll leave it up to you to decide where and when we meet. Know that, if you don't want to, that's fine as well. I'll understand."

"Okay. I'll let you know. Thanks so much for everything today. The workshop was great, but I especially liked the follow-up after coffee!" said Gabby cheekily.

Laughing, Mick blew her a kiss and walked toward his car.

Chapter 6

Packing Bags

Monday passed in a blur. The events of the last few weeks had Gabby pondering many avenues that her life could take. The thought of just getting through the day at work gave her a headache. Needing some time to herself, she phoned her manager at work the next morning and explained that she was not feeling well. Instead, she got in her car and just started driving. Before long, Santa Monica Boulevard was in front of her and the beach that she so loved to visit.

Contemplating the many thoughts that filtered through her mind, she bought a takeout coffee and just sat under a tree on a bench. The waves gently rolled in front of her as the familiar sounds of the beach filled her senses. Many times she had come here over the years to take a breather. The hot liquid provided soothing relief as she reminisced about her trip to England so many years ago. She began to chastise herself for going against what she had wanted to do with her life. Instead, she had chosen to please her parents by studying accounting and then working in a bank.

At that time, in England, she was certain that her life should go in the direction of being a yoga teacher, one of the many passions that she followed consistently throughout high school. Then her thoughts drifted to PJ, her first real relationship. Or was it? PJ was everything she wanted in a partner. He was sensitive, caring, in tune with her and had the same interests as she did. They connected on many levels, but Gabby had in the back of her mind that it was a holiday romance. Again, she chastised herself for thinking this. After she agreed to take a detour, to meet him in Cape Town, South Africa on her way back home from England, he invited her to come and live with him. The time they spent together was magical. There was so much she loved, but then she remembered his mother's unfriendly ways, and even though PJ stood up for her and showed his love for her so strongly, there was something that just didn't feel right at the time.

Tears streamed down her cheeks remembering that time in her life. Her heart ached to be loved like that again.

She toyed with the idea of making the wrong decisions and that she was now paying for it. Then, in an instant, her thoughts focused on Mick, then Anthony, then PJ, and it was a process of going back and forth in her mind among the three men. It all became too much, and without spending one more second in confusion, she walked down to the sand and began a walk along the water's edge. With each lap of water, washing over her feet, she could feel the pull of the waves as they went out to sea. Simply imagining her worries being taken away, she continued to walk until she felt more at ease.

Doing some simple yoga poses on the sand, she centered herself on the present moment, and then it all became clear. The cloudy thoughts had dissipated, and her heart felt sure about what she wanted and needed to do. It was time to look after herself first and foremost. She had to do what made her happy. This included changing jobs. If there was anything else that emanated from the positive steps, then that would be an added bonus.

A smile touched her mouth and without hesitation, she sent Mick a text message.

"Looking forward to catching up on Saturday. I'm here now! It's lovely. Have a nice day. Gabby x"

Within thirty seconds he replied, "Can't wait, Gabby, see you at the promenade 5 p.m. on Saturday. XO."

Once she had rationalized the situation in her mind at the beach, things didn't seem so confusing in her daily life. The rest of the week, although mostly dull, had an element of excitement. In her lunch hour each day she bought some new clothes as well as buying groceries to keep at home for Anthony. She stocked up on all the snacks she and Dianne would need on their trip. Picking up a map from the local travel agent, Gabby thought, *I bet Dianne will balk at the idea of using a real map when we've got a GPS!*

Things at home were very icy. Anthony had recovered from his cold, but Gabby was still sleeping in the spare room.

"I might as well stay here because all my clothes for the trip are laid out," she told him.

Gabby felt awkward around Anthony. She knew that their marriage was in dire straits, and even the sight of him repulsed her. Trying to act 'normal', she made conversation and pretended to care about what he would do while she was gone. He was somewhat distant himself until Thursday night just before they were to leave for the restaurant on her birthday.

"Gabby, I've been feeling like we are drifting apart lately."

"Have you?" said Gabby. "Actually, I have too. We don't seem to have anything in common anymore." Phew, she actually said it!

"No, we don't. I was hoping this road trip would give us some distance to think about things, and when you get back, maybe we could make an effort to get back on track."

Stumbling for words, Gabby couldn't think of the right thing to say. "Yes, maybe."

Her mind was whirling with thoughts.

A few friends, including Dianne, got together for dinner to celebrate Gabby's birthday. After toasting the birthday girl and a safe trip for Gabby and Dianne, Anthony remained in a quiet, reflective mood all night. Dianne could hardly wait to catch up with Gabby, so as soon as she saw her head off to the restroom, Dianne excused herself from the table.

"What's going on with you and Anthony? I've never seen him looking so glum! You don't seem to care either. Why do you look so happy and springy?" asked Dianne inquisitively.

"I don't know," said Gabby with an enigmatic smile on her face.

"What's that supposed to mean? Hey, you've got something going on, haven't you? Oh come on – spill the beans."

"Di, Anthony and I haven't been happy for ages. You know that, right?"

"Yes, but..."

"Well, I think we are finally doing something about it," rationalized Gabby, touching up her lipstick in the mirror.

"You mean you're separating?" Dianne was shocked, and she didn't hide her emotion.

"Well, no, not yet anyway, but...I've got lots of things going on, and with the road trip coming up soon, we have decided that the distance apart will do us good."

A woman appeared from one of the cubicles, obviously having heard the conversation and gave them a questionable look as she washed her hands.

"You're kidding. So Anthony is in agreement?"

"Yes, he said it himself before we left this evening."

"Okay, but you said you've got lots of things going on. What exactly do you mean?"

"I mean, I've done a lot of soul-searching these past few weeks...months, and I know in my heart that Anthony and I have come to the end of our relationship. It's sad in a way, but I figure it was to be expected."

"What on earth do you mean? I don't get it."

"I mean, Anthony and I were never really meant to be together. I was pushed into doing accountancy and working in the bank by my parents, and everything I did, I did for them, not me. The whole thing was an awful mistake."

"And you're only realizing this now?"

"No, it's been coming. I've tried to make it work over the years, but there's only so much you can do. Besides, he repulses me now. I can't even sleep with him."

"Gabby! You've kept me in the dark all this time!" Dianne's voiced raised to an uncomfortable pitch.

"Sssh! Not really, you just didn't read the signs, and I never advertised it. Anyway, I believe that it's my turn to start afresh. A new beginning and a chance to fix the mistake I made of going into the wrong career, which led to...well, which led to all this!"

"Gabby, there's something you're not telling me, I know it."

"Okay, here's how it goes. I'll keep it short because everyone is probably wondering what's going on....the Lotus Yoga Center is taking me on."

"Yes, I know, but..."

"Sssh, let me finish. The yoga teacher that I will be assisting is Mick. Mick Doherty."

"And?" Dianne was bursting with curiosity.

"Sparks have been flying between us, which worried me to begin with, but after a lot of soul-searching, I think there's something there..."

"You mean romantically?" Dianne was hopeless at being quiet and sensitive, and Gabby's news had blown her away.

"Yes."

For the first time, Dianne was silent. Words escaped her, and she could only stand in the ladies' bathroom with her mouth agape.

"I cannot believe it! No wonder you look like there's sparks flying off you."

"Well, we'll see. I'm meeting him on Saturday at the pier."

"This has happened so fast!"

"I know, and I'll fill you in on the details another time, but...do you mind if I tell Anthony that I'm coming over to your place on Saturday, to talk about the road trip?"

"I don't know, Gab, this is all a bit risky. You're still married to Anthony."

"I know. It's just a get-together, nothing else. I need to know for sure if I should take the job or if I'm just looking for a way out. Please, agree?"

"The things I do. Who would have thought we would be discussing this in the restroom in our late-thirties!"

Both women burst out laughing at the thought.

Sensing that everyone was thinking they were in the restroom for an unusually long time, Dianne made up some excuse that they were talking about what clothes to take on the trip. They all laughed knowing this was a predictable conversation, especially when Dianne was involved.

The excitement of the trip grew. Bags were being packed; the Jeep was mechanically serviced and new tires fitted, thanks to Dan's connections who also cleaned and polished it. Maps were bought as a fallback measure if the GPS failed, and snacks galore were packed in a special box. Dianne and Gabby were taking their iPads as most of the accommodation was to be organized on the road. Dianne had found a website that mapped out exactly the roads taken and all the hotels and motels along the way. This would come in very handy; they could call ahead of arriving in any given town to find accommodation.

Friday saw the last day at the bank for Gabby. A day she couldn't wait to finish, but she politely accepted all the gifts and good wishes from everyone. *Phew, that's one part of my life over with. Now for the new beginnings!* she thought to herself driving home. She hoped she had taken the right path.

On Saturday, Gabby was busying herself cleaning the house from top to bottom. She had made a few meals and put them in the freezer for Anthony. The cupboards were stocked with everything you could imagine. Casually mentioning that she was meeting Dianne to discuss the finer details of the trip, Gabby scrambled to explain when Anthony asked why they hadn't already done that.

"Well, we haven't had much time to get together. Last weekend she and Dan went away to Baja, and I was tied up, and the week has just flown – as you know."

"I suppose. Why don't you ask her over here for a change?"

"Oh, umm, well, I think Dan was dropping by, and she didn't want to miss him to wish him good luck in the game," Gabby lied through her teeth.

Anthony accepted this and went about his own business while Gabby showered, dressed and did her hair. She took a lot of trouble making sure her legs were shaved and smooth, underarms waxed, eyebrows plucked, hair washed, makeup flawless, perfume applied in all the sensual areas imaginable. She pondered the thought of what the evening could bring.

"Are you going to Dianne's place or meeting somewhere else? You're dressed to the hilt."

"Oh, umm, Dianne said something about going to a café near Dan's place, I think. Okay, better go now! See you later on. Did you want anything I can pick up on the way back?" she asked fully aware the cupboards were stocked up enough for the next three months.

"No, that's all right. Have fun planning." Anthony plonked himself in front of the TV and surfed the television channels.

"Will do." She planted a kiss on Anthony's cheek and ran out the door. The drive to Santa Monica Pier took about twenty minutes. The feelings of excitement had turned to anxiety, but now she felt at ease as she parked the car, checked her makeup, and made her way to meet Mick.

The breeze was gentle on Mick's back. The temperature was mild. Walking the promenade at Santa Monica, he contemplated the evening. He began to wonder what Gabby would be wearing, what perfume she would have on, and would her hair be up or down? Months had passed since he first saw the image of Gabby in a meditation; he knew that being with Gabby was inevitable. The fact that she was unhappily married seemed to make this meeting even more interesting, although he felt torn by the pain she would have to deal with if anything was to come of their union. It wasn't his intention to break them up. That is why waiting so long and pushing aside any feelings was so important to him. There was no doubt about it, they had been brought together. It seemed they were destined to find each other.

"Well, hello there," said Gabby spotting Mick leaning on the rail facing the beautiful water of the Pacific Ocean. He looked casual and boyishly good-looking with a tan-colored jacket over a pale blue polo shirt. His dark blue jeans fitted his slim hips well.

"Hi!" He kissed her on the cheek and noticed her outfit. "You look lovely."

"Thanks, you look great too!" she said as she breathed in the slight scent of cologne.

They walked side by side along the promenade chatting about how beautiful the weather was, how the water looked amazing, the restaurants looked tempting, the sunset taking their breath away. Shutters on the Beach looked inviting. On entering the restaurant, they were escorted promptly to a cozy table for two. As they sat down, the warmth they felt for each other enveloped them both. The warmth of Mick's hand over Gabby's made her feel so safe and happy.

"So, how have you been? You're looking really lovely."

"Thank you. I've been flat-out actually. My last day at the bank was yesterday, thank goodness!"

Mick planted a kiss on Gabby's cheek without warning.

"What was that for?"

"Happy Birthday! I thought of you all day on Thursday, and I sent you birthday wishes all day long. I hope you got them!"

"Oh, thank you." Gabby blushed, "Yes, I think I got them."

Mick reached into his pocket and pulled out a black velvet pouch. He handed it to Gabby.

"This is for you. I wanted to give it to you on Wednesday night, but after the class was canceled, I thought tonight would be the best time. Hope you like it!"

"You shouldn't have!" said an excited Gabby kissing Mick on the cheek and opening the pouch. "Oh Mick! It's beautiful! You really shouldn't have gone to so much expense and trouble."

"Gabby, I wanted to buy you something that you could take on your trip so you would know that I care for you. It's an exciting time, and I thought the crystals complement you."

"They are so beautiful, Mick."

Gabby put the earrings on, and Mick helped her with the chain and pendant.

"They complement your hair color and features, Gabby."

"What type of crystals are they?"

"It's called citrine. It will help give clarity of thought, open the mind to new thoughts, protect from negative energy, and increase self-esteem. It's also known as a lucky stone, not to mention abundance."

"Sounds perfect. Thank you so much!"

She kissed Mick, this time on the lips. Her heart beat fast as this was a bold step for her to make, but her heart felt right about it.

They ordered a seafood platter to share. Talking about the yoga center monopolized the evening's conversation, which led to the position that Gabby was taking.

"I hope I will be of some help to you at the center," said Gabby, showing a little nervousness.

Mick detected this and placed his hand on hers.

"You'll be fine. I know you can do it, and if you ever feel like you are over your head, just let me know. No worries, okay?" He was very kind and calm as he spoke.

Gabby had decided on the way to Santa Monica that she would be open and honest about her marriage.

The gift from Mick, and now his hand on hers, made her feel a little self-conscious. It seemed she was floating in an act of feeling free and yet still so attached to her current life.

"Thanks, it's a big step for me to change careers and so soon after making the decision."

"Yes, some big decisions, definitely."

It was clear that the evening had come to an appropriate time to leave the restaurant.

"It's such a clear night," said Gabby, stepping out onto the boardwalk, where many people were enjoying the evening.

"It is. Let's go for a little walk," suggested Mick.

"That would be nice."

He held out his hand, and she gladly took it. It felt warm and inviting just like him, she thought.

Walking along the boardwalk, the sound of the people on the Ferris wheel at the pier became part of the background noise.

"Are you okay?" asked Mick.

"Yes, I am. I've had such a lovely time with you."

"But? I can feel a 'but' coming."

"No, no, sorry. I'm just unsure of what I'm doing. What I mean is, I spent a lot of time soul-searching in the last few weeks, and I listened to what I felt my heart was guiding me to do. Now that I'm here with you, in this gorgeous setting, and everything seems so perfect, I find I'm being so shy and coy about everything. It's very annoying."

"It's just your ego mind. A completely natural thing to happen, given that you are in the middle of a very important time of your life."

He led her down the boardwalk as they looked in on all the other restaurants and cafés. The atmosphere here always had a magical feel. Silence between them felt comfortable and not awkward at all.

"You know, I do understand your situation. It's all right to feel unsure. That's why I wanted to get together with you tonight, before you head off on your trip. I wanted you to know how I feel, but under no circumstance would you *have* to do anything. I'm not like that at all. In fact, I respect you so much that if you didn't want to see me again, I would still respect you for making that choice. Truly, this is how I feel."

He stopped walking and faced Gabby. As he lifted a stray hair of hers away from her eye, his expression deepened. "I wanted to tell you this when we had coffee the other day...but I lost my nerve."

"Oh, sounds very serious. Please, tell me now," said Gabby, as her heart sank. She expected him to tell her something had come between her getting the job.

"Well, I wouldn't say serious in that way – but definitely important...You see, Gabby, it was no coincidence that you and I connected. I have seen you many times unexpectedly in my meditations for over a year. It baffled me for so long, but then I became used to it, and I actually looked forward to it! You see, we always became a couple, together. Every meditation I did was different, but that was the one theme each time."

He shifted from one leg to the other, gazing back toward the ocean and then to Gabby, trying to read her emotions.

"Really? How do you know it was me? We didn't know each other until fairly recently," she added, quite intrigued by this suggestion.

"I didn't know it was you, I just knew what *that* woman looked like in each meditation. It was more a feeling than anything else. Then one day, you walked into the yoga center when I was at reception. I've never felt that way before. You looked carefree, beautiful, full of energy, but it was that same feeling that I got from the meditations. I knew you were the same woman. My heart sang!"

Gabby listened intently. What she was hearing felt foreign, like she had missed something very important or mis-interpreted a very important fact.

She too, looked to the ocean for answers. What Mick said sounded strange, yet she felt a very similar feeling, she thought. It reminded her of the strong sensation when she attended the yoga workshop, before they met for coffee.

"You were in many of my yoga classes, and I was so drawn to you. I never had the nerve to approach you. Plus, you were always in a rush to leave at the end of the session."

"I'm lost for words, Mick," said Gabby.

That's okay, I understand how this may sound odd to you. You probably think I'm some kind of weirdo," he joked, with a halfhearted laugh.

"No, I don't..."

"I don't want to scare you off or put pressure on you either. I just felt it was the right time to share this."

Gabby turned to Mick. His eyes so kind and gentle. His face was boyishly good-looking, with *that* hair that swept across his forehead. She felt like running her fingers through it, touching his face, tracing his lips with her fingertips. Her whole being felt like being one with him. As she stood and looked into his eyes, she felt it again. The feeling that she experienced when she focused on the present and felt what her heart truly desired. It was Mick. A bright and warm space was there in her heart, just for Mick.

"What was that for?" he said as she kissed him tenderly on the lips.

"It's for being you. Thank you for all that you said. I appreciate you being honest, and I too respect you for giving me that freedom."

"Does that mean you will take the job?" he winked.

"It does. It means that I am 100 percent committed to the job and lots of other things as well." She winked back, this time the shyness not so prevalent.

"I'm liking what I'm hearing. Shall we continue walking?"

"Sure, I'd love to, but maybe we should turn around. I think we've come to the end of the boardwalk now."

"Well, if you're up for it, I just live about 200 yards that way." He pointed toward the road, away from the beach.

"Really? That's close."

"It is. I took a leisurely walk down to the promenade." He kept his expression relaxed and waited for Gabby's response.

Gabby looked to the dark sea rolling in. The bright Ferris wheel in the distance and the sounds of people enjoying themselves still. As if the activity around her would tell her what to do, or at least she could will it to advise her.

"Okay, let's go," she said finally.

They walked hand in hand to Mick's apartment. Gabby wasn't sure what to expect. She just kept on reminding herself of the heartfelt feelings that leaped into her awareness whenever she focused on her heart center. It felt right to be with him.

As Mick opened the door to his apartment, still holding Gabby's hand, her free hand found its way up to the chain and pendant, then fingering the earrings before relaxing down by her side.

Whatever happened from this point on was her choice. She made this contract with herself and was fully aware of the consequences. As she entered the apartment alongside Mick, noticing the corner table lamps left on, making it look very inviting and cozy, nothing could have swayed her away from here.

Chapter 7

Say You Want a Resolution

In Miami...

"Hi, Virginia," said Hamish timidly.

"Hello," Virginia replied, dreading this phone call. She sunk further into her office chair and cupped her hand over her mouth and the phone.

"I just wanted to see how you were doing."

"I'm fine!"

"And how are the babies doing?"

"They are fine, Hamish." She peeked over the partition that divided her office space from the other journalist and discovered that the desk was empty.

"Do you have an obstetrician appointment soon?"

"Yes."

"When is it?"

"Actually, it's this afternoon if you must know..."

"Would you like me to come with you?"

"You're kidding, aren't you? What's the point, Hamish? Is there really any point?"

"Ginny, I know this must be very upsetting for you. I am so sorry. Really sorry that you found out."

"What do you mean...so if I hadn't found out, would you have been sneaking around behind my back anyway? You disgusting bastard! You would have pretended everything was rosy, meanwhile you would be sleeping with Monique! How could you even have the nerve to call me! You really disgust me – I do not want to talk to you. And don't show up at the doctor's because I will announce to everyone there what a lying, cheating, disgusting creature you are and tell them everything!"

"Okay, okay. It's just...can we meet up afterwards, please?"

"What on earth for?"

"I want to talk to you."

"No, Hamish."

"Please."

"No."

With that said, Virginia hung up the telephone and tried to carry on with a story she was working on for an upcoming Sunday edition of the Miami Herald on bringing the outdoors indoors. Her mind was definitely not focused, and she couldn't stop thinking about the phone call. *So what if he wanted to come with me to the obstetrician's? That doesn't mean anything,* she reasoned with herself. *Should I go? Maybe I should just meet him, and then that's it. No. I can't, how will I face him? I'm a mess, I look huge, and he'll probably compare me to the bitch! No, I won't go!*

Virginia wrestled with the thoughts running through her head. It wasn't easy to concentrate anymore.

Her desk phone buzzed and startled her out of the dilemma. It was Marni, her managing editor. "Virginia, how's the feature coming along?"

Apart from being Virginia's manager, she was also her mentor and friend. Marni was in her late forties, had short, brown hair – always combed perfectly into place – with clear-rimmed glasses and wore skirt suits and heels. She had experienced everything from the bottom of the ladder up. Personally and professionally, Marni had a world of experience and always kept her door open to everyone, especially Virginia.

"Can I come in for a minute, please?" said Virginia.

"Sure, come in."

Virginia was at her office in seconds.

Marni gestured to Virginia to take a seat. "How are you?"

"I'm fine, thanks," said Virginia unconvincingly.

"Really? You look a bit pale," remarked Marni.

"Well, I'm a bit tired. This whole situation has got me feeling like I'm never going to be able to cope! I just had a call from Hamish, and he wants to come to the obstetrician's appointment this afternoon! How could he even think that I would want him there, after what he's done?"

"Do you think he's trying to apologize and work things through?"

"I don't know, Marni. I feel sick at the thought of even seeing him."

"You know what I think? Tell me to shut up if you want..."

"No, go ahead. Tell me what you think."

Marni stood up from behind her desk, walked to the door, and closed it. Her expression was one of scheming and her movements quick. She was enthused by what she was about to say.

"Well, I think that this whole fling with what's-her-name..."

"Monique," added Virginia.

"Yes, this whole fling with Monique is just that. A fling. A fly-by-night, wham bam thank you ma'am kind of fling. In fact, I bet you, Miss Monique got sick of being the *other woman* and has left him stranded."

"What makes you think that?"

"Well, because I know Hamish, and I know how the two of you really love each other and how much both of you wanted to have children. I think that the affair was just a lot of stress relief, not that I condone his behavior! That is disgusting, let me just clarify that, but I really do think that it was a mistake, one that he will regret for the rest of his life. Nevertheless, I think that it was a stupid, idiotic mistake, and I bet he is regretting it so much. I would bet the affair has fizzled out already."

"Yes, that's probably why he wanted to see me."

"And that's why you need to put your pride aside and think of your babies first and foremost, and then think of the lives you will be bringing into this world. Sure, Hamish screwed up, but he is the father of the babies and your husband, and you know he wanted these babies as much as you do. Just think about it..."

"Yes, I guess you've got a point, but–"

"No buts, Virginia. I am on your side here, but don't forget I've had a lot more experience than you. When Robert left me for that witchy woman, Suzanne what's-her-name, I thought it was the end of the world. Sean was only five years old then. He really sensed the tension between Robert and me. It was about six months after that I pulled myself together and put Sean first and foremost in my mind. I began a different thought process where everything I did, I would put Sean first and, sure enough, things seemed to get brighter and more positive because I was doing everything for him, the most important person to me. It was after that realization that Robert saw me in a different light. He saw the more independent Marni, the creative Marni, the Marni that he fell in love with, and that's when our relationship really deepened. Having lived apart, but in unison with each other for Sean's sake, we became really deeply enriched by the togetherness we shared. When we got back together, the marriage we had was so much better in all kinds of ways. Look, all I'm saying is that Hamish and you deserve to give this marriage another go."

Virginia was in deep contemplation taking in Marni's words because she knew in her heart that this was true.

"Now, I know you've got the appointment, but why don't you just meet him afterwards and then see how things go? Phone me after, if you need a sounding board. I'm always here for you."

"Okay. Thanks, Marni," said Virginia, very relieved. "Oh, and I'm nearly finished the feature. I've just got to finalize the stockists and get some photos."

"Great, I'm looking forward to seeing it. Now go! Call him!"

"Okay, okay...Thanks again."

Later that afternoon...

Virginia spent most of the day processing what Marni had said. She didn't feel she was ready to phone Hamish straight away, but she would definitely do it soon.

Waiting patiently in the waiting room, she really didn't want to do this by herself. This was what her life was going to be like from now on. It left her feeling empty and alone. Just as the receptionist called her name out, the elevator door opened and out walked Hamish. A feeling of panic, and at the same time relief, overcame her.

"What are you doing here?" questioned Virginia, annoyed at Hamish's blatant disregard for her wishes. She wasn't ready for this, now, in this moment.

"Well, I know you said you didn't want me here, but I couldn't let the appointment go without trying to be a part of it." Hamish was forlorn. His expression showed deep concern and anguish.

"You shouldn't have come, Hamish. I'm not ready for it yet."

Dr Van der Rych was showing his face outside the door as if to say 'hurry up', and so in the rush of the moment, both Hamish and Virginia walked in and sat down. Both of them were aware of the speedy way in which the obstetrician's visit would go.

The uneasiness was felt in the air and detected by the doctor. His first question to Virginia was loaded, to say the least.

"How have you been, Virginia?"

"Good, thanks, doctor," lied Virginia through her teeth. Her hands were knotting in and out of each other.

This was not going as it usually did. Dr Van der Rych knew his patients well, and he knew that Virginia McDonald was a very relaxed, organized person and, whenever she had an appointment, would be quick to take out her very long list of questions to ask so that she didn't forget anything.

Sensing the tension, he began by motioning to Virginia to take herself over to the examination table. While his wife carefully positioned herself on the uncomfortable examination bed, Hamish swiftly followed and sat next to the monitor.

"So, let's see what these little ones are up to today," said Dr Van der Rych cautiously.

As he put a blob of ultrasound gel on Virginia's swollen abdomen and placed the ultrasound pad over the top of it, the cold sensation made Virginia shiver.

Straight away the two little bodies showed up on the overhead monitor. It was at times like this that Virginia liked to hold Hamish's hand as they watched their two babies playing inside of her. The baby on the right always seemed to be sucking a thumb. The one on the left appeared more placid, happy to just chill out and go with the flow. Hamish and Virginia had decided early on in the pregnancy that they would wait to find out the sex of their twins, although Virginia had a sneaking suspicion she knew.

As the monitor showed the little hands and feet, the baby on the right seemed to be almost trying to face them so that they could get a better look.

Virginia kept her thoughts to herself, but she couldn't help but think that he or she looked like Hamish, in a fuzzy, blurry sort of way.

Forgetting their current situation for a minute, they both relaxed and asked questions as though they had nothing at all worrying either one of them.

"Doctor, I've been getting a sharp pain quite low down whenever I take a longish walk. Is this something I should worry about, or is it normal?"

"Really?" interjected Hamish showing concern for Virginia and their twins.

Dr Van der Rych was in a quandary about the unusual behavior of his patient, so he took the next step to ensure everything was all right.

"Virginia, it is very important you don't stress yourself too much. By that I mean, try not to get yourself into situations where you feel that you can't control your stress levels, anxiety, and any situation that pushes you physically. It is fine to exercise, beneficial actually, but overexertion could tire you out unnecessarily, and that is when you put yourself and the babies at risk."

"Doctor," Virginia began, stumbling over her words and worried about the situation, "Hamish and I are having some difficulties."

"I see," said Dr Van der Rych. "I did sense there was some tension. Look, from where I stand, the two of you have been blissfully happy, and you have been blessed with two healthy babies. The situation is in your hands to smooth out any problems and prepare yourselves for the most magnificent event in your lives. I suggest you do everything and anything it takes to settle any difficulties because, once these babies are born, your lives will never be the same, and I mean this in a good way. A busy way, but a good way. Babies change the dynamics of a marriage. They change everything, and all that was once an organized, neat, quiet household will be a pleasantly busy and chirpy little family nest."

Both Virginia and Hamish were sitting in silence as they absorbed the words coming from the doctor.

"Thank you, doctor," said Virginia. Wiping the gel from her abdomen with a tissue the doctor had given her, she clumsily sat up.

"Let me help you," offered Hamish.

Slipping on her shoes, she looked into Hamish's eyes. Eyes she hadn't been able to face until just now. There was softness in them. She longed to trust him again, but it was too late. Or was it? She had been betrayed, and nothing could turn back the clock.

Leaving the obstetrician's office was awkward, to say the least. Virginia couldn't face another uncomfortable situation with Hamish, so she thought of something to excuse herself from having to have a coffee with him. "Marni wanted me to come back to the office to finish off a piece due tomorrow, so I'll see you later."

Hamish could see the nervousness and the obvious mistrust she felt toward him, and this really made his heart sink. *How could I have done such a stupid thing and ruin the trust forever*, he asked himself.

All he could manage was, "I understand."

"Okay, bye then." Virginia half raised her hand in a wave and turned to walk to her car.

"Hang on, Ginny," called out Hamish. "I know I've probably wrecked everything we had, but I really am sorry. It was so stupid of me, I...I just don't know why I did it. Please, please, find it in your heart to forgive me. I will do anything, anything at all, to make it up to you," he begged.

This pulled at Virginia's heartstrings so strongly. The hatred she felt toward him, yet the love she still yearned to feel, were tearing her in two. His face looked drawn and sallow, like he hadn't slept, and his mouth quivered as he spoke.

Not knowing what to say and how to react, she just shrugged her shoulders and made a gesture to the effect of saying, "Well, you made your bed. Now lie in it." She turned her body toward her car, desperate to climb into its safety.

"Ginny, please listen to me. I mean it when I say I'm sorry. I can't expect you to just forget everything that happened, but I beg of you, please give me another chance." He stared down at the ground, his face looking tortured. "I've stopped seeing her. I promise...I will do whatever it takes. I've looked into some couple counseling sessions and made an appointment on Monday afternoon. Please, please could you think about coming with me?"

"I don't know, Hamish, I'm so stressed out," she managed. "Plus, I think it's fairly clear exactly who needs the counseling!"

"This is exactly why I want to start counseling straight away. You shouldn't be having this stress, not at this stage of the pregnancy, not ever!"

"Well, Hamish, you should have thought about that sooner, shouldn't you! Jeez!" she fumed. Now Virginia was angry. The range of emotions she experienced was uncontrolled, to say the least.

"What do you say?" he persisted, his eyes pleading with her.

Virginia replayed in her mind what Marni and the doctor had said, and she knew in her heart that this would be the right thing to do. She thought of her two babies and how she would cope. She could see and hear the sincerity of his plea.

"Okay, I'll come. What is the address? What time exactly?"

"Thank you, my darling." He kissed her tenderly on the cheek. A spark of hope lit his eyes now as they crinkled up at the corners, and a tear slowly escaped from one, down his cheek.

"It is on Ambrose Street, Dr Philip Green. I'll text you the exact address. The details are on the business card in the car."

"See you then." Virginia wanted to burst, but kept her cool.

"Bye, Ginny – I love you."

Turning to face her car, she held it together as it took a momentous effort to unlock the door and get inside. Then she let out a huge sigh before bursting into tears.

Chapter 8

Phoenix, Here We Come

Gabby was awake before her alarm sounded at 4 a.m. Finally, the day had come to begin her journey to Miami. As she lay in bed, she realized this trip wasn't just a trip to Miami, this was a pivotal process of her life journey. From this point onward, her life as she knew it would never be the same.

"Don't forget to call and let me know how you are," said Anthony, looking rather anxious in his robe and slippers.

"We will. Have a peaceful time without me. Bye, now," waved Gabby as she slowly reversed down their driveway.

The sun hadn't quite risen and the streets were empty in the surrounding suburbs.

"I can't believe we're finally leaving! It feels like we've been planning this trip for about six months!" said Dianne excitedly.

"I know what you mean!" agreed Gabby as she traced her fingers along the necklace Mick had given her.

Their windows were down, letting in the fresh morning air. It was 5 a.m., and the Monday morning traffic heading out of Los Angeles was manageable. Any later and the girls would find themselves in sheer gridlock.

"It's funny," said Dianne out of the blue.

"What is?"

"Well, we're going to drive across the country to help Virginia out because her husband cheated on her and she's pregnant with twins, and it's taken us so long to get organized that they're actually getting back together. It's funny, don't you think?"

"I know what you mean, but things are still shaky, and Virginia is still shaken up by it. I am so glad things are looking a bit more positive than they were," added Gabby.

"Yep. It is so good that she's agreed to Hamish's suggestion of counseling. She's so excited and really wants to keep in contact right throughout the trip. I think she asked me about five times whether we'll phone, text, email or Facebook her!"

"She said the same thing to me. I think we had better keep her in the loop," laughed Gabby.

"I'm so ready for some excitement, Gab. With all the juggling of the Dodgers' cheerleading team and the Starlets, I am so ready to get out of California!"

"You *are* excited, aren't you?"

"Sure am! And you know what? Nothing, I repeat nothing, is going to stop me from enjoying myself."

Dianne twirled her long, blonde hair and brought it all around to one side of her face. She continued to twirl and twist it as they traveled the outskirts of Los Angeles.

"So, we're going down I-10, right?" asked Gabby, wanting some reassurance.

"Yes, I'll turn my iPad on and head to the Maps. There should be our route already programmed in."

"I'm impressed. You did some preparation."

"Well, we did spend Saturday night discussing the finer details, didn't we?" Dianne teased.

"Oh, yes. I nearly forgot."

"How was your date with Mick?"

"It wasn't a date! It was a catch-up. It was very, very nice," said Gabby with a slight smirk.

"Well, come on now, I've been waiting to hear about this 'sensitive' yoga teacher since you told me about him in the restaurant the other week!"

"There's nothing to tell, really. We had a nice meal, walked along the boardwalk and...not much else," insisted Gabby, trying to change the subject.

"Ooh, you'll keep, Gabby Drayton! We've got a whole month for you to tell me the juicy details of your sordid affair!"

Gabby looked at her friend and sighed, quietly wanting to tell her everything, but knowing they had the whole trip in front of them to discuss all the details. She turned her attention to the road and happily drove on.

The morning radio show hosts provided so many laughs with the competitions and general chat that the girls felt content with just listening, letting the entertainment take over.

As they traveled through San Bernardino Valley, Dianne was gazing out the window being melodramatic about how Dan had introduced her to his family during the week and how she felt a bit awkward with them.

"They're a bit, how shall I say it...simple, with no finesse, no class. That's it, they're simple. I don't mean it in a backward kind of way, but it's just things I take for granted with Mom and Dad."

"Like what?"

"Well, they're not polished, they don't have any class. I can't pinpoint it, but every so often they will say something, and I'll think how strange that is. His mom is the worst. She has a gripe over everyone, even in her own family. Makes me wonder what she says about me."

"Well, they couldn't be worse than Anthony's parents. His mom is such a bitch, but his dad's okay. I think it's by association that I don't rate him."

"You're too funny! By association? So just because he's married to her, he automatically becomes the enemy?"

"Of course!"

"You know, I can't help thinking if I ended up marrying Dan, how the hell would I get on with his family? Seriously, once you're married, that's it, isn't it. You're stuck with them."

"You're telling me! I've had to put up with Anthony's parents for the last few years. I dread when the phone rings thinking it's going to be one of them."

"Jeez, Gabby, I didn't realize you felt that way. You shouldn't be living like that. What does Anthony think about it?"

Gabby reached over to the volume dial and turned the radio down a touch.

"He doesn't see anything wrong with how his mom and dad are. Typical guy."

It was clear that the focus was now on deep relationship issues. With no one but themselves in the car, not a restriction in place, the conversation grew serious. With the windows up, air-conditioning on, and now music softly playing in the background, the hint of David Bowie's "Changes" struck a chord, which was uncannily appropriate for the conversation at hand.

"So, what do you do in a situation like that? I mean, it's not like you can totally ignore that he has a family. If he's neglecting how you feel, do you go on like that forever?"

"Well, I don't plan to."

Dianne practically spun around in her seat, "What do you mean?"

"Well, I haven't felt like I'm in the marriage for months now, actually more like a year or so. Nobody's noticed, but I haven't worn my rings for months." She lifted her left hand up off the steering wheel, clearly bare of any rings.

"I can't believe I missed that!"

"Yeah, people take it for granted. I have just gone through the motions, and really, the thought of going on this trip has kept me going lately...and now the prospect of a new career and Mick, of course!" said Gabby with a smile.

"I knew it! You have been cool as a cucumber all this time! So, tell me what's happening. I'm dying to know!" Dianne was so eager to hear all the details. She positioned herself giving Gabby all her attention.

"Calm down. I feel like a teenager all of a sudden," said Gabby, laughing. "Well, as you know, you and I got together to go over the trip details, remember?" She winked at Dianne.

"Yes, yes. So what happened? And who gave you the necklace and earrings? Don't tell me..."

"Yes, it was Mick, for my birthday." Gabby brought her hand up to her chain and earrings.

"Oh my...they are beautiful. I did notice them this morning, but with all the excitement forgot to mention anything. Didn't Anthony notice?"

"No, he didn't. He was probably half asleep. Well, after the dinner, we walked along the boardwalk, and he invited me back to his apartment."

"Oh, oh. Something tells me my romance novel is about to be put to shame!" beamed Dianne, her smile gleaming from ear to ear.

"You are so funny! Anyway, we walked back to his place, which is about two blocks away, and it was just like the other time. The energy between us was amazing. When we got inside the apartment, neither of us said anything. We just took off our clothes and made love. It was beautiful."

"What, just like that! Oh. My. God! I don't believe it! You, Gabby Drayton, bank accountant, married to Anthony Drayton, bank manager, are sleeping with dream-babe Mick?" Dianne didn't hold anything back. Like a teenager, she drooled at this information and craved some more.

"Yep!" Gabby proudly said, purposely ignoring the 'married to Anthony' remark.

"Well, I don't know what to say!"

"Don't say anything! Hold that thought." Gabby spotted a lone gas station as they veered onto the off-ramp from the I-10, and drove through the outskirts of Palm Springs. "I think I'll stop here to top up with gas rather than leave it too long, okay?"

"We've only been driving for a couple of hours! But, it's fine by me. I think I need to get some fresh air after that little humdinger!" Dianne was full of made-up words when she didn't know what to say.

While Gabby topped up with gas, Dianne walked into the shop and got the key for the restrooms. As usual, she looked amazing in her signature white attire. White denim cut-off shorts, showing off her tanned and toned legs; white off-the-shoulder clingy top, showing off her tanned shoulders and shimmering white-gold chain and earrings. Her gorgeous, long, blond hair, held back by sunglasses propped on top of her head, was cascading down her back.

The shop was small, so seeing two tattooed, unsavory-looking men scouring the pages of a girly magazine felt a bit claustrophobic. Dianne paid for some chewing gum and a packet of soy crisps while asking the attendant where the restrooms were. Out of the corner of her eye, she saw the two guys watching her. Not taking much notice, she walked toward the door when the taller of the two made a comment asking where she was heading to.

"First stop, the restroom, second stop ... well, you know, just around." Dianne almost blurted out their destination, but quickly changed her tune when she felt their gaze was somewhat creepy.

Meanwhile, Gabby had filled the car up with gas and headed toward the shop to pay.

The attendant was preoccupied looking out of the window toward the rear of the block when Gabby attempted to get his attention.

"Excuse me, I'd just like to pay for the gas, please."

Expecting service straight away, being the only customer, Gabby thought the attendant was being plain rude by ignoring her presence at the counter.

She waited patiently for what seemed like about five minutes. The attendant was just not moving his focus. Gabby became impatient and made her way over to the window.

"Excuse me!"

"Is that your friend, ma'am?" The bald, overweight man turned around with a concerned look etched on his face.

Gabby couldn't see Dianne from where she was, but she assumed he was talking about her.

"If she has long, blond hair, dressed in white, then yes, she's my friend. Where did she go?"

"Ma'am, I'd watch out if I were you."

He gestured in the direction of the restrooms, somewhere toward the back of the building.

"Those two may have taken a liking to your friend, ma'am."

Gabby's heart palpitated at the thought of the warning. She still hadn't had the chance to pay for the gas.

"Can I please pay for this now?" she said in an urgent tone.

Slapping a fifty dollar bill down on the counter, she ran out the door. The restrooms were located adjoining the main building. Her heart was thumping as she ran. The door was still closed, and from the corner of her eye, she saw the two figures getting into their utility. Her intuition was telling her one thing, that those guys were up to no good, but her head was telling her to back away. Something triggered her to reach into her back pocket for her mobile phone. In one instant, she took a photo of the back of the utility as it sped out onto the road.

Walking a few steps back to the restrooms, she could hear Dianne whispering, "Gabby?'

"Yes, I'm here. Are you all right?"

"Yes, yes, I'm fine, but is the coast clear? Can I come out?"

Dianne finally opened the door, relief etched on her face.

"What on earth was that about? I came in here, and then all I could hear was someone standing out near the door, and I just knew it was those dropkicks. I didn't know what to do. Thank goodness you came when you did. There's only so much shuffling noises you can make to make it sound like you're actually doing something!"

"I didn't like the look of those guys, Di. Did you talk to them at all?"

"No way! They asked me where I was heading, and I just said, first stop restroom, second stop–"

Gabby interrupted, "Tell me you didn't say where we were heading!"

"No, I didn't. I was just fairly vague."

"I really hope you didn't say anything, Di. Something didn't sit well with me, so I took a picture of their car with the license plate as they drove out."

"Boy, you're really scaring me, Gabby. Let's get out of here!"

"Yeah, I'm getting the shivers too."

Relieved to be back in the safety of their car, Dianne remotely locked all the doors, started the car and drove off, turning onto the I-10 on-ramp and back on track.

The silence that prevailed after stopping at the gas station ended when Dianne turned up the volume of the music. The Rolling Stones sang "Start Me Up". She had her foot on the gas pedal like she was a woman possessed. Realizing her speed, she backed off the pedal and glanced over at Gabby, who was gazing out at the desert scenery.

Gabby was still thinking about the situation at the gas station and how those guys made her feel. She just couldn't pinpoint what it was about them.

"What's up?" asked Dianne turning down the volume of the music.

"You're probably going to think I'm over-reacting, but my gut instinct is usually pretty spot-on."

"What do you mean?"

"I think there's something serious going on with those guys."

"What makes you say that? I mean, beside the fact that they look like criminals," half joked Dianne.

"I'm sure I read about two drug carriers in Miami who raped a woman, killed her husband, and held their teenage daughter hostage for drug money. The husband had some inside knowledge of the dealers' whereabouts, and they framed him."

"Come on, Gabby, Miami is drug central. That wouldn't be anything out of the ordinary, and why would those guys be in a gas station near Palm Springs?"

"I don't know, but I'm going to try and find that article. Can you stop the car so I can get my iPad out of the bag in the back, please?"

"Sure. There's a pullout up ahead."

Gabby was determined to search for the article. She opened the trunk and saw that the bags had toppled over each other. Straightening the bags up, she pulled out her iPad, and then something made her look into the trunk again. It looked different. She did a mental checklist of all the bags she knew they had, but she couldn't pinpoint what was missing, or what was different. Closing the lid, she made her way to her seat in the front.

"Get it?"

"Got it. I'll just turn it on, and you can keep driving."

"So, looks like we're about three hours away from Phoenix. Can you look up the accommodation website too, please? I'm dying to get out of the car and relax, take a bath, and change clothes. Just looking at the desert makes me feel dusty and dirty!"

Dianne's mobile phone rang. Noticing the caller ID was Virginia, she answered it and put it on speaker.

"How are you, missy?'

"Hi! I hadn't heard from you guys, and I knew you'd be driving now. How's it going so far?" asked Virginia.

"Good so far. Although, some suspicious-looking guys we bumped into have given us the creeps. They looked really shifty."

"Di!" said Gabby, wishing she hadn't told Virginia, unnecessarily worrying her.

"What? You're kidding! What happened?" questioned Virginia.

Gabby piped up. "How are you, Ginny?"

"I'm really good, thanks. What's this about shifty, suspicious guys?"

"Nothing really. We just stopped for gas near Palm Springs, and these two, shall we say, awful, suspicious-looking men followed Dianne to the restroom, and there was something fishy about the way they acted."

"Oh! So nothing happened then? You're both okay?"

"Yes, we're fine, thanks."

"So has it been fun? Where are you now? I really wish I could be traveling with you guys. But then, what would you be coming to Florida for?"

"That's right! We're really looking forward to seeing you."

"Me too! Oh, the babies are doing just fine, I have to say. I look like Ten Tonne Tess now. Can't wait 'til I finish work. My ankles are swollen too, and they look disgusting, but there's still a lot of time to go."

"So, is everything still going okay with Hamish?" inquired Dianne, as ever subtle as a sledgehammer.

"Yeah. He's being quite sweet and understanding. He really feels so bad and guilty about the affair. The counseling we've been going to has helped both of us, I think."

"That's excellent, Gin. So happy for you."

"Thanks. Listen, keep in touch, okay? Send me text messages, and let me know where you're staying."

"Thanks for calling, Gin. Take care. See you soon!"

"Just so you know, we've just passed Blythe, and we'll be in Arizona very soon," piped up Gabby.

"Okay. Bye, guys. Travel safe."

"Later..."

As soon as she had hung up, Dianne's phone rang again. The caller ID was Dan. She was happy to see his name and answered straight away.

"Hello, sexy," chirped Dianne.

"Hey, how you doing?"

"Great, thanks. I'm just driving at the moment, but you're on speaker, so it's okay. We've had the music blaring, there's heaps of desert and cactuses out here, and Gabby and I are reliving our school days with our chit-chat. So how have you been? I've missed you."

"I've missed you too, babe. At training last night, coach reckoned he could tell I was pining for you because my speed was ten miles off the usual."

"Aww, that's so cute!"

"Not too cute where I'm concerned. I had to work extra hard for the rest of the session."

"Oh, you'll be fine, babe. I'm only a phone call away. We'll be in Arizona soon and will stay in Phoenix somewhere. Do you want me to call you when we get in? It might be late, though."

"Definitely, babe. Even if it's late, just let me know. I'll be waiting."

"Cool, hon. I'll see what time it is, and if it's too late I'll text you."

"Sounds good. Just going to get something to eat now. You take care, okay?"

"Okay, baby. Thanks for calling. Love you."

"Love you too. Bye, my sweet."

Gabby gave Dianne a look, making fun of the two love-birds.

"I bet, if it was Mick, you'd be all sweet with him!"

Gabby thought for a second and said, "Yeah, probably!"

The girls happily enjoyed the next few miles feeling like they were still in their twenties and traveling the world. Besides cactuses and the odd roadkill, there was not much in the way of interesting things to look at. Finally, a bright blue sign with a star read, 'Welcome to Arizona, The Grand Canyon State'.

"Yeah!" screeched Dianne.

"I second that. I'm a bit over being in the car for now. Shouldn't be too long now for Phoenix."

Gabby sat cross-legged with her feet up on the seat, browsing her iPad and chewing on some peppermint candy. She sighed and began a conversation about Mick. Dianne teased her and reminded her that she was still married. Not to dampen her spirits, but to keep in mind that Anthony would be waiting for her, and she would have to break the bubble of marriage sooner or later. The dry, desolate scenery was conducive to her mood. Her mind flitted from life with Anthony and then to Mick. The dinner date they went on was still fresh in her mind, and a sense of excitement filled her whenever she thought of him.

Sensing Gabby's melancholy, Dianne brought up the subject which was most likely on Gabby's mind.

"I wonder what Anthony's up to."

"Did you have to bring up his name? I don't want to think about him. Besides, he himself thought we needed a bit of distance."

"Yeah, distance...not pressing the delete button completely!"

"Yes, yes, I know," shrugged Gabby in disgust at the thought as she browsed her favorites on the iPad.

She regularly browsed the many newspapers in the country ever since Virginia had started reporting after university, and she still kept an eye out from time to time. Skipping her usual *LA Times* and *New York Times*, she clicked on the *Miami Herald*.

Scouring the first three pages which had the Highlights, Breaking News, and Community News, she then spotted the article titled, "Escapees Bound for LA, Drug Smugglers Origin Miami."

Clicking on the link, she read the article intently. Taking in the details of the story, the description of the escapees and the crimes committed, she noticed there were mugshots of the two men, as well.

"I don't know how you don't feel sick reading in the car," remarked Dianne noticing Gabby was so engrossed in whatever she was reading. "I would feel so off even reading a paragraph while the car was moving."

Gabby totally ignored or didn't hear what Dianne said.

"Listen to this, Di. This is the article I told you about. 'Escapees Bound for LA, Drug Smugglers Origin Miami' is the title. I'm sure these are the guys we saw. It says, 'A recent escape from a Miami prison by two drug smugglers sentenced to 25 years has sparked a nationwide search. The two men, Garth Mahoney, 27, and Derek Driscoll, 28, sentenced for drug trafficking heroin and cocaine from Los Angeles to Miami in April were reported missing at 6 a.m. local time. Los Angeles detectives uncovered a multimillion dollar scheme in which high-profile night club owners in New Orleans and Miami were taken into custody for orchestrating the smuggling of over 500 kg of heroin and cocaine. Two business owners of local nightclubs have been questioned in conjunction with the racket. The two men in question are believed to be armed and dangerous. The suspects are of Caucasian appearance, between 5'10" and 6 foot tall, of medium build. Garth Mahoney has a tattoo of a red star behind his left ear and Derek Driscoll has tattoos of eagles the length of his right arm. Both men have sandy brown, medium-length hair. If anyone has any information regarding the whereabouts of the two men, please call Crime Stoppers at 555-67487 or your local police station.'"

"Couldn't be...could it?" questioned Dianne, unbelieving.

"I'm telling you, there was something about them that didn't sit well. It wasn't just the fact that they looked rough. I'm fairly sure I saw a tattoo on one of them. The look in their eyes was evil. I could tell even from where I stood. I can picture them now, especially the taller one. He looked at me as he walked to their car. Oh, my God, the car! I took a picture of their car with my phone just as they were pulling out of the driveway of the gas station."

Gabby frantically pulled out her iPhone and searched for the picture. There it was, the back of a white utility, although slightly blurred from her hurry to take the picture inconspicuously, with the registration plate reasonably visible.

"Look, Gabby, I highly doubt it. Didn't that article say they broke out of a prison in Miami? Surely, how would they get to Palm Springs? When was the article written?"

"It was about a week ago."

"Well, they would be long gone by now. We're almost in Phoenix now, they were probably heading to LA."

"You may be right. Hey, I better see what accommodation we can stay at." The conversation took a 360 degree turn. Di was relieved at the distraction, although the thought of being trapped in that restroom, with escaped criminals outside, unnerved her as well.

Chapter 9

Distractions Are a Good Thing

"What about this one? Comfort Inn West Phoenix. It looks fairly new and has a fitness room, pool, and hot tub. It's right on our way in too, so it won't be hard to find."

"Sounds great! Especially the hot tub," Dianne agreed enthusiastically.

Gabby called the hotel and booked a double room for the night. She was told to park the car in the visitor parking and walk to the office where details would be taken. They placed their breakfast orders at the same time.

Dianne could hardly wait to get out of the car and get into the hot tub. She found it hard sitting still at the best of times, let alone sitting in the driver's seat and not being able to move. Immediately after unpacking their entire luggage, the girls took a walk down to the local shopping area to stretch their legs and have an early dinner. There was a diner advertising all-day breakfast, and vegetarian and organic foods. Gabby was keen to try the organic food, so they seated themselves at a nice corner table and began to relax.

"How can you eat that!"

"What do you mean? I could say the same about your oily fish burger and fries!" Gabby retaliated.

"Yeah, but tofu and lentil burger? Yuck!"

"You should try it. It actually is really tasty."

"No, thanks. I'll stick to the grease, thanks. Mind you, I'll be hitting the 'fitness room' in the morning to work it off."

"See, I don't have to worry about that, so I can sleep in!"

"Hmmm."

Gabby thought she would send Anthony a text to tell him they were in Phoenix. She thought she should do the right thing and stay in contact with him. He texted her back immediately, saying he hoped they were having a good time and to take care and don't forget to check the tire pressures before heading off again.

"Well, at least he is looking out for you, Gab. It's a bit late for me to call Dan. I'll send a text too."

"Yes, I know," Gabby responded. "Now I might call Mick."

There were three other tables which were occupied in the small diner: a young couple, about twenty-three years old, enjoying milkshakes; two older ladies; and another man in his late thirties, sitting by himself. They all seemed to fit into the diner like they were regulars. The waitresses seemed to know them, or maybe they were just being overly polite. The girls ordered a coffee each. Gabby talked to Mick while drinking her soy latte, while Dianne studied the menu and checked her phone for a text from Dan.

"The drive hasn't been too bad actually. Time seems to have flown, especially from Palm Springs to here," she informed Mick.

"That's good. I remember the last time I was in Phoenix. It was so hot I could hardly breathe outside. There was a yoga convention in the town hall, and the air conditioning was playing up. Needless to say, there were a lot of sweaty bodies around."

"Eeww, that wouldn't have been very relaxing. When was that?"

"Actually, it was probably around August last year. Peak season."

"Red River Valley" set the tone of the music playing in the background; there was quite a bit of country music playing.

While Gabby was engrossed in her conversation with Mick and sipping on her coffee, Dianne's curiosity got the better of her, so she got up from the table and began looking at the artefacts and interesting pictures decorating the walls of the diner. She noticed Native American headdresses, armor, and feathers, as well as team jerseys of the Cardinals, Diamondbacks, and Suns. There were dream catchers and crystals hanging in the corners of the building, with a huge cactus sitting on the front counter. Sensing someone was standing behind her, Dianne turned around to find the man she had noticed earlier eating alone. He smiled at her with his perfect, wide grin and said hello. "Hi, there!" said Dianne, slightly put off by his close presence.

"They're interesting, aren't they?" he said, pointing to the artefacts on the wall.

"Certainly are. The headdress is amazing."

"I'd love to know the history of it." He leaned closer to it.

"Yeah, it would be fascinating," said Dianne, almost taken aback by the presence of this man.

"Are you in town for long? I'm guessing you're not a local," he inquired.

"No, not a local. Just passing through. We're going to see our friend who lives in–"

Dianne stopped herself, thinking of what Gabby said about the two men at the gas station. "...just close by actually. We haven't seen her for a while."

"Sounds like fun. I'm actually not a local either. Just passing through on my way to New Orleans for a working holiday."

"That sounds lovely." Dianne had to hold her tongue again about going to New Orleans, which was one of their stops.

"So, it looks like your friend is going to be tied up on the phone for a while. Would you like to join me for a coffee?"

"Oh, um, sure, I guess. I've just had one, but please, go ahead and enjoy one..." spluttered Dianne as the waitress placed a glass of cold water in front of her.

"My name is Troy. Pleased to meet you." He held out his hand to shake hers.

"Oh, um, Dianne. Pleased to meet you too."

They sat down at the table he had already occupied. Dianne fidgeted with her chain and earrings, still wondering if she should have accepted his offer and told him her real name. She thought to herself, *Gabby is going to kill me!*

The waitress took his coffee order. Gabby still hadn't noticed Dianne at the other table. She was totally focused on Mick. Her animated conversation had grown louder, and her laughter could be heard by all in the diner.

"So, is the friend you're visiting a school or university friend?"

"She's a school friend. How did you guess?"

"Just a wild guess. I like to people-watch, and I usually make up what I believe to be their life stories. You know, I'll look at someone, see their mannerisms, how they relate to others and then make up my own little story about them."

"Wow! Quite the story-teller then? The three of us went to school together from the time we were about eight years old. We've stayed really close."

"That's nice. Are you from LA?" asked Troy, curious to know more about this beautiful woman.

Dianne thought the conversation was too one-sided, so she decided to change the pace.

"Yes, LA. So what's your story? Where are you from, and why are you going to New Orleans for work?"

Running his fingers through his sexy, brown hair, he smiled right up to his eyes. "I live in Malibu. I'm actually researching in and around New Orleans for the plot of my next book. I go by myself, so I can get a real sense of the place," offered Troy, leaning back in his chair, totally relaxed. Chatting to perfect strangers had become a part of his life as a writer.

"Ah! That explains why you enjoy people-watching," surmised Dianne.

The waitress brought his coffee. Dianne became transfixed by Troy. She couldn't take her eyes off his handsome features and his cute dimple. The information he had given her could have been made up for all she knew, but she felt fairly confident he was not a criminal. She was quite intrigued by him. His hazel eyes seemed to dance upon her when he looked up from his coffee cup. She noticed he had one dimple on his right cheek, which made him look boyish. His hands were definitely not those of a person who did manual work for a living. He had long fingers with neatly trimmed fingernails. The skin on his hands was smooth. Dianne couldn't take her eyes off his hands; they seemed very artistic.

Willing herself away from thoughts of his hands, she murmured, "Sounds fascinating. So you're a writer? How many books have you written?"

"This will be my fifth. I'm fairly new to the art, but enjoying it immensely."

"Five books! That's not so new, in my opinion. So, why New Orleans?"

"Well, I'm starting a trilogy based in New Orleans about the seedy lifestyle, drug dealing, and musical interests that New Orleans is famous for. Not to mention the other side of New Orleans – the old houses, wise, old oak trees, Creole culture, and so much more! I hope to take the story to Detroit in the third book. Not too sure where I'll go for the second, at this stage."

"Fascinating. I'm lucky if I can throw five sentences together!" joked Dianne.

Troy laughed. He found Dianne very attractive and her carefree way interesting.

"So, are you staying nearby? Maybe we can catch up before you head off."

Dianne, not used to making up stories, had to remember her story of seeing a friend in Phoenix. She felt like telling Troy the truth, that they were headed to Miami and stopping at New Orleans on the way.

"Oh, um, yes..." just as Dianne was about to speak, the background music in the diner stopped, and Gabby's voice seemed so loud that Dianne and Troy could hear everything she was saying to Mick. She ended her conversation saying she would call him from New Orleans once they settled into a hotel.

Dianne felt like shrinking into her seat. She could see that Troy had heard this comment, and he looked at Dianne with a questioning look on his face.

"Is your friend traveling on to New Orleans after seeing your school friend here in Phoenix?" He didn't wait for her answer. "Shame you aren't going with her. I would have loved to catch up with you." Now he was teasing and flirting with Dianne.

"Look, Troy. I have to be honest with you. I told you we were meeting a school friend, which is true. The school friend is actually in Miami, and we're traveling through New Orleans on our way. I'm so sorry I told you that, it's just that you have to be careful about what you say to people."

"True. That's all right. You did the right thing, I guess. I hope I don't look like an ax murderer on the run, or maybe I'm taking on the characters in my books!" he joked.

"No, I definitely wouldn't think so!"

Dianne felt awkward and just wanted to vanish. If it wasn't for Troy's good looks and lighthearted view of things, she would have. Instead, she toyed with the idea of reciprocating his light mood.

Having finished her conversation and her coffee, Gabby looked over at Dianne sitting at a table with a strange man. She gave her a quizzical look and then walked over to them.

"Hey. How's Mick?" asked Dianne as if it were perfectly natural to be sitting with a complete stranger.

"He's good. Sorry I took so long on the phone. What's happening?" asked Gabby, clearly wanting an introduction to the handsome stranger and wondering what on earth Dianne was up to now.

"Gabby, this is Troy. Troy, this is my good friend Gabby." They shook hands, and Troy offered her a seat.

"Nice to meet you. Dianne tells me you two are headed to New Orleans on your way to Miami. Sounds like an awesome road trip."

"She did? Yes, we've been looking forward to it for some time now. What about you? Are you a local or traveling?"

"Actually, I was just telling Dianne I'm on my way to New Orleans to suss out the scene for a new book I'm writing."

"Oh, really?" Gabby wasn't about to trust the handsome man just yet.

"Yes, my bus leaves tomorrow morning at 11 a.m."

"Your bus? You didn't drive?" said Dianne in disbelief.

"Yep. As I said, I like to experience every single aspect of a place and its people, including actually traveling to a place. I think that it is the only way I can write bringing the true essence of a place to life. Mind you, the desert is somewhat of a test to this theory. It seems to go on and on with not that much change of scenery. I mean, the mountains in the distance are gorgeous, but there's only so many cactuses you can look at, isn't there?" said Troy with a cheeky wink. "I am re-thinking my choice of transportation!"

132

Gabby, feeling there was a suitable pause in the conversation, jumped in and said they should head back now if they were to feel refreshed enough for the long drive.

"It was really nice to meet you," Troy stood up and shook Dianne's hand gently.

"Yes, lovely to meet a real-life author," Dianne blushed. "I'll look forward to reading your books. Good luck with it all. You never know, we might bump into each other in New Orleans."

"Could I..." Troy found it incredibly hard to say goodbye, mesmerized by Dianne and her open charm, but he swayed himself from asking for her cell phone number. Instead he shook Gabby's hand, "Nice to meet you, Gabby."

The girls paid their bill and walked toward the door to exit the diner.

"Take care driving!" he said as they walked out the door.

A few steps onto the footpath and tension arose.

"Di, you really surprise me sometimes," said Gabby as they walked toward the Comfort Inn. "I just don't know how you can be so open with a complete stranger!"

Dianne stayed silent. She knew her friend hadn't finished.

"What on earth are you doing? Are you trying to get us killed? Why did you tell him where we were going?"

"Whoa! Get us killed? Gabby, settle down...I said that we were visiting a school friend in Phoenix, until you opened your big mouth and told the whole world you would call Mick from New Orleans!"

"Oh," replied Gabby sheepishly.

"Yeah, exactly! Troy heard it too and asked if you were heading to New Orleans alone after we had visited our 'friend' in Phoenix."

"Oh. Sorry, I didn't realize. The music was loud, and then it suddenly stopped. I guess it was then?"

"Yes, it was. Anyway, he seems like a decent guy. He lives in Malibu, and he's a writer."

"Is his name Troy Taylor by any chance? I read a book about two years ago by a Troy Taylor, set in New Orleans, about the hauntings and history of the area. Great read. I wonder why he is researching it again?"

Dianne didn't answer, preferring to gush over Troy. "I didn't get that far. Troy is all I got, and let me tell you, he is so gorgeous. Did you notice his eyes? And he's got a divine dimple on his right cheek. Oh my goodness, there's something so intriguing about him, I..."

"What about poor old Dan?" interrupted Gabby.

"What about him? He's in LA and I'm here! Gosh, nothing happened. I just think he was so interesting and oh so handsome! Although it is odd that he has already written a book about New Orleans, because he said he is going to research the place for his next book."

Gabby thought the same thing. She often wondered how her friend could be so naive at times.

"Oh well, I hope he doesn't turn out to be a murderer or something. This trip is already giving my imagination the creeps after seeing those guys at the gas station."

"You're being silly, Gab. Forget about it and just enjoy yourself."

"This room is okay," said Dianne as they entered the hotel room. She kicked off her shoes and flopped on one of the queen size beds. "Do you want to try out that hot tub? I think after all that driving, my body could do with a soak." She didn't wait for an answer and instead fished her swimsuit from her luggage and headed to the bathroom to change.

"Yeah, I think it might do me good too."

The warmth of the water, coupled with the bubbling sensations massaging their aching bodies, was just what the doctor ordered. Of course, the bottle of wine that Dianne managed to convince Gabby to bring did the trick as well.

"So how is Mick? Is he missing you?" said Dianne, resting her head back on the padded edge of the tub.

"He's good. Yes, he is missing me! He went to the yoga center today and held a workshop on hatha yoga. Apparently Kara, the owner there, was really keen for me to start up as soon as I get back from the trip."

"That's great. I can't believe you'll be working with Mick." Dianne took a sip of her wine, relishing the way it made her feel.

"What about you, missy. What's with the flirting with Troy?" Gabby repositioned herself, making full use of the footrests in the tub.

"Nothing wrong with that. I was just bored when you were on the phone for so long. Anyway, I'm not married or anything!"

"Low blow, Di. You know the situation with me." Gabby was hurt by the comment.

"Sorry, Gab. You know me, just teasing. I hope we do bump into Troy, he is so intriguing. The whole writing thing is refreshing to me. You know, something that is totally different to anything sporty or athletic."

The girls had forty-five minutes in the hot tub before deciding it was time to head off to bed. They showered off and went back to their room. They drifted off to sleep, and the next thing they knew was someone knocking on the door, saying breakfast was here.

"Thanks!" shouted Dianne, "Just leave it on the step please."

She got out of bed, opened the door, and brought in the tray of dry cereals, cold toast, jams, peanut butter, and a pot of tea.

Gabby was sound asleep still as Dianne put on her gym clothes. She left a note on the tray for Gabby to see when she woke that she was going to the fitness room and to go ahead and have breakfast.

Dianne closed the door quietly behind her and walked to the fitness room situated above the office of the small hotel. She didn't have high expectations of what the room might offer, but she knew that these places would surely have a treadmill and some weights. A dull noise was coming from the fitness room. Surely no one else would be up at this time to exercise, she thought. Putting the key in the lock and pushing the heavy door open, she got the shock of her life.

"Well, well ,well, here you are!" Troy was sweating away on the treadmill. He looked happy to see Dianne turn up in her white Adidas running tank top and white cycling shorts.

"Oh, I guess we stayed at the same place last night then?" she gushed.

"Looks like it. Damn it, had I known, I could have sneaked into your room," he said, winking. "What time are you headed off?"

"Well, as soon as we're ready, I guess. Gabby is still asleep. What time is your bus again?"

"11 a.m. I thought if I'm going to be seated on the bus for so many hours, I should get some exercise now. How did you sleep?"

"Like a log. Gab and I indulged in the hot tub before bed, and we drifted off to sleep like there was no tomorrow!"

"So that was you too out there! I could hear voices and the constant bubbling of the tub from my room. I think I dozed off to the rhythmic bubble tune."

"You could hear us?" questioned Dianne, worried he might have heard the conversation."Well, I couldn't hear exactly what you were talking about, but I did hear some giggles."

"Sorry, hope it didn't disturb you. I thought I'd grab a bit of exercise before eating my 'gourmet' breakfast, waiting for me in the room."

They took it in turns to use the treadmill and spotted each other on the limited selection of weights. It turned out that Troy was quite the fitness fanatic and not bad-looking in shorts and a sporty tank top. Dianne eyed his lean torso while on the treadmill. His arms were long and muscular, shoulders quite broad, like a swimmer's. The tan he sported was probably due to the fact he lived at Malibu and frequented the popular beach, she surmised.

"Thanks for the company. I'm glad you were here. This little 'fitness room' as they call it just wouldn't have been as inspiring!" he said as he wiped his brow with a small towel.

"Ditto to you, too. Thanks. I guess I'll be seeing you around. Which room were you in last night?"

"Room 20. Just over there." He pointed across the center parking lot.

"We are in 17, just down from you. I'll come and say goodbye to you when we're leaving, okay?"

"That'd be nice! See ya, Dianne."

Both of them walked back to their respective rooms. Dianne couldn't believe he stayed in the same accommodation and used the fitness room at the same time she did. What a coincidence. She was beginning to enjoy bumping into him now.

An idea came to mind as she was nearly at her front door, but she would have to run it by Gabby first.

"You wouldn't believe who stayed at this hotel last night and used the fitness room this morning with me."

"Don't tell me the two crims we ditched at Palm Springs."

"Nope. Troy."

"What! You're kidding."

"Nope. Guess which room he's in."

"Don't tell me next door."

"Nope. The one that overhears everyone in the hot tub!"

"You're kidding! Did he hear us?"

"Yeah, he did, but he couldn't make out exactly what we were saying. Or so he says."

"He didn't know it was us though, did he?"

"No...Thank goodness he couldn't hear us properly...how embarrassing would that be."

"Yes, you were gushing over him, weren't you?"

"I'm going to ask you something, but please, just think about it without jumping to conclusions or saying no, okay?"

"Something tells me I'm not going to like this," said Gabby stretching her body into some yoga poses.

"Don't be so negative! I was thinking we should offer Troy a ride to New Orleans."

"Don't be ridiculous, Di. He could just be a very well-dressed murderer. They come in all shapes and sizes, you know."

"You know as well as I do he seems to be genuine. Look, he doesn't catch his bus until 11 a.m. Why don't you think about it while you are getting ready, and then we'll make a decision?"

"There's not much to think about, but if you insist."

Gabby got out of bed and showered, while Dianne ate her breakfast. She hoped like hell Gabby would think it was a good idea. Thinking of positives she could win her over with, she came up with the fact that he could protect them, should something untoward happen. It would also be less likely any weirdos would approach them, if there was a male with them. If he was the author she thought he was, then he'd probably make an interesting companion with interesting stories on the long, boring desert roads. Happy with her thoughts, she relaxed back into the vinyl seat and watched a bit of *USA Today*.

Chapter 10

Hitching a Ride

"I didn't bargain for picking up hitchhikers, Di," said Gabby, brushing her hair and trying to get ready as quickly as possible.

"But Troy isn't a hitchhiker. Come on, you know he'll make a good traveling companion because he's a writer, and I'm sure he could tell us some interesting things about his travels. Besides, you're so worried about those two crims on the loose. There's less chance anyone would attack or follow us if we had a male with us."

"Did you mention anything to him that would give him the idea of coming with us?"

"No. I just said I would come around and say goodbye to him when we're leaving."

"I don't know," sighed Gabby. "I guess he seems to be legitimate. Perhaps I should Google him. If he's the author I thought he was, then maybe he can come with us."

Gabby pulled out her iPad and searched for Troy Taylor. There were pages of hits for his name. Gabby wanted to find a picture of him to match up to the stranger in Room 20. She clicked on one of the links, and sure enough, a picture of author Troy Taylor popped up, sporting a goatee and looking very ruggedly handsome.

"Okay, so it looks like he could be *the* Troy Taylor," she conceded. "Sometimes authors put a short biography and picture of themselves in the back of the book. This picture looks like one of those." Gabby was satisfied with the confirmation that the mysterious stranger in Room 20 was certainly the author she thought he was.

"Di, I guess you might have a point about having a male with us," said Gabby, not making eye contact now. She busied herself putting some clothes into her luggage bag.

"So you're saying you are okay with him coming with us?" Dianne's expression showed absolute excitement.

The timing was impeccable as Dan called Dianne to ask if the girls were definitely coming to see him play in Dallas.

"Sure, we'll be there. We've got to find a place to stay overnight, but that shouldn't be a problem if we book ahead," assured Dianne gazing out into the parking area toward Troy's room.

"Can't wait to see you, babe. If you call me when you get there, I'll arrange for tickets to be picked up at the front office, okay?" Dan was determined to make it inviting for Dianne.

"Sure, hon. We're leaving Phoenix shortly, so just going to fill up with gas, check the tires and all that stuff before heading down the interstate." Dianne twirled her hair, slightly distracted.

"I'm assuming Gabby knows how to check the tires? I sure as hell know you don't!" he said in jest, knowing that Dianne was renowned for asking either himself or any other male to help her with her car.

"Yes, she does, cheeky!"

"And don't forget to let me know where you are, okay?" he persisted.

"Okay, will do. What are you doing tonight?" asked Dianne feeling a bit guilty that they were taking Troy with them.

"Oh, coach wanted us to go out to some new place that's opening up especially for us to have some dinner. Some sort of promotional thing. Should be okay, I think."

"Well, have a great time. I think we'll be eating on the road, with the mileage we've got to cover. Should make it by about nine tonight, I think."

"Okay, babe, I'll let you get going. Don't forget to text me and let me know where you are – or I'll worry. Drive safely and I'll talk later. Love you."

"Love you too, hon. Bye."

The girls packed up their gear and had it all ready to load in the trunk. Dianne sauntered down the corridor and up a flight of steps to Room 20. She tapped on the door, and Troy opened the door wearing a light blue, short-sleeved Tommy Hilfiger polo shirt, unbuttoned so just the top of his chest hair showed. He was wearing jeans and dark brown leather shoes. Having just showered, his hair was still damp, and the slight hint of his cologne drifted to Dianne.

"Hiya. So you're heading off now?"

Damn that irresistible charm, thought Dianne.

"Yes, we're just packing the car now. Troy, Gabby and I were just talking and thought we'd offer you a ride to New

Orleans, if you wanted it. That's if you don't mind stopping along the way, and of course, it won't be as inspiring as the bus ride, but–"

"That'd be great!" interrupted Troy. "Thanks! Are you sure, though? I wouldn't want to intrude."

"Don't be silly. I wouldn't be asking if it was an intrusion."

"Well, I insist on paying my way. I'm more than happy to share the gas costs, and I wouldn't dream of having the front seat! Unless of course it was going a begging." Troy's rugged boyish looks were intoxicating, to say the least. Dianne clapped her hands with joy and coyly smiled at him, batting her long, dark lashes.

There was something about him that made Dianne's heart skip a beat.

Their new passenger promised to be an interesting addition to a potentially boring drive.

"I'm looking forward to hearing your playlist," said Troy.

"I hope you like it," Dianne openly flirted.

Meanwhile, Gabby continued to arrange the additional bags in the trunk of the car. As she opened the trunk of the Jeep, she noticed that there was a powdery substance on the base and assumed it must have been something of Dianne's.

"These are the last to go in," said Troy, plonking two bags into the small space that was left in the trunk.

Troy added, "Thanks, Gabby, for the offer to drive me. As I said to Di, I insist on paying my way."

"No worries, Troy."

Gabby, Dianne, and Troy walked to the office together to settle their hotel accounts. It felt as though another journey was just beginning now that Troy had become part of the road trip.

"So, Troy, what sort of books have you written?" inquired Gabby, peering into her rearview mirror at him as he was gazing out the window.

"I started off writing mysteries, and then I discovered the hauntings of New Orleans, which intrigued me. That's actually what led me to want to write a trilogy, focusing on the seedy side of New Orleans and carrying through to Detroit. As I mentioned to Di, I haven't decided on where the second book will be based, but I'm sure to get inspiration while I'm in New Orleans. What do you do, Gabby?"

"Well, as of last Friday, I am unemployed! I resigned from my job at the bank, and I'm in between jobs now."

"So, what position did you hold at the bank?"

"I was the branch accountant. I can't believe I stayed at the bank so long. It really started to smother me. I am so lucky an opportunity opened up for me at a yoga center I attend regularly. It will be a huge change for me, but one I am so looking forward to." She reflected on the change, touching the necklace that Mick had given her.

"That's great. You really need to do what you love. If you don't, then half your life is wasted dreaming of what might have been."

"So when did you discover you wanted to be a writer?" questioned Di, now turning around in her seat to look at Troy.

"I've always had a knack for describing things and events so they seem more interesting than they are. In school, I guess the teachers spotted my creativity, and my parents would send in my creative writing to different magazines or newspapers in the hope that they would either print it, or better still, offer me a regular spot. Lucky for me, a local newspaper got hold of one of my pieces and asked me to do a regular column aimed at the school kids about what was making news among the youngsters. It took off, and I soon had heaps of kids writing in to me giving their views on things."

"That's great! You know what they say when opportunities arise..." said Dianne in awe of Troy's story.

"Yeah, that was definitely the opportunity that opened up everything. It was really the start of my writing career. Writing novels was something I always had in the back of my mind, and in between doing whatever it was I was doing, you know, studying, the column, sports, girls, I always would end my day by writing. It grew and grew, and eventually I had enough content to take to a publisher."

"So what did you write about?" asked Gabby.

"The writing I did at that time was mostly about teen-agers' views about current affairs."

"So how did you get into writing about hauntings and New Orleans?"

"Ah, so you've read that one? Or did you Google me to check if I was legitimate?" he said with a wink toward Gabby in the rearview mirror.

"Actually, I have read it, but you got me on the other question. I couldn't let a complete stranger share the ride and not know anything about you, now, could I?"

"I don't blame you at all."

The conversation grew still as they neared Tucson. Gabby pointed out the gas station coming up and said to the others she was going to stop.

Where Troy was concerned, the stop was perfectly timed. He welcomed the opportunity to stretch his legs and buy some snacks and a drink for the next leg of the trip. Gabby's offer of dried fruit and sugarless sweets somehow didn't tempt him one little bit.

Di welcomed the chance to stretch as well, so she accompanied Troy into the small shop. As they went off to buy their snacks, Gabby did a quick check over the car and decided she had better clean the windows, at least. The dry, dusty desert air had left a film on the Jeep. Where the windscreen washers had cleared the glass, there was a sweeping arc of clear glass and dust everywhere else. Gabby decided to clean the windows after refueling.

"I can do that Gabby," offered Troy on his way back to the car as he noticed Gabby about to start cleaning.

"Oh, thanks, that would be great."

"I'll give you a hand," Di suggested.

It seemed obvious to Gabby that Di was thoroughly smitten with Troy. There was an undercurrent running strongly between them, and Gabby sensed it. It reminded her of the warmth and electricity that ran between her and Mick.

With the window cleaning taken care of, she concentrated on topping the gas up. The dry heat had parched her mouth, and as she waited for the old pump to fill up the tank, her thoughts settled on drinking an ice-cold drink as soon as she could. In a way, veering off the interstate was a relief, but the area they had come to was very dry and quite desolate with small houses dotted here and there. There was no one to be seen, except for a lonely dog walking by itself over to the opposite side of the street. A small, rundown white cottage was situated on the corner, with not much of a yard. A broken picket fence surrounded the property, and a white utility was parked in the driveway.

The relentless heat, coupled with the slowness of the pump, seemed to bring on random thoughts. Her mind jostled with the long trip ahead, Mick, Virginia, and the two suspicious characters that they had come across in Palm Springs.

Still gazing and in a dream-like mode, tilting her head away as much as she could from the gas fumes, she noticed the front window of the white cottage was open and a dirty lace curtain flapped in and out. She thought the occupants must have had a fan on inside the room for it to be flapping around like that. The other window of the house seemed to be closed, but the curtains were open, and Gabby could make out a wardrobe on the right, a door straight ahead, and what looked like a headboard against the window. To her surprise, someone walked into the room, and she could make out it was a male. Checking the pump to see how much gas had been filled, she felt like an intruder, spying into someone else's bedroom. So, lowering her head, she gazed at the numbers ticking over on the counter and then closed the tank.

Walking toward the shop building to pay for the gas, it was a habit of hers to turn around and check the number of the fuel dispenser, however, in this tiny gas station, where there were only two pumps, this was hardly necessary.

In the corner of her eye, movement at the house caught her attention. A man walked out of the house, and as he got into the white utility, seemed to keep his gaze on Gabby. She felt awkward about it and pretended she was looking at something else.

A dry sensation parched Gabby's mouth. The feeling you would get if you had stage fright and were just about to go out on stage. Or the feeling you would get if you were to make a speech about the most controversial topic around, only to find you lost your notes. No, this wasn't happening to Gabby. She was simply filling up with gas and paying for it. It was the fact that Gabby had suddenly remembered what it was that had kept her transfixed on the small, white house across the road.

The white utility, now with the man sitting inside it, was the one she saw at the gas station in Palm Springs. The same white utility she took a picture of with her iPhone. Her heart pounded loudly in her ears, and her head said, *Get the hell out of here!* She briskly walked to the door of the building, paid for the gas and searched the shop for Di and Troy. They weren't to be seen. The shop was so small, with just one rack of goods in the middle, but she still paced about it looking for the others. Quite frantic now, she raced up to the counter and asked the attendant where her friends had gone. Based on their description, he knew straight away who she was talking about and said that they had decided to go to the convenience store just behind the lane.

Gabby's heart was racing even more now. It would take a lot to rattle Gabby as she always kept a calm perspective on things, so the fact that she was not calm and her heart was thumping so hard, and her intuition screaming at her, meant that there was something very wrong. Walking out of the gas station store, she pretended to look down at her keys, but her sunglasses covering her eyes allowed her to peer over the road. The man was still sitting in the utility! Why? Something was strange about that. She was sure that was the same vehicle.

Breathless, Gabby had the convenience store in sight and ran into the doorway, waiting for the sliding doors to open. The sound of Di's voice was distinctive, so she knew which direction to head to locate them in the store.

"Gabby! Are you okay?" asked Di, half smiling but noticing how pale Gabby looked.

"No, I'm not. Hurry up and get back to the car. I've got to get back now. Just hurry, okay, I'll explain later!"

Troy and Di looked at each other, then grabbed what they wanted, paid for it all, and hightailed it back toward the gas station where the car was. Di knew that something would have to be wrong for Gabby to be so flustered and agitated.

Gabby had moved the car to the side and had the engine running, waiting for her passengers to hop in, so she could step on the gas pedal and get out of the area.

"What on earth is wrong?" asked Dianne. "You're scaring me."

Gabby busied herself peering into the rearview mirror, checking the side mirrors, and looking very anxious.

"Remember those two guys at Palm Springs?" she managed to say, still looking agitated.

"Yes," Dianne responded. "What about them?"

"The car across the road was the same one from Palm Springs," said Gabby.

"Wait a minute. Which car..." Dianne realized what Gabby was referring to just as soon as the words left her mouth. "No! The same guys?"

"Yes, I'm sure it is them."

Just as she explained this, an arm pulled in the dirty lace curtain of the front room and slammed the window shut. As if her breath had been taken away from her, she motioned with her hands to look across the road. Di looked over in disbelief. A man walked from behind the house and got into the passenger side of the utility. A man with a dirty blue tank top and tattoos up his arm.

"Oh. My. God! That's them! The guys from the gas station! Gabby, what on earth are they doing here?"

Stunned into mounting panic, she said, "I don't know, Di, but I have a really horrid feeling they have recognized us."

"Did anything happen that I should know about, girls?" questioned Troy, now just as concerned as the girls were. He repositioned himself between the two front seats, waiting for an explanation.

"Those guys followed Di to the restroom and lingered there before getting in their car and heading off. It's not like they actually did anything, but more the feeling they gave us. They really spooked me, and…"

Dianne shifted in her seat, relating the incident to Troy.

"What about that article, Di, where's that? The description of them is there, as well as the mugshots," interrupted Gabby.

"Quick, get my iPad out and search the history for it. I'm going to have to drive out of here so they don't get too suspicious."

"Well, can you head on to the I-10 as soon as possible? They're less likely to try something on the open road." Troy was now increasingly worried, not knowing what he was getting himself into.

Gabby drove as calmly as possible, considering her heart was nearly jumping out of her chest. Checking all mirrors for signs of the white utility, she wiped her palms on her top to stop them slipping on the steering wheel. There was no sign of the white utility. Relief flooded through her briefly. They neared the oncoming ramp to enter the I-10, and from the next side road, about two minutes behind, approached the white utility. Gabby's heart surged into full-on pounding now, her mouth as dry as sandpaper, her face pale.

She couldn't help wondering why they bothered her so much, when nothing actually happened.

"I'm too nervous to read this, Gab," said Dianne.

Gabby asked Troy to read the article. Her hands were shaking as she handed him the phone and iPad, over her shoulder. Troy took the phone and began his search.

Both Di and Troy were hard at work looking for the information Gabby had requested.

"Found it!" Troy announced and he read the article aloud. "The two men in question are believed to be armed and dangerous. The suspects are of Caucasian appearance, between 5'10" and 6 foot tall, of medium build. Garth Mahoney has a tattoo of a red star behind his left ear and Derek Driscoll has tattoos of eagles the length of his left arm. Both men have sandy brown, medium-length hair."

"I'm sure that's them, Di. The one I saw today getting into the utility looked like he had tattoos on his arm. It was from a distance, but I am 99% sure that was them. Especially because he looked like he was staring at me."

"Is this the photo?" asked Troy holding up the phone and stretching it out into the front area for the girls to see.

"That's it. Can you zoom in on the license plate?"

As the girls waited for the picture from Troy, Gabby spotted a white vehicle entering the I-10 a fair way back on the ramp in her rearview mirror. She kept an eye on the road and an eye on her side mirrors.

There were a few cars in-between them in both lanes, which made it hard to see clearly in the mirror.

"Oh-oh, I think they're on the interstate now. Can you zoom in and get the license plate, Troy?"

"It looks like 2RDF785 to me. Not sure though, it's pretty blurred."

"Show me, please," asked Dianne stretching out her hand to the back.

"I think it could be 2PDR783. Looks definitely like a California plate though, doesn't it?" She showed Troy again.

"Yes, definitely California plate."

Troy became increasingly worried with the situation.

"Can you show me, please?" asked Gabby, trying to drive, keep an eye on the utility, and look at the picture.

Troy held the phone as close to Gabby as possible. "Hey, we don't want to have an accident so just a quick look, okay?"

"Gabby, I don't understand why you are so freaked out by these guys. Sure, they were creepy looking, but they didn't even do anything!" said Dianne who had calmed down after the initial shock.

Gabby couldn't get a good look at the picture. Troy's hand was bumping it, and she was focused on driving.

"Why would they want to follow us? Do you think they're annoyed that their little rendezvous at Palm Springs didn't work out? They didn't even really say anything other than asking me where we were heading, when I was in the store."

"So did you tell them anything?" asked Troy. "I think you're probably being paranoid."

"Well, yeah, I did. But nothing very specific."

"A bit like what you told me in Phoenix, hey, Di?" joked Troy.

"Hey, come on now. I've explained that numerous times. Gabby was on my back, and still is, about that!"

"It's most likely a coincidence," said Troy at a loss with the whole situation. Feeling a bit uneasy, he decided to keep an eye out himself for whatever this utility had in store for them. The atmosphere in the car was quiet. All were in their own worlds pondering the events of the last few minutes.

"Maybe we should call the police or something," offered Dianne after a few minutes of general silence. "If it is the same guys described in the newspaper article, then any information would be useful, wouldn't it?" She fidgeted with her chain and earrings as if keeping her hands busy would make her feel more at ease.

"And tell them what? That we think a couple of rednecks tried to get cozy with you, but we managed to steer them away. Then they happen to be in Phoenix where we think we see them across the road from a gas station. I don't think the cops will be bothered unless they have some hard evidence of suspicious behavior."

Gabby was disturbed by her own words. Something just didn't sit right. She had a bad feeling even though she didn't really know if the white utility behind them on the I-10 was the same one or not. Her mind focused on the road and then wandered, always going back to the memory she had of the two men near the restrooms in Palm Springs.

The time seemed to drag for them. Besides listening to the music, the scenery was not too exciting, and each small town that was named on the interstate signs gave Troy fuel for a bit of fun he decided to invent so the girls would relax a bit. For each town name, Troy would make up a poem which would amuse the girls and also impress them with his expertise.

Casa Grande, Casa Grande, how quaint you are to me,
For each day my love grows and sets me free,
Casa Grande, Casa Grande, your soil is so rich,
Harvesting my crop and leaving seeds in the ditch,
Casa Grande, Casa Grande, please show me your ways,
For without your safe haven, I shall have to count the days.

Chapter 11

Being Followed

"Guys, I hate to break up this cozy little reverie, but our friends in the utility are driving up closer to us in the next lane," announced Gabby, interrupting Troy's poetic attempt to lighten the mood.

"You're kidding! I kind of forgot about them for a while. Damn! What if it's them? What should we do?" Dianne was really worried now since Gabby had put the fear in her.

"Just be natural. Do what you do for any other car that drives up past you. You either ignore them completely, or a casual glance over and then back. There really is no need to do anything. The only thing you could do is casually see if you recognize them. I'll concentrate on the license plate, okay?"

Troy was strong in his advice, even though there was no evidence in his mind that the guys were guilty of anything. Still, this was his ride, and he preferred it to be a peaceful ride.

"Di, I don't think you should look over at them. It was you who actually spoke to them, so they are most likely to remember you. I think the less you are visible the better," Gabby decided.

"Girls, please don't take this the wrong way. I really think you a making more of this than it deserves. From what you have told me, they loitered around the restrooms for a while, then when Dianne didn't come out, they took off. Seriously, I can't see what you are making so much fuss about...unless, of course, there was more to it that you haven't mentioned. In which case, I would be grateful if you filled me in, since I am now part of this expedition."

Troy had some regrets about taking this trip with Dianne and Gabby. He retreated into the back seat and reflected on the possible implications to his career, should something actually happen.

"Troy," said Dianne seriously, "I think I know how you must see this situation, and trust me, I would normally have the same view, but it's just that I've known Gabby for a long time and usually, when she gets a feeling like this, it's better to take heed. There is no rational way to describe it, other than to just go with it."

Gabby's heart was beating harder, and she could see the utility in her side mirror now. Announcing to the others that they were nearly in view, she gripped the steering wheel hard and kept a constant gaze between the road, the rearview mirror and the side mirrors.

It was Troy who managed an audible sound at this time. His no-nonsense approach taking on a more pragmatic turn made him think of the possibilities, should the two men really have it in for them. "Have you thought of what you will do if they are following us? Seriously, I think we need to call 911 as soon as possible if they try anything, don't you think? Actually, I vote we call 911 anyway. If you think they could be the escaped criminals described in the newspaper, then it's our duty to tell the police."

Now it was Troy's turn to be serious.

"Not yet," said Gabby still distracted by the vision of dirty oyster white weaving in and out of her mirrors.

"Can I ask why? If you are so worried about them, why not call the cops?"

"Look, I can't explain it, but I just need to know I'm not just imagining it all."

With a look of exasperation, Troy let out a sigh. That nagging regret reared its head again. Sure, Dianne was taking his interest, but being involved in whatever these guys were following them for surely wasn't worth the risk.

Keeping to the speed limit, it was obvious now that the utility was going to pass them. The traffic on the I-10 was quite constant, with most cars sticking to the speed limit and the occasional overtaking.

"Here goes, guys," announced Gabby. The utility was finally on its way past them.

Dianne's heart was pounding in her chest. Gabby bit her bottom lip, and her knuckles were turning white with the fierce grip on the steering wheel. Troy waited in anticipation, sitting straighter in the leather back seat and peering out through the window to his side.

As the white utility edged closer, Troy could see the bonnet first, directly in line with the backdoor window. The utility sped up slightly and stayed at a constant speed. Both Gabby and Troy gingerly turned their heads ever so slightly and caught a glimpse of the driver's arms holding the steering wheel. They were tattooed. The only clothing that could be seen was a dirty blue tank top.

Gabby let out a gasp at the sight of the tattoos. Her heart was now pounding so hard she could hardly breathe or concentrate on the road. Keeping the car in the middle of the lane took an extraordinary amount of effort. Even her peripheral vision was distracting her now. Her eyes were looking straight ahead, though not really seeing what was in front of her. Knowing that to her side was someone staring at her, she could only think of trying to remember their faces from the gas station and the description in the newspaper article. Dianne sat uncomfortably in the passenger seat, peering through the side of her sunglasses, past Gabby, and she edged herself up slightly to see through Gabby's window and down at the utility. Catching a glimpse of the top of the utility and a man's arm, she sank back down in her seat for fear of being recognized.

Wiping the sweat from her palms on her top, Gabby was exasperated by the situation. "Oh no, they're not budging. What do I do? I think they are purposely driving close to us."

As Gabby said this, the passenger of the utility wound down his window and looked directly at Gabby. She turned her head, acknowledging his look. They exchanged glances, and Troy managed to get a good look at the man, etching his face into his brain for future encounters, or whatever the situation may hold for them.

The passenger of the utility was clearly getting frustrated with the driver. His face was unshaven; his hair was a sandy brown, wavy mess. Ruddiness flushed his cheeks, almost as red as the tattoo that seemed to color behind his ear and down his neck.

"Di, didn't the article say one of the men had a distinguishing tattoo behind his ear?"

"Yeah, I'm pretty sure it did. Don't tell me he's got one?" Dianne said in a quiet tone, almost as if they could hear her.

"It looks like they are going to keep us close to them. Gabby, how much gas do we have in the tank?" asked Troy.

"About a quarter of a tank. Why?"

"Because we're going to have to stop for gas eventually, and so will they..." His voice trailed off as the utility pulled up again next to them.

There seemed to be some tension between the driver and the passenger. It was as if they were arguing about something, given their expressions and aggressive hand movements.

"Why do you think they are trailing us? We haven't done anything. All we did was get away from them at the gas station in Palm Springs." Gabby was racking her brains to figure out why two supposed crims could be so interested in them.

Something she had thought of earlier, but kept to herself, reared its ugly head. She had to get it off her chest at the expense of hurting Dianne, insinuating she might have been the cause of the whole situation they were in.

"Dianne, did you flirt with these guys in the shop? Did you tell them anything else? Anything that might have got their back up?" Gabby's tone was accusatory, terse, and her features now so serious. It was quite unlike Gabby, but it seemed the situation had brought out a tense and worried side in her.

"No! How could you even suggest it? Like I said before, I just said something like 'First stop restroom, second stop... just around...' They didn't even say anything to that. The next I knew they were hanging around outside the restrooms." Dianne was exasperated at the thought that Gabby hinted she might have been flirtatious with the men and led them to think they could intimidate them by bullying them on the road.

"Well, I don't know why you had to say anything at all!"

"Gabby, honestly, this whole thing has been blown way out of proportion! Look, I've been happy to support your intuition, but for goodness sake, get a grip!"

Dianne settled herself in the seat, her body facing the door and window as much as possible. The monotonous scenery proved very tiring, but her thoughts circled her mind, keeping her entranced for miles.

The next two hours were tense, to say the least. Dianne was annoyed with Gabby for thinking she had flirted with the men. Gabby was on tenterhooks while she concentrated on the road, the gas tank, the white utility, and the tattoos.

It was Troy who broke the silence, shifting in the back seat and shuffling through his bag to locate the much-needed candy that they bought at the gas station.

"Here you go, girls, I think we all need a bit of sweetness right now."

The girls looked at Troy. His head was stuck right in the middle of the two of them, with the funniest look on his face. He offered the packet to Dianne first, then Gabby.

The girls looked at each other and burst out laughing at his oddball look and the kind gesture.

Di made use of the map which was neatly folded in the glove compartment and informed everyone that Lordsburg was the next big town they would drive through.

It was getting to be a little hair-raising for Troy, and after passing by two gas stations, Gabby agreed to Troy's pleading to stop at Lordsburg, on the outskirts of New Mexico. It looked like a lonely town with not much in the way of shops, or people, for that matter. The only gas station driving through was an old one with a single pump and a driveway in and out. Gabby pulled up next to the fuel dispenser. Troy offered to get out of the car and fill the tank, while the girls took in some relief from the tense situation they felt on the interstate. The white utility had somehow slowed back in the lane it was traveling in and eventually was not in Gabby's line of sight in any of her mirrors. The exit ramp to Lordsburg proved to be a welcome sight.

It was about ten minutes before they were back on the road. A joint decision was made about their accommodation in Las Cruces. Still in New Mexico, but in comparison, the journey from Lordsburg to Las Cruces was much more peaceful than their last leg of the trip. The utility had not been spotted for a while now, and a sense of normality had returned in the car.

Quiet contemplation seemed to be prevalent now. Besides concentrating on driving, Gabby ran through the events at the gas station in Palm Springs and just out of Phoenix. Her mind strayed from the guys' faces to the uneasiness she felt, to the newspaper article, and then did the whole thought process over and over again.

Dianne contemplated her actions in Palm Springs, arguing in her mind that she may have teased the guys with her carefree attitude. She then changed that thought pattern and reasoned that there was absolutely nothing wrong with what she said.

Thinking once again of the possible mistake he made by accepting this ride, Troy hoped that this would all blow over, the guys they thought were following them would get bored of the chase, and all would be back to normal.

The Hilton Garden Inn Las Cruces on Don Roser Drive was a delightful sight for the travelers. The large, white, Spanish-style complex and the friendly staff at the drive-in entrance in front of the hotel couldn't have been a more welcoming sight. The bellhop kindly took their luggage up to the room on the 2nd floor as they wandered the expanse of the entry foyer, the inviting sitting room, and the large bar area. An eclectic mix of Spanish and Moroccan décor seemed to permeate the building. The terracotta floor tiles and the huge vases, filled with palms strategically placed, gave a sense of openness and a carefree holiday atmosphere. The dark brown, rustic leather sofas in the sitting room and the stark contrast of the white walls and cream furnishings were pleasing to the eye.

"There must be a mistake. I booked one double room and one single room," Gabby argued with the hotel receptionist.

"I'm sorry, ma'am, the hotel is fully booked, and the only room we have available is a double room."

Gabby turned exasperatingly toward Troy and Dianne motioning with hands outstretched for their input.

"How many beds are there in the room you have available?" asked Troy trying to figure something out. It was late, and after the stressful trip they had had, the last thing they wanted to go through was being stranded for the night.

"Two queen-size beds, sir," said the hotel receptionist with an air of annoyance in her voice. Clearly she was tired of the fuss, especially at this time of night.

Troy turned to the girls and suggested that they take the room. He reasoned out the situation with them and whispered to them that he didn't mind sleeping on the sofa. If the hotel knew he was planning on doing that, they wouldn't approve.

"Well, okay, if you're sure," agreed Gabby.

"Sure, fine with me, but I feel bad about you sleeping on the sofa. Maybe we can work something else out..." offered Dianne.

"Settled! We'll take the room, thanks." Troy was clearly jubilant at the arrangement now. The hotel receptionist knew what was going on, but frankly, she couldn't care less as her shift was coming to an end. He handed over his credit card and picked up the keys.

Once in the room, Troy checked out the sofa and then the cupboards for spare blankets and pillows. Di sat on the end of the queen-size bed nearest to the sofa and suggested that she and Gabby share a bed so Troy could have the other one.

Gabby was not fussed and continued setting up her iPad and phone for charging. She was so exhausted after that afternoon's events that she just wanted to shower, eat and sleep. Dianne and Troy were keen to try the restaurant in the hotel, so Gabby was left to order room service.

After a quick trip to the bathroom and a slick of lipstick, Dianne was now ready to walk downstairs with Troy to the Great American Grill restaurant. Spotting the Pavilion Lounge Bar from the base of the steps, Di suggested they have a drink there before going to the restaurant. Troy was happy to oblige. He had been waiting for a quiet moment with Dianne and was relieved the tension from the driving was behind them, for now.

Over a Singapore Sling and a Vodka Martini, Troy and Di talked animatedly about their work. Troy's good looks and the casual way he ran his fingers through his hair every so often really ignited Dianne's interest. Her mind briefly fleeting to Dan, she remembered that she was meant to phone him when they arrived in Las Cruces.

"How about we head over to the restaurant after I visit the bathroom?"

"Sure."

"Won't be long." She shot Troy a cheeky wink and was off to the restroom.

Dianne dried off her hands and then dialed Dan's number. Checking her watch, she wasn't really sure if he would be at home or not. On the fifth ring she hesitated and thought she would send a text message instead, but at the last second, Dan picked up the phone.

"Hello."

"Hi, hon, sorry it's so late. We got into Las Cruces totally exhausted. How are you?"

"Jeez, Di, I was pacing the room wondering when the bloody hell you were going to call. Did you even think I'd be worried? I'm so tired, but I couldn't sleep because of you!"

"I'm sorry, Dan. I guess I got a bit carried away...we had a..."

Dianne couldn't think of what she wanted to say. There was the fact that Troy had joined them and also the two guys who Gabby suspected were following them. Instead she said nothing, given Dan's tone.

"Oh, nothing. We just had a long trip. Sorry."

"So is everything going to plan?" Dan changed his tone

"Yes, sort of...sorry I didn't call earlier. You sound really tired. I'll let you go and get some rest. We are just going to get something to eat and then get to bed."

"Okay, thanks. Keep in touch, let me know where you are, okay? I worry about you."

"I will, don't worry. We are heading off early in the morning. It's going to be great to see you in Dallas!"

It was at this moment Dianne felt in her heart that she didn't really want to go to Dallas. Dan's tone had hurt her. Her mood was deflated now.

She pondered these thoughts for a moment, checked her face in the mirror, regrouped her emotions, and tried to connect to her true feelings for Dan. Slightly confused over the way she was feeling toward Troy, she put those thoughts aside and joined Troy at the bar.

"I was coming in to get you if you didn't surface soon!" Troy put an affectionate hand on Di's back as they walked to the restaurant in the hotel.

After enjoying a bottle of wine, dinner and dessert, as well as each other's company, Troy and Dianne decided to head back to the room. The hotel floor proved too slippery for Dianne's slingbacks as she took one step into the quiet foyer and slipped over onto her side. Clearly the alcohol masked some of the pain she felt. As Troy lifted her up, nearly toppling on top of her, they both burst out laughing at each other and, in a tipsy state, hobbled their way back to their room.

"Shh, Gabby's asleep," said Di fumbling her key card into the unlock position as Troy mentioned something about the way hotel doors weren't meant for sneaking in because they always made a loud opening and closing sound.

Kicking off her shoes, a sharp pain jolted right up Dianne's leg from the fall.

"Ouch! I think I've done some damage."

"Does this hurt?" Troy began prodding different areas of Di's leg, shifting the angle at which she had it.

"Yikes! Are you trying to hurt me?"

"Sorry. We should put some ice on your leg – but I'll need you to pinpoint where the pain is coming from."

As Troy gathered her up in his arms, she protested at first, but relaxed when she saw the mischievous look on his face.

"Now, oh clumsy one, how does this feel?" He kissed Dianne's ankle.

"Mmmm, not too bad." She could see where this was going, and suddenly the shooting pain had nearly disappeared.

"Okay then, what about this..." Kissing her calf, he then gently trailed kisses up and over her knee, up her thigh, over her hip, stomach and cleavage.

"Whoa, mister! I don't recall the pain going this far."

"Relax please, I'm Dr Troy now. You will lie back, relax, and let me heal you."

They both broke out in fits of laughter at Troy's impression of a doctor and his less than shy approach, before shushing each other to keep the noise down, as Gabby was fast asleep.

"I like your bedside manner. Maybe you can do more of your healing on me, doctor?" Di whispered.

It didn't take much more than an instant, and Troy had catapulted himself over Di next to her on the bed.

His bare chest revealed a smattering of dark hair which Dianne found irresistible. She cuddled up to him, nuzzling herself into his chest. His heart was beating quite fast, as was hers. His relaxed smile showed he was happy to be where he was. "I really enjoyed tonight," said Troy, running his hands through his tousled hair. "Even the finale in the front foyer was entertaining."

"Yeah, apart from the finale, as you call it, it was really nice. I have to say, the trip so far has been quite eventful. I would never have imagined anything of the sort."

"I have the same thoughts. I set out to experience the journey from Malibu to New Orleans and, boy, what a journey so far!" He kissed Dianne, surprising her as she began to speak.

"Hey, you!"

Dianne was so entranced by Troy. Not only by his boyish good looks, but the way he could capture a subject and talk about it so animatedly, bringing it to life. She felt as though she could gaze into his hazel eyes and stare at his dimple forever. As Troy kissed her ever so gently on the lips again, she let out a quiet groan and let him kiss her. The feelings that began in the restaurant resurfaced and ignited the passion within her. They slid down the bed together, now facing each other, legs entwined. As light as a feather, he ran his lips along her jaw and again planted soft kisses on her open mouth. Their tongues found each other, and their bodies closed in a tight embrace. Arms and legs were writhing slowly and passionately. A muted groan of pleasure from Dianne, when Troy stroked the side of her breast, brought them both back to reality and the fact that they were not alone. Gabby lying fast asleep in the next bed was what kept them from taking the next step. A step both of them were eager to take together.

"Gorgeous," said Troy looking down into Dianne's eyes as he swept back her blond hair from her eyes.

"You are not so bad yourself!" Di put on an air of casualness, feeling slightly awkward.

"Do you think Gabby will be upset if she finds me sleeping in your bed?" said Troy, with a mischievous smile.

"This is actually your bed! Remember I was bunking with her. I think she'll learn to get used to it!"

Dianne closed her eyes and inhaled the faint hint of Troy's cologne. The only thoughts that filtered through her mind were of Troy consuming her and that he did.

In the quiet confines of the queen-size bed, their bodies continued to writhe, entangle, entwine and intrigue each other. Tasting the sweet saltiness of each other's skin, feeling the soft skin between them, arousing each other, they made love to the sweet rhythm of their own heartbeat.

Chapter 12

Dodgy Dodgers

"Franco, my man, how are things in Miami?" asked Dean Fraser. The Dodgers' head coach leaned back in his black leather reclining chair, feet comfortably up on the edge of his mahogany desk, with his phone poised between ear and shoulder. Pleased with himself that he had found the perfect carrier for the latest assignment, he relaxed knowing that his 'friend' would come to the party and all would be good.

"Deano, would you believe it? I just thought about calling you! You read my mind," said Franco, a man in his early fifties, shaved head, olive skin with an athletic figure.

"So then, I heard all is well?" Dean was referring to the recent news of the escape of two drug couriers sentenced to twenty-five years. He absentmindedly picked up a pen and drew circles on a notepad.

The two couriers commissioned by Franco who were 'let out' of Miami prison were officially on the run. Their deal carefully structured by Franco Natelli and Dean Fraser with the more than capable assistance of the Miami Chief of Police, Joseph C. Toohey.

The deal: Garth Mahoney and Derek Driscoll had been informed of their fate, should they choose to accept the terms and conditions stated. Should they choose to decline the offer, their life on the inside would not be worth living. Is it any wonder they chose to accept it?

The mission: In a time frame of four weeks from the date of their 'freedom', Garth Mahoney and Derek Driscoll were to travel to Los Angeles from Miami, identify the chosen 'anonymous' carrier, and orchestrate the delivery of the 'goods' to Miami.

"You ready? We'll go down NW 41st Street and see what we can find," said Garth checking around him for possible cars to hijack. It was 3 a.m., and the outskirts of Miami were dark, except for the traffic lights and occasional street lamp. The smell of freedom was intoxicating, and the promise of cash, the icing on the cake. On a side street, roll-up doors to a large, underground parking garage took up most of the side of the building. Opposite was a lone, white utility truck, parked in the driveway at the back of an office block.

"What do you think?" Garth eyed the utility and motioned to Derek to keep watch.

With one swift motion, the utility was opened and hot-wired into starting. Both of the men were in the car now, with no turning back.

"You'd think they would fly us over to LA," joked Garth at the enormity of the task at hand, having just changed the license plates.

It was sheer luck that they were 'chosen' by their boss to fulfill this assignment. Others would balk at the idea of traveling so far. For Garth and Derek, the adrenaline rush of pushing themselves and others to the limit to carry the goods and, in the end, see the cash in their hands, was exhilarating. Not to mention the freedom.

The stressful road trip took them three days. They managed to keep off the radar by keeping a steady speed and stopping at the designated gas stations, as planned out for them prior to the job. Their boss looked after them by planning out the route, gas stations, and accommodation. He had 'friends' all over the country looking after him. The information about the carrier was given to them in minute detail:

Dianne Grayson

Very attractive

Long blond hair

35 years old

5 foot 9 inch tall

Wears white all the time.

Tan with athletic toned body.

Lives at 5250, Unit 6, Hampton Drive, Santa Monica.

Drives a white BMW, California registration plates, 6FGR999.

Works for the LA Dodgers as head cheerleader coach as well as her own business, coaching cheerleading to young girls. Business name, Starlets.

Currently dating Dodgers pitcher, Dan Schleberg.

The route of Dianne's trip was also mapped out for them, thanks to her beloved boyfriend, Dan, and his ever-so-willing coach.

Planned stops are:

Phoenix

Las Cruces

Dallas

New Orleans

Tallahassee

Miami

"Shit! Why the hell did you have to hang around the restrooms, you moron! I had it covered!" Garth Mahoney was livid. The stop at a Palm Springs gas station was an unplanned one, but to their horror, the girls also stopped there, and Derek couldn't keep his eyes off Dianne as she sauntered into the store and swayed her hips in front of them.

"You and your need for Playboy! Damn it, Driscoll, if you've screwed us up, you are going to pay for it. I never should have listened to you. Bloody hell."

Garth had a gnawing feeling in his head that they had screwed up. The blonde girl came face to face with them, and Derek acted like a complete idiot, making him so easy to recognize by following her, even though he himself hung around for a moment or two as well. He didn't know if it was just a guilty feeling, or whether the girls had actually recognized them from the news.

Deciding on the former option, his mind couldn't help settling on the other girl with brown hair, the way she eyed him.

So far the trip had gone to plan. The girls had been in their sight and now were headed to Phoenix. Setting up for the night in a dump of a place, the two escapees had a takeout hamburger and fries for dinner. The text from their boss in Florida said that the accommodation that the girls were staying at was the Comfort Inn West Phoenix. They followed the girls as they walked from their hotel to the main strip of shops and coffee houses. Waiting discreetly across the street, they watched them have a meal through the glass and waited patiently for them to finish. This job entailed a lot of patience, but Garth and Derek were more than happy to oblige, given the cash they would get for their efforts.

Seeing that the girls were back at their accommodation, the two men headed off back to their dump for the night, taking it in turns to keep a lookout. On the move early to stake out the Comfort Inn once again, they confirmed that the Jeep was still there as they set their sights on a vantage point across the nearby park and kept watch.

"Any movement?" asked Derek walking toward their car with a packet of chips and a coke.

"Yeah, Dianne must have found a place to exercise. She's come out of the room all sexy and sporty. I'd say she's sweating it off a bit before the car ride," said Garth looking straight away at the male that was accompanying her.

"Sure as hell would like a piece of her. Mighty fine specimen, I must say. Did you say her boyfriend's the pitcher for the Dodgers?"

"Yep! But my guess is he won't be for long," said Garth knowingly. "There was talk that he was getting the where-abouts of Dianne straight from the horse's mouth, so to speak. Mr Dan Schleberg is getting a bit from both sides." He chuckled to himself at the thought.

"Hang on, who's that?" Derek pointed with his chin in the direction of Dianne and Gabby, and the young man loading their luggage into the car.

"Shit! That's the guy she came out of the exercise room with. Damn it! They must be taking him with them. Shit. Shit. Shit."

"Well, they're still going the same way though, so it doesn't really matter, does it?" asked Derek.

"I haven't heard anything different, so I suppose so. Shit! And put a bloody shirt on, will you, your tats are going to get us into trouble," yelled Garth, annoyed with Derek's inability to be incognito.

"I'm sick of how hot this shitbox is! Trust you to jump a car with no air conditioning. I've gotta take this bloody shirt off," announced Derek as a statement that he wasn't listening to Garth and his whining about wearing a shirt.

"Well, keep your arms in, will ya!" conceded Garth.

"Jeez, you are feisty today, aren't you? Didn't sleep well?"

"What do you reckon! The bloody hellhole was covered in fleas and shit." Garth was irritated by Derek and the fact that they goofed up by stopping in Palm Springs, plus the less than luxurious accommodation they had found themselves in.

"We've gotta get to this place in Tucson. There's a gas station across the road. We'll fill up and have a bite to eat there. Boss said there's a house unlocked for us to make ourselves comfortable. Mind you, how the hell does he think we'll have time to do that, I have no idea."

Filling the car up and heading over the road to the little white cottage, they parked the utility out front. A fleeting thought crossed Garth's mind that the front of the house was probably not the best place to park, but considering the short time they would be there, all should be okay. They walked to the back of the house where the back door was left unlocked. Always suspicious, even though he trusted the boss's contacts. You can never be sure who you'll find in a dump like this.

They took it in turns to shave their beard stubble and cut each other's hair. Blunt scissors weren't the best for this job, and the shoulder length hair that they both sported was now a ragged crop.

"Hurry up!" shouted Garth from the utility, directing his voice inside the white cottage through the open windows.

"Hang on, the bloody windows are open," Derek shouted back and closed the windows to the front bedroom.

Wearing a faded blue tank top with his shirt hung around his hips, he walked around from the back of the house toward the utility parked in front. His pockets were full of loose change, and he struggled to fish out the coins before getting into the car. Doing this, he glanced into the distance at the gas station and noticed Gabby.

Picking up the coins that had fallen to the ground, he took his eyes off her for a moment, and in an instant she was gone. She must be in the shop.

"You're not going to believe this," stated Derek, turning to Garth in the driver's seat of the white utility.

"What?" said Garth half expecting some catastrophe.

"The chicks are over the road," he said motioning toward the gas station.

"What? Crap!" Garth shouted as he turned his mirror in that direction. "Well, did they see you?" He was livid now. Their cover could be blown and the cash down the drain.

"Nah, I don't think so."

"Are you sure? We can't afford another foul-up!"

"Cool it, man, you're way too stuffy about this. The chick was just looking into space as she filled the gas. Far out, you are so freakin' on edge."

"Look, we've gotta be more careful. From now on, we're not stopping anywhere different to the plan, okay?"

"Okay, okay. Jeez!"

As they sat in the truck, Garth waited for the Jeep to pull out of the gas station driveway. They waited until the car was comfortably out of sight, but still within distance of following them, to start the engine of the utility and head on toward the interstate.

"I'm pulling over. You take the wheel. I've got to check our next stop that's planned and call the boss," said Garth in a bossy tone, completely ignoring Derek's perplexed look.

"Okay!" Derek hissed at Garth's tone and his bossiness.

They spotted the Jeep ahead on the I-10. Derek kept them in sight at a safe distance. The pressure was off for the time being because they knew the girls were headed to New Orleans. Confirmation of this from their boss seemed to put Garth in a better mood when he found out the details. For some unknown reason, Derek decided to put his foot down on the gas and scoot up beside the girls. Garth gave him hell.

"What the hell do you think you're doing?" Garth said through gritted teeth. He was beyond angry now. His whole plan was going to be screwed up by the moron driving the car.

"Lay off. I know what I'm doing. If we're bold enough to drive up next to them, they're not going to think we are following them, are they?"

"Are you kidding me! How the hell do you think that? Honestly, you're such a bloody loser. No idea." He shook his head at the complete lunacy of his so-called accomplice.

"Think about it, Mahoney. They see us right next to them, they don't get suspicious. If we front up, they would think that we're just two perverts trying to get an eyeball of them."

"So why are you so worried all of a sudden? I bet you did get busted, didn't you?" Garth resigned to the fact he was doomed with the worst accomplice in town.

"I said no, didn't I!" His mouth etched into a straight line, knuckles turning white on the steering wheel, he was two cars behind them on the right lane. He knew in his mind that Gabby did recognize him. This was his way of reasoning that the screw-up would blow over.

Chapter 13

Take Me Out to the Ball Game

The wake-up call from reception was unwelcome and a rude awakening for a still-sleepy Gabby. Clutching her pillow, she reached lazily over to the telephone, clumsily put it to her ear, and answered.

"Hello?" yawned Gabby into the phone.

"This is your wake-up call," said a recorded voice at the other end.

"Thanks," said Gabby unnecessarily. It was all Gabby could manage, given the time and sleepy state she was in.

Stretching her arms over her head and yawning, she realized that the sleeping arrangements had been changed. Catching a glimpse in her peripheral vision, which incidentally had summed up all her thoughts from the previous evening, she noticed Troy was in bed– with Dianne. *Surprise surprise*, she thought.

Stillness from that side of the room meant that they were most probably asleep, given the loud ring of the telephone and the lack of movement or sound from them. Feeling as if she was intruding on their privacy, she faced the opposite wall. It didn't take long though for her curiosity to get the better of her, and she peeped over to her left. A scattered cushion sat in the middle of the carpeted room, two mugs cluttered the bedside table on the far side, and a tangle of white sheets creased and folded itself among two bodies, modestly covering what looked like the two of them sleeping with arms and legs entwined.

Gabby lay back down thinking of the situation they found themselves in. From what started as a journey to visit a dear friend in Miami, the trip had taken on quite a different turn of events. She wondered how Virginia was, since there had been no recent updates on Facebook or even any texts from her for a couple of days. Closing her eyes and recalling all of the events of the last couple of days, she thought of Mick. How she wished he were here in this bed with her. His loving arms wrapped around her body. She missed the smell of his cologne and the sparks that ignited whenever they were in close proximity of each other. She missed the long, interesting conversations they had and the shared love of yoga, meditation, and making each other laugh. Her thoughts then surfaced on Anthony. Her heart was no longer in tune with Anthony's, and she dreaded the fact that she was going to have to tell him that she no longer loved him. Looking at Di and Troy blissfully asleep, she couldn't help but compare the feelings she had for Mick and the heartache she would cause Anthony. *Oh dear, what a tangled-up predicament we are in!*

Edging herself out of the comfortable queen-size bed, she collected her clothes and headed to the bathroom for a quick shower. The warm water soothed her melancholy mood. The drive ahead entered her mind. Remembering the two men acting suspiciously on the I-10, she concluded in her mind that any criminal in their right mind, especially if they were on the run, wouldn't take a chance to be found out by blatantly showing themselves so openly.

After agonizing over the whole situation last evening, Gabby finally put her mind at ease by deciding that the two men were probably just interested in Dianne, having seen her in the Palm Springs gas station dressed alluringly in her signature white attire. They were probably really bummed that Gabby had 'saved the day' and they couldn't get a bit of action from Dianne.

Satisfied with this thought, she dried herself, applied sunscreen and makeup, and towel-dried her hair. Her favorite black-and-white crinkle skirt and white V-neck tank top showed off the citrine pendant and earrings that Mick had bought her for her birthday. That seemed like so long ago after all the traveling they had done. A thought crossed her mind as to the awkwardness of Di and Troy waking up together in front of her, so she quickly decided to head down to the central atrium café for an early-bird breakfast.

"Good morning, sleepyhead," said Troy looking at Dianne, still with her eyes closed but stirring in the comfort of his gentle touch on her shoulder and face.

Dianne stirred still feeling drowsy, probably due to the fact she had just woken up, but more likely because of the alcohol last night.

"Mmmm, is it morning already?" she said in a groggy tone. Then she realized she was naked and became embarrassed and shy about the situation.

"Oh, ummm, gee, I must have fallen straight to sleep last night," she said, pulling the sheet even further up to her chin, scanning the room for her clothes, and then realizing Gabby was not there.

"Didn't you sleep well?" asked Troy, tracing a stray strand of hair away from her forehead.

"Umm, yes, but..."

"Don't be embarrassed. Last night was fun," he winked.

Dianne didn't take long to relax. With Troy's eyes and one dimple staring back at her so longingly, it was a quick fix to make her feel comfortable.

With a big stretch and yawn, she said, "Actually, I was dreaming of being on an island, surrounded by white sand and crystal waters," said Dianne.

"I hope I was there with you."

"Ummm," said Dianne stretching again. "Yes, I think you were!"

"Good answer. I slept so well."

"So did I."

"It's because you were sleeping by my side," he said with the most adorable grin.

"I think we might have embarrassed Gabby though. She's nowhere to be seen. I hope this doesn't cause any hassles now, you know, with me hitching a ride and all."

"Don't worry about Gabby. She'll come around. I know she will understand our situation."

"Oh! You sound very confident." Troy's interest had been piqued.

"I'll explain later."

Springing out of bed, there was no shyness about being naked. He grabbed his clothes and headed for the shower.

"Hey, where are you going?" said a pouty Dianne, still looking every bit as gorgeous even though she had just woken up.

"Shower. As much as I'd like to loll around with you, my dear, I don't want Gabby to come back in, get mad at me, and then decide I can't ride with you guys. See ya." He scooted off to the shower while Dianne had one last stretch, savoring the thought of last night and waking up to Troy. *Boy, this is one mixed-up adventure*, she thought.

The familiar sound of the proximity key unlocking the hotel door sounded, and both Dianne and Troy silently braced themselves for the conversation about to take place.

"Good morning, all!" Gabby said cheerfully, putting down her key and mobile phone on the dresser.

"Morning," said Dianne rather sheepishly waiting for something to be said.

"Look, Gabby–" piped up Troy poking his head around the bathroom door, looking very cute.

"Don't worry, Troy," Gabby interrupted, knowing that Troy would be feeling awkward. "I know you two have found each other, and really, I'm totally all right with it. Don't sweat, okay."

Looking across the room at each other, Dianne gave Troy an 'I told you so' look.

"I'm not judging you and Dianne. After all, she is my best friend. I'm sure the two of you have discussed things, and I just wanted you to know I am okay with it." Gabby was speaking from experience and would never again allow true feelings to be stifled.

"Sure, umm, thanks," is all Troy could muster before closing the bathroom door again with a sigh of relief.

"Okay," Dianne said as if she needed time to digest what Gabby just shared. "So, did you have breakfast downstairs?" she added as a change of pace.

"Yes. You better hurry if you're going to eat there. We really need to be out of here by 6:30 a.m. at the latest, okay? It's going to take us a good nine or ten hours to get to Dallas."

"Sure. We can do that," yelled out Troy, eager to please and grateful of the peace still among the threesome.

A couple of hours had already passed since leaving Las Cruces. The road had been comfortable. Gabby had The Rolling Stones on a random play. Troy asked the girls if they minded putting his iPod into the dock for a change in musical tastes. Dianne was eager to hear the music he listened to. As she put the device into the dock, Troy instructed her to pick a playlist called 'Writing.' Within a couple of seconds, soothing music began to play, filling the car with a lovely female voice singing about no more crying and about the sun shining.

"Hello?" answered Dianne as her mobile phone pinged into vibration mode, shaking her out of the lovely mood of the tune.

"Hi, babe. Thought I'd surprise you!" said Dan, being overly chirpy.

"Oh, hi there. How are you?" Dianne was surprised by Dan's call as his name didn't show up on her caller ID. She could hear the beautiful tune in the background, and curiously it seemed to be about songbirds doing what they do best, singing like they knew the score.

"What's up? You sound a bit vague."

"No, no, I'm just concentrating on the map. Gabby's got me working as navigator," she lied, turning her head toward the door and speaking softly, trying hard not to be heard over the music.

"Oh, okay. Thanks for the call, by the way, last night. Sorry if I sounded weird, I was just so tired. I've been kind of busy with training and workouts. Coach has been on edge this week, and he's taking it out on us. Hey, babe, you there?"

"Yes, yes, sorry...umm, maybe I should go. I need to make sure we take the right turnoff for Dallas." Dianne could hardly get her words out. She sounded very un-Di-like. The beautiful song was now crooning about loving someone like crazy, like never before. *Oh, how beautiful this song is*, she thought. *Damn, I'm missing it.*

"Well, okay, you sound really distracted, so I'll let you go. Take care and make sure you call or text me where you are. Okay?' insisted Dan, clearly getting annoyed with Dianne now.

"Yes, I will. Sorry, I'm just..."

She didn't get to finish her sentence because Dan had hung up on her. Flustered by the call and overwhelmed by the beauty of the song playing, she sank back into her seat and mused on the meaningful lyrics. How is it that just one song could evoke so many feelings and make her feel so alive!

"What did Dan want?" asked Gabby

"Oh, nothing really. I couldn't really hear him over the music...Troy, that song was so beautiful!" She managed to change the subject. "Who sings it?" Dianne turned her body fully around to face Troy in the spacious back seat. He was beaming his perfect white teeth at her with his dimple in full 'I'm so into you' look.

"I thought you'd like it. It's one of my favorites, Eva Cassidy. Her voice is so soulful and gentle, and I love writing to it."

"It's the most beautiful song I've ever heard!" batting her eyelashes at Troy, Dianne was overawed by this man. She wondered what their sleeping arrangements would be in Dallas. Oh no! Dallas...arghh, Dan! Her thoughts were rudely interrupted by the fact that they were only going to Dallas so they could watch Dan play baseball. She didn't know who the Dodgers were playing, and she didn't really care either.

The music continued to play on a random selection. Stopping for a bite to eat at Chuy's Restaurant, one of the many diners located in Van Horn, Texas, Dianne decided to bring her iPad with her to check if there were any emails from her assistant coaches.

After replying to a couple of emails from Kristin, she opened Facebook to get the latest news feed. Dianne didn't open up Facebook on a regular basis, but used it mainly to keep in touch with old school friends. There were a couple of pictures of friends at various holiday destinations, a couple of status updates, some funny pictures and then the shock...

Dan had been tagged in someone's pictures. She looked in horror as the more she scrolled through, the more revealing the pictures were. Someone had taken pictures of Dan with one, two...maybe three scantily-clad women, draped all over him. It looked like they were taken on different days. Dan showed that he was enjoying himself in all the photos.

"What's up? You look like you've seen a ghost?" asked Gabby, returning from the ladies' restroom.

"I don't believe it. The rat! Take a look yourself." Dianne was angry. She shoved the iPad in front of Gabby.

"What! Surely he wouldn't have posted those pictures?"

"They're someone else's pictures, but he has been tagged on them. I bet that's why he called me earlier. He wanted to see if I had seen them yet. Now that I think about it, I thought it was strange that his number didn't show up on my Caller ID. He must have used one of those girls' phones to call me, I bet."

"Hmmm, something's definitely fishy."

"Well, Gabby, I don't see any point in going to Dallas now. We can go straight to New Orleans! Seems like Dan and I have officially drifted apart...way, way apart." Her face reddened, as she looked away from the table, grasping her thoughts for a solution. "There's no way I am going to drive all that way to watch him play after that!"

Gabby consoled her friend, placing her arm around Dianne's shoulders. "I'm sorry, Di. That's just awful. You deserve better than that."

Di quietly let tears flow, as Gabby comforted her. When Dianne had composed herself, wiping away tears with a tissue, she bravely said, "There's no need to go to Dallas now. No way am I going to go all that way. He can stuff his Dallas game!"

Gabby took Di's iPad once again and opened up a website showing the route from Van Horn to New Orleans. "See how far it is. I think we would be better off staying in either Austin or San Antonio."

"Anywhere is fine with me. I realize I am just as bad as he his. He is just so sleazy, though. Ewww, those pictures are disgusting!"

Troy walked toward the girls now. He noticed the angst on Di's face straight away. They sat at a table covered in green vinyl. Troy pulled up a chair next to Dianne.

The décor of the diner was 1970's retro. NFL paraphernalia cluttered the place, which almost made it cave-like. One chair was dedicated to John Madden, an NFL Legend. The thousands of pictures of sports stars, cheerleaders, and teams seemed to cover every inch of the diner.

"What's up?" asked Troy.

"Well, I hope you didn't have your heart set on going to Dallas."

"Why?"

"Cos we're not going there now." She pushed the iPad in front of Troy. He took one look at it, and although he didn't know what Dan looked like, he guessed this was him.

Sensing the awkwardness of the moment, Gabby decided to leave Di and Troy alone for a while. Finishing her coffee, she told them that she would drive to the gas station on the next block and meet them back there in about twenty minutes.

"I'm sorry."

"What for? The guy is obviously a jerk," said Troy, holding Dianne's hand and giving her some reassurance.

"To be honest, although I'm hurt that he could do that, look at the situation we're in. I was obviously having doubts about him to even contemplate being interested in you. So it probably is a blessing in disguise."

"Hey, I'm here for you," said Troy. He kissed her temple and pulled her closer. "I'm just glad we've found this out now...you know, while we can easily continue on the road to New Orleans. Oh...and also, I know you're definitely free to be with me now," he added with a cheeky grin, showing his gorgeous dimple as he smiled. "I've been thinking. Now, I don't want to barge myself into your plans, but if it's all right with you and Gabby, could I stay with you both on the road trip to Miami?"

"That would be fantastic! I'm sure Gabby wouldn't mind."

Dianne perked up with this suggestion.

She hugged him, and then they walked outside the diner hoping they hadn't kept Gabby waiting since it was longer than twenty minutes. She had obviously been through a car wash as the dusty exterior of the Jeep was now shiny and gleaming.

"Hi, guys. Is everything okay?" asked Gabby cautiously.

"Yes, thanks. All okay," said Dianne strapping on her seat belt.

"So, I guess it's okay to change our route then? I was thinking we could head to San Antonio and stay overnight before continuing on to New Orleans. Is that okay with the two of you?"

"Sounds like a plan. I wasn't really looking forward to the huge drive to Dallas," said Troy. "Gabby, I've had an idea, and I've run it by Dianne, but I wanted to ask you. Would you mind if I stayed on the road with the two of you until Miami? It's just that I think I could use the inspiration of the south, plus...I like the company." His cheeky, handsome grin was hard to refuse. With the recent upset, he decided to change his plans and go with the girls.

"Yeah, of course! We'd be happy to have you along."

"I'm glad we haven't reached the turn off for I-20 yet," he added.

"It's still going to take about nine hours, but at least we are on a more direct route."

Meanwhile, back in LA, Dan was sweating from the publication of the pictures plastered on Facebook. It wouldn't be long before the press got hold of the pictures as well as Dianne. *Damn it!* he thought. *Coach is going to be manic. Dianne's not going to want any communication for sure after she finds out.* He tried to think of ways that he could get a hold of where she was. There was too much at stake here. *Shit! Too late.* Dan's mobile phone pinged into vibration. It was his coach.

"Hey, coach," he answered as if nothing was wrong.

"What the bloody hell do you think you're doing?" barked Dean Fraser.

"Look, coach, I don't know how those pictures leaked out. If it's any consolation, I called Dianne a short time ago, and she didn't seem to know anything about them."

"Schleberg, if you screw this up, you are cut out of the deal. You realize this, don't you? Not to mention your position at the club will be up for grabs as per the contract you signed."

In an incoherent moment, Dan had an idea that he was framed. For what reason he didn't know, but he blurted out, "Was it you, coach?"

"Was it me? What do you mean?"

"The pictures? Did you arrange for them to be put up, just so I wouldn't have a share in the money?" Dan was feeling brave now, the money foremost in his mind. His position on the team and the deal was on the line now anyway. He also remembered the bribe that Dean had used as a scare tactic.

"Look, in all honesty, I knew those pictures were out there... But no, I didn't put them on Facebook. If I were you, Schleberg, I'd be thinking real hard about things before you go accusing people."

"Okay then. So we're still on then, you know, the deal?"

"Well, it all depends on Dianne, doesn't it? Sure, they have instructions, but it's your girlfriend transporting the goods. If we don't get the feedback on their whereabouts, well, you signed the contract. You did assure me they were going to Dallas, so I suggest you get on the phone, make amends, and all should be sweet. Just make sure you find out where they are staying and for how long. You tell me all the details. I arrange with my good friend, Franco, to convey the details to 'our friends', and the drugs are happily transported to Miami, where they belong. Capisce?"

The pressure was on Dan. He glanced at his mobile phone. There was a new message in Facebook. He put Dean on speaker while he checked his Facebook messages. "You can shove your game in Dallas! Yes I saw the pics of you and yes you can forget about us. YOU ARE DISGUSTING!!!"

Dan kissed his career goodbye then and there, thinking about the predicament now in place. Not to mention his relationship with Dianne. In one fell swoop, his career, his relationship, and his money flashed before his eyes.

"Look, coach, I've got to tell you something, and you're not going to like it."

"This better not have any bearing on our little gold mine, if you get my drift."

"Well, yes, it does." Dan swallowed hard. The lump in his throat felt as though it would choke him.

"Well, spit it out."

Dan's mouth was so dry he could hardly talk.

Dean was impatient on the other end of the phone. "Well, what is it?"

"Dianne's not going to Dallas. She saw the pictures. I just got a message from her..."

"Shit! Well, where the hell is she going? Did you think to find out, you moron! She's carrying half a million of our goods!"

"She didn't say. Look, coach, we know they are heading toward Miami. Chances are, they'll break journey somewhere before New Orleans."

Before he could continue, Dean had hung up. Dan was left dumbfounded, holding his mobile in his hand, numb.

This could ruin me, damn it! he chastised himself for allowing this to happen.

Reading the message from Dianne over and over, he decided he would reply to it. If he apologized and conceded that he was in the wrong, maybe, just maybe, she would at least tell him where they were stopping next. "Hey baby, I know how mad you must be, I don't blame you. Please know that I love you. I truly do. It wasn't me who organized it. You have to believe me. I worry that you are on the road, please let me know where you are staying and that you are all right. Love always, Dan xxx."

Satisfied with his message, he pressed Reply and silently hoped that Dianne would grant him the information he needed. *Please, Di, reply to me...*

Chapter 14

All That Jazz

It became clear that after nearly five hours of driving, Gabby, Troy, and Dianne were tired of the confinement and monotonous road. Currently, Creedence Clearwater Revival singing "Born on the Bayou" only added to their frustration about the long journey to San Antonio.

"I'm glad we lost those idiots in the utility," said Gabby, breaking the silence. "Guess we'll find out on the news if they were the escapees."

"Yeah. I wonder what happened to them. Probably broke down somewhere. That pickup looked like it needed an overhaul," said Troy, gazing blankly at the uninhabited scenery.

Dianne was quiet. She had been silent for most of the trip. As they were approaching the vicinity of San Antonio, where they would break journey for a night, she turned to Troy in the back seat. Sensing she needed to tell him something, he turned his body fully around to face her.

"Troy, I'm so sorry I've been ignoring you...and you too, Gabby. It's just that I can't believe the situation I've put myself in. I'm usually in control of my feelings, and I'm not used to being so scattered."

"Look, don't stress about it, Di," said Troy, stretching and yawning. The nine hours of traveling was taking a toll, not to mention his consistent aim to console Dianne. He had tried several times throughout the journey to put Dianne's mind to rest, reassuring her and supporting her.

As they pulled in to La Quinta Inn and Suites, it was very apparent this overnight stay would be very welcome.

Gabby parked the car. The conversation continued as they took the opportunity to step outside and stretch.

"Come on, let's see if there is a room for us." She led the three of them toward the reception sign.

With Troy and Dianne in tow, still in deep conversation, she took it upon herself to inquire at the reception desk.

"The fact of the matter is I cheated on Dan. He has cheated on me. I know we aren't married, but I still feel" – she was searching for the right word – "dishonest. I've been thinking, if I had truly loved him, I wouldn't have made myself so available to fall for you. I obviously had doubts."

The fact that they were in the middle of the foyer of a hotel made no difference to Dianne, who continued to vent her feelings.

Gabby turned around, "Hey guys, they have two rooms for us. A double and a single. Is that all right?"

This quietened the conversation down, and then Troy piped up, "Sure is."

Gabby secured the rooms, and Troy paid the deposit using his credit card this time. It seemed that he had become emotionally and physically tired and wanting his own space, so the single room worked out perfectly.

"I suppose," replied Dianne as Troy attended to the deposit.

As they took the elevator to the 11th floor, Gabby reflected on what Dianne had been saying. She admired her friend for speaking from the heart and expressing her true feelings but knew the next step of this journey was going to be trying, to say the least. She too looked forward to a quiet evening relaxing before another long day of traveling.

The next morning...

"If you both don't mind, when we get to New Orleans, I would really like to have a bit of time to myself. I need to gather my thoughts so I can move on." Dianne shifted in her seat, feeling uncomfortable with the way things had turned out and what the future held.

"Sure, Di, whatever you need to do." Troy squeezed her shoulder showing her as much affection as possible being restrained by his seat belt. The room arrangement had provided some much-needed alone time, to collect his thoughts. Before drifting off to sleep, he couldn't help but be concerned by the possibilities that lay ahead. His public profile was going to be tarnished, if the mention of the involvement regarding a well-known baseball player and his girlfriend saw the light of day.

"I've always wanted to see New Orleans," added Gabby, lightening the conversation. She relaxed in the passenger seat, while Dianne took the wheel. "I wouldn't mind going on one of those tours around the plantation houses. I hope there is a funeral procession on when we are there. I've heard they are such a lively spectacle! After another huge drive, I think I'm going to need a few interesting things to do as well as some down time."

"A funeral procession? Interesting things?" shrieked Dianne. "I think I've had enough depression for one trip, thanks. Personally, the funeral procession doesn't sound like it's going to be on my bucket list."

"No, no. They are truly meant to be a celebration. People wear colorful clothes, and the music is so upbeat. New Orleans isn't your ordinary type of place, Di. I'd also like to explore some of those mystical voodoo-type places. Sounds creepy, but I'm so fascinated!"

Troy totally understood Gabby's interest. "You read my mind. I've got some places along those lines to research for my book too, so that would suit me fine. In fact, if both of you weren't in too much of a hurry, I'm happy to spend three nights there."

"Hmm, three nights? What do you think, Di? We should call Virginia and see how she is. I haven't heard from her in a couple of days." Gabby was happy she wasn't driving this leg of the trip, but was sick and tired of being confined. The suggestion of three nights appealed to her.

"Yes, okay. I'm keen. I'd love to have a good look at everything after I've had a day to myself." She resigned to the fact that her traveling companions were in need of rest to break up the journey.

"Great. Troy, do you mind giving the hotel a call to see if we can extend our stay to three nights, please? It looks like we'll be there just before check-in time. Hopefully that won't matter."

"Sure."

They were staying at the Hyatt. It was agreed that they would splurge on the accommodation this time.

They continued on the I-10 and entered the outskirts of New Orleans. Not long after, the scenery changed. Older style houses with small front yards seemed to be scattered throughout the Lafayette district. Using the GPS, Dianne drove cautiously through the central business district until the parking garage of the Hyatt was in view. A massive sigh from her really brought home the stress of the drive.

Their room was plush. Two king-size beds occupied one side of the grand room, and a single bed tucked away in a nook looked very cozy. There was a finely appointed bathroom, kitchenette, and a spectacular view of the Mississippi river from the oversized lounge area. The fittings and fixtures, décor, and ambiance were top class.

Placing their bags in the luggage area, Troy suggested they have a bite to eat in the coffee shop in the lobby. As they stepped out of the elevator, a stocky middle-aged man seemed to be waiting around the elevator lobby, and on seeing the three of them exit, he looked quite agitated and pulled out his mobile phone, seemingly to dial a number. His arms and hands were covered in tattoos.

"What was that about?" Troy noticed him ogling Dianne and protectively put an arm around her as they walked to the coffee shop. "You've got to stop looking so beautiful. All these crazy people are attracted to you. Look at me, I'm crazy..." He pulled a funny face and Dianne, for the first time in about eight hours had a laugh.

"Can I take your order?" asked the waitress, giving Troy an eye of approval.

He was oblivious to the attention, and like a true gentleman, he gestured to the girls to give their orders first.

"I'll have the vegetable frittata and a skim soy latte, please," said Gabby.

"The Caesar salad with a tropical fruit juice, please," added Dianne.

"The house hamburger with salad and a regular cappuccino, please," Troy put his lovely smile on full show, obviously sensing the admiration from the now-blushing waitress.

This was good. Enjoying the food and company, free from the constraints of the car and concentration of the road. Even Dianne had relaxed more now. It seemed the stop was very timely.

Meanwhile in Los Angeles, Dan saw a window of opportunity to regain his good standing with Dean Fraser. After receiving a reply from Dianne via a private message on Facebook, he noticed that Dianne must still have the setting on her phone turned on, showing her location. He clicked on the small balloon icon, which brought up a map of her current whereabouts. He zoomed in, and to his surprise, it zoomed right into the actual street she was in. Bingo! He sat for a moment, thinking what he should do. Deciding to tell Dean Fraser that he knew where the girls were, he thought more about the 'reward'. *This could put me back in business. I think an extra 50 percent would do the trick.* He smirked to himself.

As if on cue, Dianne replied to Dan's earlier text message. "Dan, I got your message, but it's too late. I have been unfaithful too, so it seems we must not be meant to be together. If what we had was true love, then we wouldn't have strayed. It is best we don't contact each other again. Good Luck. Dianne"

Wounded by Dianne's message, Dan took himself down to the Dodgers Club. Dean Fraser was pleasantly surprised at the information that Dan offered. Relieved by the discovery, Dean conceded to the fact that he had a lot at stake and cut Dan back in on the deal, not that he had officially cut him out.

Dan fidgeted with his watch and looked around Dean's office, waiting to discuss the coming events.

"So you're set to do this?" asked Dean, directing his voice into the speakerphone.

"Couldn't be more set if I tried," the voice on the other end replied. "Dianne's a piece of work. Can't wait to see her strut her stuff down Bourbon Street," he laughed.

Dan became agitated and stood up, facing the speaker-phone. "Hey, listen here. Keep away from her! Touch her and I'll knock your block off!" His face was red with anger.

"Whoa! Back up, Schleberg! Murray is on assignment. Remember, we are all in this together. Keep your cool, man! Your girl will be fine. Besides, it's only until the others get back on the track after heading to Dallas," said Dean in a calm voice. "Won't she, Murray?"

"Yeah. Real fine," replied Murray, his tone derogatory, like a child being told what to do and then grudgingly agreeing.

Meanwhile in New Orleans, Gabby walked to their room with Dianne, while Troy headed off to tour one of New Orleans' oldest cemeteries, reportedly best explored from dusk to dawn. The research for the book he was writing involved visiting some of the less likely places that the girls were interested in. It was now about 6:30 p.m., the long car ride was put behind them, and Gabby was now comfortable sitting on one of the king-sized beds, ready to call Mick.

Dianne had a quick shower, changed into some white jeans, a white off-the-shoulder top, her favorite pumps and jewelry, which included a long gold chain, dangly earrings, thick gold bracelet, and a couple of rings. She unplugged her mobile phone from its charger and was ready to go.

"Where are you going, Di?"

"I'm just going to head down toward the French Quarter. There are heaps of boutique-type places that I can browse through and apparently a marketplace called Riverwalk. Then I'm just going to have a bite to eat, and maybe, if I'm lucky, I can find a jazz/blues club or two." She winked at the irony of what she suggested, given they were in the jazz and blues capital of the world.

"I'm really not that keen on you going by yourself. Promise me you will stick to decent-looking places? Maybe I should go with you?"

"That would defeat the purpose of having some time to myself, wouldn't it?"

"Yes, but why can't you wait until tomorrow to spend some time exploring by yourself. It will be much safer. Please, Di. Who knows what could happen."

"I've got a good idea. How about we agree on a time that I will be back?" Dianne was determined to start her soul-searching straight away. "How about 10 o'clock?"

"10 p.m.? Will you take a taxi back, then?"

"Yes, definitely. I wouldn't walk around that late."

"Okay. Can you text me at about 7 p.m. and let me know how you are, please?"

"Sure. Can do. Listen, I feel so awful about this situation. I really need to get my head around everything. I've gone and complicated it with Troy now, and the last thing I want to do is hurt him."

"You've got yourself a treasure there. I think he would be happy with you being happy. So just be careful and sort out that head of yours!" joked Gabby, hoping that her friend would be safe.

"I intend to. That's why I need this little space."

Dianne walked toward the door and waved, "See ya."

"Now I'm going to call *my* darling treasure..."

"Say hi to Mick...or is it Anthony you're calling?" teased Dianne.

Without replying, Gabby threw a pillow at Di as she closed the hotel room door. Feeling a pang of guilt, she sent a text to Anthony, clearly explaining everything. "Hi. We are in New Orleans now. Staying for 3 days at the Hyatt. Car has been great, roads good and weather fine. Hope all is well. Text me back. Ta. Gab xo"

"Hello, Gabby!"

"Well, hello there! I've been dying to have some time to myself to actually call you instead of the texts." She was really excited to be talking to Mick. They had been texting occasionally throughout the journey, but found it increasingly hard to talk on the phone with the schedule they were keeping.

"I'm happy to hear your voice. I really miss you."

Gabby's heart melted. How could those four little words make her feel so warm inside? She felt an immense surge of love for this man. Someone she had hardly got to know, except for a couple of heart-to-hearts just before the trip.

"I miss you too, Mick. The trip has been great and all, I can't complain about the car, roads or weather. It's just been such a long leg of the trip."

"I can imagine. The scenery wouldn't be too interesting out there, would it?"

"No, it's not that really. It's the fact that Di has been in a really melancholy mood since Van Horn."

"Yes, I can imagine," Mick hesitated.

"Did you hear about Dan?"

Gabby, Di and Troy had avoided looking at the news. No one discussed it, but it was obvious that this could have tipped Di over the edge, had she seen articles about Dan cavorting with half-naked women on the front page.

"Yes. I did. I..." Mick seemed hesitant yet wanting to say something.

"What is it?" asked Gabby, sensing his caution.

"You know me and my senses. They never leave me alone," he joked.

"Mick, what do you mean?" Gabby sat upright. She knew there was more to this conversation. "Were there more newspaper articles? More pictures of Dan? What is it?"

"No, no. Not that I'm aware of. I'm not sure how to say this...but it's just a feeling. Well, actually it came as a vision," hesitated Mick.

"What do you mean a vision? You are sounding so mysterious."

"It's something that happens to me suddenly if I look at something, or read something, or see someone, I might get a vision or symbol trying to tell me something."

"Okay, I'm a bit confused. Can you elaborate, please?"

"Well, when I saw the article about Dan, I got a vision almost immediately of Dianne. I'm not sure it was anything to do with Dan's misadventures with the half-naked girls, but there were ropes involved, clothes torn, and loud music playing. I couldn't decipher the music, but it was significant."

"Do you think it's some kind of premonition?"

"I'm not sure. It could possibly be."

"Hmm, I hope it's nothing we should worry about. Did you get any feelings along with the visions?"

"Well, yes. I got a constricting feeling in my throat. Which could mean that someone needs to communicate in some way, or a feeling of being constricted in a situation perhaps..."

"I don't know what to say..." added Gabby. "Is this to do with Dan? Di?"

"Well, I...I don't know. Look, in my opinion, err on the side of caution is my motto. Keep an eye out, and don't over-stress yourself thinking about these things. They might not mean anything sinister," said Mick. "It might not be anything. But I will try and get some further insight and let you know, okay?"

"Okay. I'll take that on board."

They chatted for the best part of two hours. She loved how easily they could talk to each other. A text from Troy said he enjoyed the cemetery so much, and was going on a walking ghost tour, and wouldn't be back until 9 p.m. at the earliest. Gabby responded saying that she was staying in the hotel relaxing and Di had left earlier to do some browsing and to get a bite to eat, perhaps in a blues bar. She told him that Di had sent her a text at 7 p.m. saying she had bought them a gift each and couldn't wait to see their faces. Troy responded, saying that he couldn't wait to see Di and hoped that the time alone had helped clear her head.

Gabby ordered room service, had a warm shower, and watched the end of "Shawshank Redemption", one of her favorite movies. It was 9:45 p.m., and feeling the effects of the long trip, she decided to go to bed. Leaving a note for Troy and Di on the dresser near the front door, she said she was sorry she couldn't stay up any longer and hoped they had a nice evening. She signed it off with a big smiley face. From her bed, she sent Di a text message as well and then put her phone on vibration mode next to her bed.

Troy arrived later than expected. It was now 11:30 p.m. He was sure that he would have been greeted by Di, but was disappointed since she wasn't back yet. He took the opportunity to have a shower, catch up on some emails, read the paper, and watch some mindless infomercials on television with the sound turned down. 12:30 ticked over. Worry about Dianne started to fill his mind. He called her mobile and received her voice mail message. Leaving a short message, he continued watching TV. When he had no reply, he sent her a text message asking if she was okay and where she was. Still no reply. The time seemed to drag as thoughts entered his mind of what she could be doing and what could have happened. She could be dancing up a storm at some blues bar and have forgotten all about the time. She could have been kidnapped, and who knows what could have happened.

Damn it, he thought. *I should have gone with her.*

1:30 a.m. ticked over, he began pacing the room and then went over to Gabby and woke her up.

"Gabby, Gabby, wake up."

"Hmmm, what's up?"

"Di's not back yet. It's 1:30. Did she say where she was going?"

Taking in what Troy said, Gabby took a moment to register this information. She immediately sat up in bed and looked at the digital clock.

"Oh my God! She said she would be back by ten! I didn't stay up because I just–"

"Did she say where she was going? Anything?" interrupted Troy.

"She told me she was walking down toward the French Quarter, I think. There was some market place that she wanted to look at."

"Anything else?"

"Yeah, she said she was going to get a bite to eat and was hoping to go to one of those blues type places. She said she would be back here by 10 p.m. Oh my God, Troy, I hope she's okay."

"What about that text she sent you – did she say where she was?"

"No, only that she had bought us gifts."

"Crap!"

Gabby grabbed her mobile phone off the bedside table to search for the text from Di. Finding the text, she read and re-read it, hoping to get some sort of answer. Then she thought of what Mick had said earlier.

"What's up? Can I have a look?" Troy took Gabby's phone to read the text message, but noticed that Gabby had gone as white as a ghost.

"You okay? You don't look too good."

"I feel sick. Oh my God. I talked to Mick earlier, and he had seen an article about Dan in the newspaper about his fling. He said that while he was reading the article he got a vision, firstly of Di, then of ropes and torn clothes or something. He wasn't sure whether that had something to do with Dan's fling with the girls or what."

JOURNEY OF LOVE AND BETRAYAL

"Jeez! What are you saying, Gab? Quick, we need to call Mick back. Do you think he can do something to find out where she is?"

"I don't know, Troy. I'll phone him. What's the time again?"

"Now, it's 1:45. Oh God, I hope she's all right."

"Hello, Mick, I'm so sorry."

It was 11:45 p.m. in Santa Monica and Mick was lying awake in bed, unable to get to sleep. "Gabby? Are you okay?" Mick said, alarmed.

"Yes, yes. I'm so sorry to bother you at this time...it's just that Dianne hasn't come back yet after saying she would be here by ten. It's now 1:45 in the morning, and Troy and I are really worried."

Mick was silent, which made Gabby feel even more anxious.

"Look, Gabby, remember what I said. Don't let what I said earlier cloud your thoughts. Think positive. I'll call you back, okay?"

"Okay, can you hurry? Please?"

"I'll try."

Mick put the phone down. He didn't tell Gabby that, as she was talking to him, he saw more visions and felt immense pain. This time there was blood. He felt a sharp pain in his side, the music was clearer now, definitely a brass instrument like a trumpet. There was an image of barbed wire, eagles, and the word 'wolf' kept entering his thoughts. A feeling that he had been thrown to the ground jolted through him. There was definitely something barbaric happening to Dianne...

Chapter 15

Bars, Bourbon and the Whole Fandango

"Please, let me go. Please..." pleaded Dianne, her voice constricted by the pressure around her throat.

As she forced her head to move away from his weight, the asphalt beneath her provided no relief, in fact it increased her pain as it pulled her long, blond hair.

"Be quiet!" he yelled at her. The putrid smell of alcohol and cigarettes that emanated from his mouth made her want to heave.

She attempted again to turn her head to avoid the stench. His bulging eyes were red as they looked her up and down.

Sounds of the familiar blues music coming from the club and the partygoers walking the nearby streets were distant reminders that she was not going to be heard. Busy Bourbon Street, in the heart of New Orleans, was only a short walk away.

"You whore! I mean it. Shut up." He slurred, showing his intoxication.

A garbled sound escaped her mouth as the tremendous pain accelerated through her ribs, forcing her to curl up and shield her body. Her beautiful face was now scratched, bruised, and pinned hard against the asphalt, her hair fanned out, partially covering her face, allowing her to see her attacker through it.

"You can thank your boyfriend for this. If he didn't threaten me, you wouldn't be here," he said, fumbling with something behind his back.

Dianne kept still, fear running through every cell of her body as she peered through her hair and noticed him retrieving a piece of rope. She shifted slightly, giving a moment's relief to the pain in her face.

"What do you mean?" she gasped, wanting to believe this was all a mistake and that he had the wrong person.

"Your boyfriend, he's not who you think he is, love. Got yourself in for a ride with that one, I can tell you. Drugs are going to cost him. It's a wonder you're still carrying it..."

Annoyed with himself for divulging more than he wanted to, he grabbed her wrists together, attempting to tie them.

"Let me go…" she pleaded in a distorted way, holding off the nauseous feeling as his hand pushed down on the side of her throat and neck, before she managed to squirm into a different position.

"You're a wriggler." Using all his force, he coerced her onto her back.

"Get away from me!"

Mustering all her strength, she managed to edge herself back. The rough surface close to her body provided a safety net. Observing the disgusting sight in front of her, she was thankful that he was severely intoxicated and not using his full power. In a moment's flashback, she was reminded of a video she used to show her cheerleading girls: if they were being harassed or attacked, they should look the attacker directly in the eyes.

She knew that for as long as she lived, those eyes would never leave her memory. She could see them watering, an image ingrained in her mind forever. While she tried hard to keep her focus, her next step was to try and question him.

"I'm sorry, I don't know what you mean." Barely getting the words out, she managed to start to engage in conversation. His eyes looked fiery at the gall to question him.

Her idea had the desired effect, and soon enough he was answering her and, at the same time, she was being spared any more pain – for now.

With his oversized belly hanging over his belt and a tattoo of a wolf occupying the whole of his right forearm, she now had a clear image to identify him. As he lifted his hand to his bald head, she noticed each of his fingers was tattooed with what looked like barbed wire. Momentarily freed from his hands, the thought of running away crossed her mind, except that now she was confused. He knew something, and she couldn't let it go without more information.

"The deal. You know, Deano and Dan got that deal going. Your boyfriend's been tracking you, darling, because of you and your girlfriend going to Miami..." Annoyed with his own loose tongue, he stopped short, and his dirty, rough hands wiped away saliva that had escaped from slurring his words. Clearly the alcohol had slowed him.

The realization of having said too much angered him. With a second wind, he jolted Dianne to her side, kicked her in the stomach so she was forced to surrender, ripped off her white top to expose her lacy bra, and then pulled open the button at the top of the zipper of her jeans.

Now Dianne knew that this lunatic had the right person, though she couldn't fathom what his reasoning was all about. Thoughts of, 'The deal, Deano and Dan, going to Miami...'

stung her mind, and now she was faced with battling for her life.

Strength that she was not even aware she possessed overwhelmed her entire body, giving her an edge as she lifted her legs kicking her attacker in the groin with her high-heeled pumps so hard that he doubled over and vomited.

"Argh! You're going to pay for that!" he grimaced, momentarily bending over, holding his groin.

Like a wild animal hunting his prey, his rage became uncontrollable as he began to tackle her again, despite the intense pain. This time, he attempted to force her down, and she struggled beneath his heavy weight, her hands still tied together.

"That's for being so pretty!" He slapped Dianne on the cheek, saliva and vomit dripping from his chin. The veins in his neck protruded and made him look even more beastlike.

"No!" she shouted, seeing him raise his hand for another painful blow.

"That's for kicking me." Then another slap across her face, this time slicing her lip with his ring.

"Please stop!" Once again pleading, she felt the warmth of blood now trickling down her chin as her hair stuck to the sticky mess on her cheeks.

"Not until I get what I want," he said with an evil glint in his bloodshot eyes.

Bourbon Street was buzzing with the sounds of music playing at every club. Thousands of people walked the streets in party mode, intoxicated and boisterous. She thought to herself, *Why don't they walk down here?*

"Help me, please!" pleaded Dianne, she didn't know to whom, but her instincts were to plead for help.

She started to sob. "Please let me go. What do you want from me? I don't know you..."

His drunken state was not going to help him now. Besides feeling the effects of at least a dozen or so drinks, Dianne's shouts for help were going to attract too much attention.

"Just you wait, you little bitch," he said, stumbling to his feet. "Your new boyfriend is going to die if you even think of telling the cops..." he trailed off and threw up again. "Franco will see to that."

Dianne listened to him in disbelief. At this moment, all she cared about was that she was alive. She watched him stumble away, vomiting and yelling obscenities at her.

Watching his grotesque body move away from her, her thoughts now centered on the pain which was excruciating in her stomach and ribs. Barely able to move, her hands trembled up to her bleeding lip. The blood seemed to have congealed, and just the look of it made her feel nauseous.

New boyfriend, thought Dianne. *He must mean Troy! Oh no!*

Then images of Dan flooded her mind in a blur, coupled with the words from her attacker.

In a state of utter pain and confusion, she attempted to regain some composure, but she couldn't move nor think what to do. She was grateful to be alive. Mouthing the words, "Please help me," just a tiny voice was audible.

The stabbing pain took hold as she stole one more look up the darkened alley, which was now so empty, and then Dianne collapsed.

5:30 a.m.

Meanwhile, at the Hyatt Hotel, Gabby and Troy gave a detailed account of everything to the police. They felt useless. Deciding to walk the walk that Dianne most probably took, they scoured through everything they could see for any clues at all. Being so early in the morning, none of the businesses were open yet.

"Can you call Mick back? Surely he would have found out something by now."

"No, I won't phone him. He will call when he's ready. If I phone him, I could disturb his thoughts."

"It's just killing me! You should have insisted she took one of us with her!" Troy was fraught with worry and now took it out on Gabby.

Minute by minute, Troy questioned his involvement in this road trip. Niggling thoughts of his professional profile being sabotaged plagued him. Torn between his feelings for Dianne and these thoughts, he found himself in an uncomfortable position.

They continued to look in every garbage bin they passed, every gutter, every shop entry in the hope they were open or she may have taken refuge inside. Taking a few of the side streets off Dauphine Street, they scoured everywhere.

"Why don't we drive around the area?" said Troy, searching for new ways they could try to locate Dianne.

"Might as well. By the time we walk back, I'm sure Mick would be calling by then." They took a different route back to the Hyatt, and Gabby's phone rang just as they were approaching the hotel. She answered it on the first ring.

"Hi, Mick. Please tell me you know something..." Gabby put her phone on loudspeaker, so Troy could hear as well.

Mick always spoke in a gentle way. He was calm but firm and knew that what he had experienced was definitely something to do with Dianne.

"Gab...the visions I'm getting...I am sure it is Dianne. I think she has been attacked, perhaps beaten. Her hands may have been tied, and from what I felt, I suspect she has some injury to the stomach or ribs."

"Oh God!" Gabby sobbed now. She felt responsible for letting Dianne go by herself.

Troy put his arm around Gabby and drew her in close to him.

"Anything else, Mick? We've reported it to the police, but if there's anything else that we could tell them..." Troy trailed off now, the agony of knowing she was hurt or worse was too much to handle. "You're not making this up, are you? I mean, you are pretty good with this, aren't you?" Troy wanted to believe that Mick could help with his psychic abilities, but at the same time, wished it wasn't true.

Silence grew as Mick realized that this would have been hard to hear. He let it brush off him, used to people who didn't believe him.

"I have a feeling the attacker might have had a tattoo, because an image of a wolf kept appearing. It was quite strong, in fact, and perhaps another tattoo of barbed wire.

JOURNEY OF LOVE AND BETRAYAL

The music I heard became clearer to me, and I am positive it sounded like brass instruments, maybe a trumpet or saxophone."

"She must have been in one of those jazz clubs." Gabby was numb now.

"Anything else?"

"What I am sensing is that she is still alive. I am positive about that."

"Oh, Mick! Thank you! Thank you so much...I wish you were here."

"I do too, Gab. Just know I'm here for you if you need me. Just call, okay?"

"Okay. Bye then."

"Bye, my sweet. Take care and call me."

With the information Mick gave them, the call to the police department was a lengthy one. Officer Hardy was mostly interested in how someone could see and sense all these images and feelings without even being in the same state. It took a great deal of patience to run through everything with such a skeptic, along with more paperwork to be completed.

Time ticked away, and they decided to drive around the streets in neighboring areas. She could have been dumped somewhere...waiting around seemed pointless.

On entering the underground car park of the Hyatt, Troy had a thought that they should call Dan and see if Dianne had tried to contact him, or if he had any clues to where she might be.

Entering the parking garage from the elevator, Troy and Gabby stopped in their tracks when they saw the tailgate of the Jeep was slightly open. With the events of the last few hours unfolding, anything out of the ordinary shocked them.

"Oh my God," whispered Gabby.

They looked at each other and cautiously approached the car.

"Stay here, I'll have a look to see if there's anything or anyone around," offered Troy.

Peering into the trunk area, there seemed to be nothing untoward. The rest of the exterior seemed to be intact. Troy opened the tailgate fully now, inspecting the space. Some of Dianne's candies had been spilled on the carpet and a couple of CD cases, which were cracked, were up behind the rear pull-down seat. There was an umbrella and a couple of canvas shopping bags. Apart from that, nothing seemed out of place.

Gabby waited away from the car, but the suspense was too much. She joined Troy at the rear of the vehicle.

"Do you think this has something to do with Dianne? Or were we just careless when we unpacked the car?" she said as she too gave the car a once-over.

"Doesn't look like there's anything suspicious to me. There's no damage to any of the doors. Like you said, we may have been hasty and just didn't lock it properly."

Troy became silent as he remembered that it was he who brought the last of the luggage into the hotel suite. *Surely I locked the car*, he thought.

Taking the western link through the city's business district area, Troy set the GPS to Kenner, and Gabby carefully followed the directions. Once they were out of the central business district, Gabby stopped the car so that Troy could continue driving while she phoned Dan.

Since the number was not recognizable, Dan answered the phone in a gruff tone.

"Hello."

"Dan? It's Gabby...Dianne's friend..."

Dan hesitated. Half expecting him to hang up, Gabby prompted him.

"Oh, hi Gabby. How's the trip going?" he put on a fake greeting, trying to act as calm as ever.

"Dan, something's happened to Di...she's gone missing..."

"What! Where?"

"Well, we're in New Orleans, and she was quite upset about the photos of you..." Gabby hesitated bringing this up. "She didn't speak to us at all from the time she found out until we were nearly in New Orleans."

"Jeez, Gabby. I didn't put those photos up..." He was grappling for some sort of explanation, but was failing miserably.

"Well, anyway, I'm not calling to chastise you, it's just that we thought you might have heard from her. Did she call you or send you a text? Any information would be helpful..." Gabby nearly lost her composure again but kept herself strong.

"Yeah, um, sure. She sent me a private message through Facebook. She was pretty pissed about the photos."

"Can I ask what she said?"

"Well, it was something along the lines of, I can shove the game in Dallas and how she saw the pictures and thought I was disgusting."

"Is that all? Do you know if anyone would purposely want to hurt her?"

"Gabby, like I said, she was really pissed with me...look, a girl like Dianne, you know, so beautiful is always going to be a target."

"What! So just because she's beautiful, she should expect to be kidnapped or beaten?" Gabby was volatile now. *What a pig,* she thought. "Just tell me, please, Dan, is there anyone, anyone at all, who could have something against her? You're both in the same industry..." Gabby was angry and pleading at the same time.

"Not against *her*..."

"Sorry? What did you say? You know something, don't you?"

"Honestly, I don't know anything about Dianne's disappearance..." he trailed off. Now his thoughts steered to the conversation Dean had with Murray, the guy hired by Franco to trail the girls in New Orleans. Dan had threatened this guy Murray. He thought to himself, *Shit! That son of a bitch has done this...*

Troy stopped the car at the nearest side street. "Look, bud, if you're holding something back, you're only hurting Dianne. Come on, just tell us who you think it is..."

"Who the hell are you? Gabby, who is that? I thought you were alone?"

"It's a friend of ours, Dan. He's helping me look for Dianne."

"Look, I don't know who you are, *bud*, but Di's my girl and I..."

He trailed off once more. It was so obvious to Gabby and Troy that he knew more than he was letting on. She was desperate to get whatever information it was that she knew Dan had.

"Dan, Di was so upset when she saw those photos. Can you imagine how she would have felt? She felt so embarrassed knowing all her friends and family would see them. I've never, in the entire time I've known Di, seen her so withdrawn. You know yourself, I'm sure. Di is usually so bubbly and always cheers everyone up."

There was silence, because Dan knew this too. Gabby gave Troy a look that said, I think he's going to crack. She motioned to Troy not to say anything, for fear of him riling Dan.

"There's someone I know...he's a friend of my coach. I might have irritated him a couple of days ago, and he threatened to...well, he said he thought Dianne was a good sort. Look, I can't talk, I've gotta go..."

"Please, Dan, don't hold out on us. Please! I'm begging you, what's this guy's name? And why would he be in New Orleans just as we are here?" Gabby was clutching at anything she could to get answers.

"He's working with Dean, my coach. Look I can't talk, I've really got to go…"

"Just one more thing, please? What's his name?" There was no holding back now. Gabby had to get as much information as possible. She had to try everything for the sake of her best friend.

Dan hesitated. The thought of how he had betrayed Dianne ran through his mind like a train speeding through a tunnel, except there was no light at the other end. He was in too deep now. He wanted the money desperately, even at the expense of his girlfriend's life. This was too much for him to battle in his mind, and the guilt seemed to multiply with every waking second, but he felt as though he was in the middle of a tug-of-war.

"His name is Murray Wolfe."

Chapter 16

Questions and Answers

Gabby picked up the phone to dial Officer Hardy. She was keen to give the information Dan had reluctantly offered. Writing a list, so nothing was left out, she dialed the phone number.

"Officer Hardy, it's Gabby Drayton here. I have some more information to do with Dianne Grayson."

"More from the psychic?" he said dryly.

"No." She was annoyed at his tone, but didn't dare say anything that might put him off the case.

"I contacted Dianne's ex-boyfriend. He reluctantly offered some information on someone called Murray Wolfe, who may have had an interest in Dianne."

"I see. Just a moment, I'll get my file."

Hearing a shuffling of papers, phones ringing in the background, and general chatter, she carried on in the hope the information she was giving would help locate Dianne.

"Dianne's ex-boyfriend is Dan Schleberg. He plays for the Los Angeles Dodgers. He is a high-profile player there. Apparently Dan had said or done something to irritate this Murray Wolfe person, and Murray had implied or threatened, I'm not sure, that he thought Dianne was attractive and that he might make a move on her...I'm really not sure of the situation as he was being so vague. It seems that Murray is working with Dean, the Dodgers' coach, and I'm not even sure how he is working with him."

"I don't understand the connection here. Who is Murray Wolfe to this Dan Schleberg? And why would that person be in New Orleans with Ms Grayson?" said Officer Hardy, his casual, unfriendly attitude evident.

"That's what I don't understand. I just thought you may want to follow up the leads..."

Troy was listening to the conversation, rolling his eyes at the way the police needed the information spoon-fed to them to get going. He thought to himself that he and Gabby had acquired more clues in their investigation than the police had.

"Thank you, Ms Drayton. That information will be useful. In the meantime, if you hear from Ms Grayson, be sure to contact me immediately."

"Of course. Thank you."

"Good bye, Ms Drayton."

"Talk about getting blood out of a stone. I'm certain we've uncovered more information in the few hours since we started than they would have in a week!" said Troy, agitated.

"Don't you think the situation with Dan is really suspicious? I still don't understand why someone working for the Dodgers' coach would be in New Orleans and why they would want to target Dianne. Makes me think that Dan has done something to really annoy this Murray character, or Dean."

"I don't know. I just wish Dianne would call us. Jeez, I can't stand this. The not knowing is agony."

Checking the clock again, it was now 11:22 a.m. The minutes seemed to take forever to tick over. Dianne had not been heard from since the text message that she had sent Gabby at 7 p.m. the previous day.

"Do you think we should call her parents?" Troy asked.

"I think we should wait...wait until this afternoon. If we haven't heard anything, then at least the police investigation will be underway, and we can tell them that. Besides, I have faith in what Mick said. He is certain she is alive. It's just a matter of time before we hear from her..."

"Jeez, Gab, he better be right."

Making Gabby a chamomile tea and himself a coffee, Troy's emotions took hold. He turned his back to Gabby so she wouldn't notice, but being the sensitive person that she was, Gabby noticed and walked to the small bench area where Troy was standing. She put her arm around his shoulders and comforted him. Somehow, she managed to stay focused on a positive outcome. It was Mick's reassurance that Dianne was alive that gave her a renewed sense of faith in this potentially horrific situation.

As if on cue, the hotel phone rang. Leaving Troy at the small bench with their hot drinks, Gabby calmly walked over to the phone and answered it.

"Ms Drayton?" said a businesslike male voice.

"Yes, speaking."

"Ma'am, it's the hotel manager here, James Parker. I'm sorry if I have disturbed you. Would you and Mr Taylor meet me in my office in half an hour, please? I am on Level 2. If you follow the stairwell along until you come to a corridor leading to the seafood restaurant, my office is just on the right."

"Can I ask what this is about, sir? It's just that we are waiting for some news about a friend of ours..."

"Ms Drayton, I have been contacted by the police. Please, come to my office, and we can discuss this matter."

"Okay, we'll be there," said Gabby, putting the phone down. Her heart began to beat fast again.

"Who was that?" asked Troy, having wiped the stray tears away and composed himself.

"The hotel manager. He wants us to go to his office on the 2nd level in half an hour. He said he's been contacted by the police."

Troy rushed to get his cell phone and keys, hopeful that there might be some news. "I hope he has some positive information."

They paced the length of the hotel room, waiting for 25 minutes, before heading to the hotel manager's office. When they arrived, the hotel manager and a police officer greeted them.

"Thank you for meeting me," he extended his hand to Gabby and Troy. This is officer Smythe," he gestured toward the officer standing next to him.

"Thanks for coming down here, Ms Drayton, Mr Taylor," said Officer Smythe. "Please, take a seat."

Gabby and Troy sat in the two chairs opposite Mr Packer's desk as he sat down at the far end of the desk.

"We have some information on your friend, Ms Dianne Grayson."

Gabby braced herself. Troy reached for her hand. Neither could read the neutral expression on Mr Parker's face or Officer Smythe's.

"Ms Grayson is in Ochsner Medical Center, downtown. She has a mild concussion, is bruised and has some internal injuries," informed Officer Smythe. He shifted in his seat, taking in the expressions and body language of the two people in front of him, who were eager to know more.

"Oh, thank God she's alive! What happened to her? Do they know?" questioned Gabby, with urgency expressed in her voice.

"She appears to have been beaten and quite brutally assaulted. The assailant is under arrest."

"Can we go and see her? Is she talking?" asked Troy, his tone also urgent and relieved.

"She has been reluctant to talk, Ms Drayton. The authorities believe she is holding information back on her attacker. Her personal effects were not with her when she was brought into the hospital, but a business card from this hotel was in a back pocket of her jeans. Do you know anything that could lead us to her attacker?"

Troy looked at Gabby, each knowing what the other was thinking. "No, Officer. I don't know anything. We have been on a road trip from Los Angeles to Miami to see a friend. I don't know why this has happened or who might be responsible."

After much interrogation, Troy and Gabby were free to visit Dianne. The police would be in touch.

On arriving at Dianne's hospital bed, Gabby and Troy could hardly believe this was their beautiful friend. Her face was red and swollen. She had cuts and scratches, and her eye was black and blue. The hospital gown covered her, but a deep red line was clearly visible above the neckline of the gown.

Troy kissed her forehead, stirring her into waking. She recognized them immediately and said hello.

"Thank God you are all right, my beautiful. We've been so worried," he said gently, tracing his hand across hers.

Gabby held her hand, which was rare to see so bare of jewelry, her skin so dry and pale.

"You had us worried, missy."

"I'm okay. Lucky I insisted my girls know how to protect themselves..." She spoke softly.

"Yeah, we heard you gave the guy an almighty kick in the groin. You must have really packed a punch!"

"See, my high-heeled pumps do come in useful," said Dianne who was actually joking. It was a pleasure to see.

"Your cell phone was handed into the club that you were in, but your handbag hasn't been located."

"How did they know to contact you?" She was still confused as to the events that followed her attack.

"Well, you must have had a business card from our hotel in your jeans pocket. The manager of the hotel called us into his office and told us that the police had contacted him."

"Oh, yeah. I remember taking that from the front reception desk on my way out. Lucky I did! I do recall someone asking me who my next of kin was, or something. I said your name, and then I must have dozed off."

"I would say that you are one lucky person, Di. I can't believe you're joking about things, but it's such a relief to see you...to hear you talking," Troy was emotional, and he couldn't contain his relief. Tears welled up in his eyes as he wiped his sleeve across them.

A nurse entered the room and took Dianne's blood pressure and temperature and examined her cuts. "I'm afraid I'll need you to leave the room for a moment, please," said the nurse.

"Oh, that's okay," managed Dianne.

The nurse looked at Troy and Gabby as they stepped forward, but still gave the nurse some space. What they saw when she pulled back the gown was distressing. Dianne's rib area was black and blue.

"Oh Di, that looks so painful. Are your ribs broken?" asked Troy, wincing at the sight before him.

"One is, but mostly just badly bruised. The doctor said, as painful as it is, she needs to be up and moving to get them better faster," said the nurse. "The doctor is relentless!" she added. "You should be discharged tomorrow morning, dear."

Neither Troy nor Gabby brought up the conversation with Dan. They didn't want to rock the boat with Dianne's recovery.

After being discharged, she spent the day lounging in the hotel, getting thoroughly spoiled by Troy, and she became very protective of him. She was saying things like, "If anything happened to you, I don't know what I'd do". It was a reaction from the attack, that what happened to her could happen to Troy, or worse. She shed many tears, and it was clear that the shock was starting to surface, a delayed reaction.

Gabby thought Dianne should know that they had spoken to Dan, but she wasn't sure how to broach the subject. She asked Dianne if she had seen the attacker before.

"I don't really want to talk about it, guys," responded Dianne.

"I know, Di, but there's something you should know... when Troy and I walked around the streets looking for you, and then we drove around the area still with no clues, it dawned on us that Dan might have heard from you. I called him and asked him if he'd heard from you. He was hesitant, but it was so obvious he knew something."

"I can't believe you called him," Dianne shifted her position, grimacing in pain as she placed her hands gingerly on her ribs.

"Well, reluctantly he gave us some information. He told us you were pretty mad with him. He also said something about Dean, his coach."

"Do you know if Dean and Dan had some sort of arrangement off the field? I think there was a third party. Perhaps someone working with Dean. This person might have irritated Dan, we aren't sure. Things are a bit sketchy," said Gabby, hopeful her friend would open up.

"No. No, I don't know anything."

Dianne clammed up. She took herself carefully to the bathroom at this point. Gabby and Troy were left thinking that something was very suspicious about the whole thing. First Dan and Dean with their off-field arrangements and also this Murray Wolfe person, who attacked Dianne. They couldn't work out what the connection was.

"If she's going to get upset each time we bring it up, then I think we should lay off for a while. She's obviously traumatized," announced Troy, wanting the best for Dianne's recovery.

Dianne re-entered the sitting area of the hotel room. She put her legs up on the cushions and slid down in a semi-reclined position.

"I don't feel up to talking about all this now. Can I just watch some TV, please?"

"Sure, sorry," said Gabby switching on the TV and handing the remote control to Di. "Do you think you'll be up to traveling soon?"

"Yes, I will. I really want to get out of New Orleans. I've had enough of it. If I do what the doctor said and have twenty-four hours' complete rest, then by tomorrow morning I should be well enough to leave."

"Okay, but you've got to tell us if you're not up to it. Okay?"

"Okay, " she agreed, then stared blankly at the television.

Troy and Gabby were exhausted. Lack of sleep and all the worrying was starting to catch up now that they were all together in the hotel room. Each of them had found comfort for the time being just sitting and relaxing. Their thoughts active, with questions circulating through their minds.

"It's about five and a half hours to our next stop, so it shouldn't be too bad," added Troy. "We'll take it easy. Stopping, if you need to." He directed this at Dianne, but she was unresponsive.

Gabby and Troy walked to a takeout restaurant and picked up some food for dinner, giving Di some time on her own, which is what she had hinted that she needed. While they were out, Dianne reflected on what her attacker told her. She would never forget his face, having made a point to look him in the eye. He said that Troy would be killed if she mentioned anything to the police. She tried to remember what it was he said. Her foggy memory was annoying her. Unwelcome feelings of her struggling and being restrained entered her thoughts. She remembered him saying that this was her boyfriend's fault. He warned her about him and said something about drugs...and that it's a wonder that she was still carrying them.

It was confusing her, all the thoughts and visions running through her mind. Something just didn't feel right. This guy seemed like he really knew that Dan was involved in something big. Then it hit her. He said something about a deal that Dean and Dan had and that they'd been tracking her because they were headed to Miami.

It was after he told her this that her recollections of the attack got sketchy. She remembered being kicked in the ribs and that he tried to rip her top off and undo her jeans, but she put up so much resistance that he, being intoxicated, was somewhat disorientated himself. That was when she mustered all the strength she had, given that her wrists were tied together, and she brought her knees up toward her chest and forced her heels into his groin. He went flying.

She vaguely remembered seeing some people walking toward her, and then that was it. The next thing she knew, she woke up in a hospital somewhere feeling like she'd been hit by a train.

As she made herself walk around the hotel room just for some movement, like the doctor had suggested, she had a light-bulb moment. Finding the car keys on Gabby's bedside table, she gingerly opened the hotel door and walked, very slowly, down the corridor to the elevator. Her palms were getting sweaty, and her heart began to race at what she thought she might find. Pressing the B2 button on the elevator, it all began to make sense to her. Her ribs ached, as she protectively placed her hands around her abdomen to shield them.

Trying to remember where the car was parked took a bit of an effort, and she walked down three aisles before finding the Jeep. Her heart was now nearly jumping out of her chest. Its increased activity drew even more pain from her already sore ribs. She pressed the unlock button on the remote. The lights flashed and it beeped. Peering into the car as if to see if anyone was in there, she satisfied her curiosity and then proceeded to open the tailgate.

There was a small amount of white powder along the edge of where the carpet met the underlay. She really didn't want to go any further. Looking around the parking lot checking for people, she felt her ribs ache. Her body was still so sore, but finding out what was under the felt underlay was something she had to do.

Taking one more look around, she wedged her fingers under the edge of the underlay and lifted it.

"Please no, please no, may it not be here…" she chanted to herself.

"Oh. My. God!" bringing her hands up to her mouth, she gasped in horror at the sight before her.

Barely able to breathe from her heart pounding so much, she just stared at the hundreds of packets of white powder stashed away.

Her legs turned to jelly as she let the felt underlay flop into position. The carpet which had been rolled back had now flattened itself into its rightful place.

Barely able to hear herself think from the thumping going on inside her, she pulled down on the tailgate to shut it. Leaning back onto the car, she couldn't believe what had just been uncovered. It all made sense now.

Needing to collect her thoughts, she locked the car and took the elevator back to the ground floor. Instead of going straight back to the hotel room, she walked through the lobby to a quiet lounge area, furnished elegantly with plenty of black leather sofas, cream and gold table lamps, and lush potted plants. Taking a seat in one, closest to the fireplace, she took stock of the events leading up to this moment.

It all made sense. The two guys in the white utility that they saw in Palm Springs must have had something to do with all of this. They must have been following them as they thought. *Maybe they planted it in the car.* Assuming the utility had broken down, or the guys had lost interest in following them, they hadn't thought too much about them at all after Las Cruces.

Coach Dean Fraser had been all too keen to give Dianne time off for this trip. He also had become very interested when she told him they were going to Miami, even suggesting that he give her names of some places to stay. Then she got really angry. She thought of how Dan was so insistent she phone or text him exactly where they were staying and when they left a place.

How stupid of me, I should have known something was up, she thought. Her ribs shot pain up through her. She gave off a moan as she gripped her ribs in bear-hug style. *Who was that loser who attacked me, then? He wasn't one of the guys from Palm Springs, and why was he telling me about Dan in on a deal with Dean Fraser? Maybe Dan knows about Troy and me getting together, and he's gone troppo about it...* Thoughts whirled through her mind.

Thinking of Troy only reminded her of what the attacker had said to her, "Your new boyfriend's gonna die if you tell the police." This meant that he knew that Troy was her new boyfriend and Dan was the old one...

Her ribs were aching. Her head was throbbing, and now she was aware of the drugs planted in Gabby's car. Actually it was Anthony's car. If she told the others, they would go straight to the police, and then Troy could get killed. She thought about not saying anything. If they were smuggling the drugs to Miami, where would the crims plan to actually get them out of the car? What if they injured Troy or Gabby, or killed them? The thoughts were unbearable.

Remembering she should get back up to the hotel room before Troy and Gabby returned with the takeout food, she carefully got herself up from the sofa and walked back. Conscious of all the people in the busy hotel foyer, she managed to walk as normally as possible toward the elevator lobby. It was too late; she had been sprung.

"Hey there, what are you doing walking around down here?" Troy was so happy Dianne had been found, but so protective now too.

"Yeah, you should only be in the room walking around and taking it easy," said Gabby.

"I just felt like a change in scenery. I'm feeling much better actually. The more I move around, the less sore I feel." She hid the car keys in her pocket.

It was at this moment that Dianne decided that she would keep quiet about the fact that there were about a million plastic packets of who knows what drug in the trunk of their car. Troy was far more important to her, and they only had one more stop before they reached Miami...

Chapter 17

Secrets

Sitting in the front seat meant that Troy had control over the music. Since leaving New Orleans an hour earlier, they had listened to what he called his "Thinking" playlist on the iPod, which he listened to while plotting a story.

Classical music soothed his soul, relaxed his mind, and opened it up to the infinite possibilities of creative writing. The beautiful music seemed to resonate with the moods of everyone. Reflecting on the previous seventy-two hours was a necessary step in processing the events of the attack and moving forward.

"This music makes me feel so relaxed and peaceful," said Dianne from the back seat.

"I totally agree. I often feel like turning on some peaceful music, particularly if I'm trying to let go of the day's events," added Gabby.

"Well, my intention was to create a peaceful atmosphere and looks like I've accomplished that." Troy was pleased by his choice of music and the effects it had on the girls.

Passing through Gulfport, Biloxi and Pascagoula, they arrived at Mobile Bay. It was a picturesque setting, especially with the sun shining on the crystal water, reflecting the boats moored at the marina.

Deciding they would stop for an early lunch, they found a place to park the car and walked to a row of stores, cafés and restaurants that lined the main street opposite the bay.

Dianne was still very protective and clingy toward Troy. The attack, as well as the threat, was something that played on her mind every minute of the day. Sitting in the car meant that she couldn't stretch and move as she would have liked to, but they managed to stop every hour to have a stretch. Her range of movement was increasing, and her ribs weren't quite as sore.

Having found a lovely café overlooking the bay, they ordered some seafood for lunch to share. All seemed to be very relaxed until Dianne, who was gazing out toward the roadside, spotted a white utility that looked similar to the one that had been following them earlier on the trip. She stopped chewing and just stared out toward the road.

"What is it, Di?" asked Troy. He looked out in the direction she was facing but saw nothing out of the ordinary.

"Oh, nothing. I just got some recollections..." she said vaguely. Her whole attitude changed from that moment.

"Are you all right? Tell us, Di, we want to help you." Gabby needed Di to realize that their support was always there for her. "You are probably going to get flashbacks of the attack, which is completely normal."

The car was parked about a block away. She wanted to see who was in it. Her heart started thumping, and a thought crossed her mind. The guys in the white utility might have wanted to access the drugs now, while the car was parked. Her mind flitted from one possibility to the next. All the while, she couldn't help think of the threat.

Not wanting to alert Troy and Gabby, she forced herself to calm down and appear 'normal'. She ate some of the seafood and welcomed the cool cider to wash down the pain killers.

Gabby and Troy were aware that the relaxed atmosphere of just twenty minutes earlier had disappeared. It was back to the guarded and tense feeling among the three.

"Well, I guess we better start heading off now." Gabby picked up the check and paid for the lunch. This was the first time that she had experienced not knowing exactly what to do to help Dianne. There was obviously something she wasn't telling them, and it was painful to see her agonize over whatever it was.

As they walked back to the car, nothing seemed to be amiss. Dianne held onto Troy like she was taking her last steps; or his last steps, as the case may have been. They got into the car, and then she nervously got her iPad out of the trunk. Carefully opening the tailgate, while keeping an eye out for whoever might be around, her heart beat so fast. Being careful not to strain her ribs from the weight of the luggage, she lifted up the edge of the carpeted base ever so slightly.

From what she could tell, given that all the luggage weighed the carpet down, she noticed that the packets of white powder were still under there. Quickly grabbing her iPad, she pushed the edge of the carpet back into position and then sat in the rear seat.

"Got it."

Gabby started the engine, and they were off. It was a relief to be on the interstate. Dianne relaxed into the soft leather back seat and gazed out at the scenery. The music once again was chosen by Troy. This time he chose a playlist called, 'Chilling', and the beautiful voice of Norah Jones filled the car.

Just as the soothing music had restored everyone's equilibrium, a white utility overtook their car and proceeded in the lane next to them, but just slightly ahead. Dianne noticed it immediately and sat upright in the seat trying her hardest to see if it was the same guys. She thought to herself that it was only a matter of time before Gabby recognized them, and then who knows what would happen.

A nervous chatter took hold of Dianne. She flitted between topics including everything from the comfortable leather seats to the vast scenery they had experienced along their journey. Troy and Gabby looked at each other with a 'what's got into her' look, but were happily chatting along.

From Mobile Bay, they traveled along the interstate toward Tallahassee, Florida. It was as if a lifetime had passed since they left Los Angeles. So many things had happened. So many topics were discussed. As they pulled into the Best Western Plus, they all hoped there would be availability, since a booking had not been made in advance.

Easing into the walk to the hotel lobby, Dianne was grateful for the timely stop as the car ride was taking its toll.

"Super! They have room for us, so let's go!" Gabby was just as relieved for the break in journey.

"Well, well, well, what do we have here," said Troy, investigating the bathroom.

"What is it?" said Dianne.

Gabby joined them, and as the three of them crammed into the bathroom, it provided some much-needed light-hearted conversation.

"So who is going first?" said Gabby, looking at the enormous spa tub.

"I think the three of us could fit in there!" said Troy with a wink.

"Ha ha! Can you imagine the three of us having a spa...I'd be in fits of laughter, and that would be so painful," Dianne managed a laugh, and the smile on her face was such a relief to see.

"Okay, so who did the most driving, hint hint," said Gabby cheekily.

"Hey! That's not fair. I would have driven, if I had felt better."

"It's okay, I'm sure Gabby won't mind if you go first, Di." said Troy. "Besides, I'll make sure you are comfortable while in the spa. I'll bring you grapes, snacks, wine, chocolate, and whatever your heart desires. Hell, I'll even give you a massage!" he added with a grin.

"Sure you will," said Gabby.

"Ah, Troy, I hate to remind you, but I've got bruises on most of my body. A massage would be agonizing pain! But thanks for the thought."

It was nice to see Dianne relax. The banter was just what the doctor ordered and soon they would be enjoying a meal in the restaurant downstairs.

"I'm going to put on weight after this trip!" said Dianne, having just finished a mushroom risotto. "It seems like ages since the 'fitness room' at Phoenix!"

"Oh yeah! Remember when you walked in? I was like, 'Well, *hello,* baby'. I couldn't believe you were there too," added Troy.

"I think I was still sleeping or something," said Gabby, enjoying a vegetarian lasagne.

"You were. I sneaked out early, and lo and behold there was Troy sweating it up," Dianne winked at Troy.

Finishing a huge steak with vegetables, Troy enjoyed reminiscing, "I remember seeing you in your shorts and teeny weeny t-shirt, and I thought, *Oh my God, it's my lucky day.*"

The three of them burst into a raucous laughter at Troy's recounting of the encounter. Dianne grimaced as she held her ribs, but still managed to take part in the fun.

"What about the hot tub!" added Gabby. "Didn't you say you could hear voices coming from the hot tub?"

"That's right! How could I forget? I remember trying to read, and all I could hear were giggles and the constant chatter of female voices. Hilarious, it was the two of you. Wished I could have been a fly on the wall."

By this stage, Dianne had really relaxed. She didn't seem to be grimacing so much.

"I think the wine had something to do with the giggles," said Gabby. "Dianne insisted we indulge."

"Exactly! That's why I would have loved to have had a bird's eye view," said Troy.

Dianne rapped him over the knuckles gently with her fork.

Troy felt he had known them for a lot longer than a few days. In fact, the three of them got on so well together.

"I wonder if we would have bumped into you somewhere else on our trip, if we hadn't stopped in Phoenix and met you in that coffee shop," said Gabby.

"I've wondered that myself. I think that, yes, we would have bumped into each other somewhere along the line. It might have been in New Orleans."

He reflected on what might have been. If only he had been with Dianne, the attack wouldn't have happened. As the evening grew to a close, so did their energy, and soon the comfort of their beds would be calling them for yet another night before traveling to Miami in the morning.

Chapter 18

Stashed Away

"So what exactly did Dan say when you called him?" Dianne asked completely out of the blue, sitting in the passenger seat the next morning and feeling a lot better.

Again, Troy and Gabby looked to each other for support in the rearview mirror, and with that silence, Gabby took the lead and very cautiously explained the phone call.

"Dan was so worried about you, but there was something in the way that he spoke that didn't sound right. When I pushed the conversation, he let it slip that he and Dean had some sort of deal going, and I'm still trying to get my head around why this Murray Wolfe person was involved and why he targeted you."

Silence filled the void. Dianne had taken another verbal blow to add to what must have been the most traumatic experience.

Gabby noticed tears welling up in Dianne's eyes. The pain was so overwhelming, yet so necessary so she could travel from the dark place she was in, learn from it, regain confidence, and move on in her life. It was by no means an easy journey, but one that she could work through with the support of her friends and family.

"I don't know who Murray Wolfe is... But he had a wolf tattooed on his arm."

Troy looked into the rearview mirror at Gabby and then shifted in his seat, glancing at Di.

"Do you know anything about his involvement with Dean and Dan?" Gabby gambled with the fact that Dianne was likely to close down and go into silence again, but it was so important to try and piece the information together. Even though this guy had been taken into police custody, Dean and Dan were clearly involved in something sinister. Something so big, that Dan put his girlfriend's life at risk. It was only a matter of time before the truth was revealed, and Dan may end up in jail as well.

"It's just too awful. I can't talk about it." Said Dianne, teary-eyed. "I'm sick of this! Why did they have to target me!"

"Please, Di. I know it's painful to talk about, but it is so important. If they had you targeted, who's to say that Troy and I won't be a target, too?"

That was her undoing. Dianne lost her composure and sobbed so loud. Her face, which was still scratched and bruised, was now swollen and distorted from crying. The bright, beautiful, vivacious woman, who always had a positive thought to convey to anyone, was now broken. How she looked on the surface was only a tiny reflection of how she felt within herself.

"They're out there still," Dianne managed to say.

"Who is out there?" Troy leaned forward in his seat and stretched his hand out to touch Dianne.

"The two guys in the utility."

"What!" said Gabby.

"They are following us. I'm fairly sure I spotted them in Mobile Bay."

Gabby wanted to ask her why she didn't tell them there, but thought better of it now. This wasn't the time to chastise Dianne. Instead she kept quiet and let Troy soothe her in the hope that she would continue to open up.

"Di, did that Murray guy tell you they were headed there, or was it a coincidence that you saw them?"

"No, but I've worked it out." Her tears had dried now. She faced the window, gazing out at the cars passing in the nearby lanes.

"How? What did you work out?

Since leaving Mobile Bay, Dianne had come to the conclusion that whatever the risk of keeping her secret, it couldn't be worse than what could happen to Troy.

"Dan and Dean have some sort of deal. It's to do with drugs."

There, she said it.

Her mind visualized all the drugs stashed away just inches away from where they were sitting. The thought paralyzed her.

"Di, what is it? Do you know anything about the deal? Come on, please tell me," pleaded Troy.

Entranced by the fear that held her, Dianne didn't speak for the next few hours. Gabby and Troy were perplexed as to what they should do. Stopping each hour, so she could stretch her body, provided physical relief for all of them, but the stress of not knowing and her silence had left them drained and in despair.

The interstate provided no relief in the way of scenery. Gabby kept a close eye on the cars around them, Dianne, and the thoughts that circled her mind. She wished she could speak to Mick. She wished she had a solution.

Troy retreated with his ear plugs in, preferring to keep to himself and listen to some heavy music, for want of distraction. This road trip was once again taking its toll. His intentions were good, but now he was faced with a lot to deal with, not to mention the possibility of his public profile in disrepute.

By far, this leg of the trip proved the most taxing.

Oh shit! thought Gabby as she spotted a vehicle suspiciously like the utility they had dreaded seeing again.

Keeping her eyes peeled, she drove steadily. Now the only thing on her mind was that car. *Was it the utility?*

The last stop they were to make before approaching the outer suburbs of Miami came at a good time. Gabby took the nearest off-ramp into a suburban area. Dianne had the dire urge to get herself a milkshake.

As Troy stretched and yawned outside the car, Gabby joined him from her side of the car. "This has got to be the worst leg of this trip. I really fear for her well-being," said Gabby. "I also hate to bring this up, but I think I saw the utility on the interstate, but I couldn't slow down enough to be sure. Looks like they are definitely headed to Miami."

"Great!" added Troy sarcastically, annoyed at the situation. "We are damned if we try and talk to her about this and damned if we don't. Totally rooted!"

Troy scuffed his foot on the loose gravel, raising some dust, and walked down the pavement leaving Gabby standing by herself.

"That looks nice," said Gabby, entering the small diner where Dianne had just purchased a milkshake. "I might buy one as well."

The girls took a seat in one of the booths, Dianne still retreating into herself, not saying a word. Troy entered through the screen of vertical strips of vinyl that was supposed to keep the flies out. He joined them at the booth, noticing Gabby had bought him a milkshake.

"Thanks," he said. "I just needed to vent some steam."

Dianne felt awful about the tension she was causing. The same scenario rolled around in her mind. If she told them there were drugs in the car, then they would go straight to the police, then Troy could get killed. If she didn't tell them, then she ran the risk of those guys doing whatever they had planned to get the drugs. Either way, she saw no clear escape from this horrid predicament.

They were about fifteen miles from Miami now. Totally exhausted and just hoping that everything would sort itself out at their destination once they saw Virginia, Gabby spotted the utility again. This time, she cautiously kept her eyes firmly on their whereabouts. Troy suspected that Gabby was on to something.

Dianne, having also seen the utility nearby, nervously chatted and joked about random topics. She thought it was now or never – she had to tell them about the drugs.

"Do you mind if we just stop here for a minute?" she said, her nerves getting more and more obvious.

"Sure, but what for? We're nearly there," said Gabby.

"I just need to do something...and..."

Both Troy and Gabby were relieved she spoke. Going with the flow, Gabby agreed to stop the car. Carefully taking one of the exit roads, she parked and turned the ignition off.

As white as a ghost and sweating profusely, Dianne unbuckled her seat belt.

"Babe, are you okay? You are so pale. Gabby, look at her!" Panic was clearly etched in Troy's voice now. "She looks like she's going to faint!"

"Jeez, Di, what is it?"

"I'm going to tell you something, and you're not going to like it."

"Oh, Di, please, just *tell* us."

"Right at this moment, the white utility that has been following us from Palm Springs is hot on our tails. Gabby, I'm surprised you haven't seen it. The same guys are driving it."

"I thought I saw it...but wasn't sure. What's going on?" asked Gabby, scared for their safety, looking at Troy for backup.

Something was seriously was about to happen. Di's face was ashen. Her hands were shaking and her mouth distorted as she spoke.

I don't get it. Why? *Why* are they so interested in our whereabouts?" Gabby said, asking no one in particular, but questioning this whole scenario.

Then she had an epiphany.

At that very moment, as the words left her mouth, her curious mind put two and two together. A drug deal, Dan, Dean, Dianne – it could only mean one thing...they were carrying drugs in the car.

"Don't get out!" screamed Dianne. "Gabby! Don't get out of the car!"

"I know what's going on, Di, I've got to check the car!"

"What is it?" said Troy, raising his voice now in urgency.

"No, please don't. Not now," she sobbed again as her throat seemed to constrict thinking of the possibility of Troy being killed.

"What the hell is going on here?" asked Troy, completely at a loss.

"There's drugs in the car, isn't there?" Gabby's eyes were bulging and her nostrils flaring at the possibility. "We've got to inform the police!"

"You're kidding!" Troy really didn't have any idea.

"No! You can't tell the police. Troy will get...killed if we do. I had my suspicions, and then I found them. I just couldn't say anything to you guys because of the threat. We've got to get back on the road soon, or they'll get suspicious. I just needed to tell you before getting to our hotel."

Gabby processed all the information thrown at her. Her mind was running from one scenario to another.

"You realize they're going to be all over us. The police are probably on our tail too! Jeez, Di."

"Well, I didn't know what to do. I'm sorry."

"Now's not the time to have a domestic, girls. We should get back on the road and head to the hotel. My thoughts are, we park the car and get the hell away."

They drove in silence down through the outer suburbs of Miami. On reaching the hotel they had booked, Gabby pulled into the driveway of The Staybridge Suites. She left Troy and Di in the car and went to check in at the reception desk. She had a sinking feeling it was going to be the last minutes of freedom before something huge was coming down on them.

Unbuckling his seat belt, Troy swung fully around in his seat, now holding Di's hand.

"If I tell the police about the deal, you could get killed!" She unbuckled her seat belt, and in one quick move, she dived through the middle of the two front seats and hugged Troy, sobbing, forgetting all about her sore ribs and body.

"I'm so sorry, so sorry...because of me, they could get you." She was shaking now. Saying the words aloud made it real. Her body was now heaving and trembling, and the injuries that she had endured to her physical body were only a fraction of the emotional pain.

"Hey, come on now, baby. Did this guy tell you they would kill me, or did you guess that?" He held her tight, stroking her hair which was damp from all the tears shed.

"He told me. He said that because of my 'old' boyfriend, my 'new' boyfriend would be killed if I mentioned anything to the police."

Gabby came back to the car with the key to the hotel room. On seeing Troy turned fully in his seat toward Dianne in the back, hands held, tears flowing, she knew he must have persuaded some information from her.

"Is everything all right in here?

"Yes, we're okay." He winked at Gabby, so she started the car and drove into the allocated covered parking spot not asking any questions, but hoping for so many answers.

"Gabby, I've already told Troy this, but you need to know too. The guy that attacked me, Murray Wolfe, told me that Troy would be killed if I told the police about the deal that Dan and Dean had going."

"Oh my God! But I thought you didn't know anything about that?"

"Well, I don't know the details. But what I do know is they've been trailing us. Dan has been giving them the details of where we were headed and staying at."

Dianne had reasoned in her mind that this was the only way that she could try and keep Troy safe. By telling them about the risk at stake. "I haven't seen the utility in a while.

The only way they would know where we are staying is following us. They haven't had Dan to inform them."

Gabby shook her head. The predicament they were in now surpassed all others on the trip. Calling the police would put Troy at risk, if it were a real threat. But police protection is what they needed.

If the threat that Murray Wolfe made to Dianne had any weight to it.

Surely the police could stake out these guys, or take Dean and Dan in for questioning. The thoughts ran through Gabby's mind. She knew that the police needed to be informed, but she dared not risk putting anyone's life in danger. *There must be a way that we can inform the police,* she thought.

"Hi! I'm so glad it's you, Mick. Oh, I wish you were here."

"Whoa, Gab. What's up?"

"I don't know where to begin, but something bad is about to unfold, and I'm just not sure what's going to happen."

There was silence. Mick was always calm and thought things through in a matter-of-fact way. His approach was always: stay positive and calm, and be truthful in all your feelings, emotions, and actions. Be present in the moment.

"I was actually just calling you because I've organized a flight to Miami this afternoon. I managed to get a few days' leave from the center, and I've been missing you."

"Oh Mick! Thank you, you don't know how much I've missed you. It's just that after I tell you what has happened, I don't know if you will really want to be here."

"It doesn't matter, Gab. I'm coming over to see you."

"But do you know that we've been carrying drugs in our car, and the whole time we've been followed was to make sure the drugs arrived here 'safely'?"

"Put it this way: after all those visions, as horrid as they were, I still had the sense that there would be a positive outcome. I know Dianne has a lot of recovering to do, but I know she'll be all right. As for the drugs, I would suggest you do whatever the police need you to do. Even if it means being taken into custody."

"Well, if you're sure, I'd love you to come over. You can meet Virginia, too. Oh, I just remembered, you know how you said you kept getting the word 'wolf' in your mind?"

"Yes?"

"Well, the guy that attacked Dianne had a tattoo of a wolf on his arm, and his name is Murray Wolfe. Not too shabby, Mr Doherty." Gabby showed a hint of a smile now. Among all the stress and anxiety of the last half hour, Mick was able to put a smile on her face and give her a glimmer of hope.

"I have my moments."

Chapter 19

The Waiting Game

It was as if a time bomb was ticking away. Since Dianne had opened up to Troy and Gabby, the seconds, minutes, and hours felt like they were on borrowed time. Questions had been answered, and all the angst of treading on eggshells around Dianne was out in the open. The reason for Dianne's quiet moods and jumpy behavior was justified. Considering she had experienced a brutal attack, been physically and emotionally tortured, it showed great strength of character to speak up about the threat and the hidden drugs, especially when there seemed to be so much at stake. She cared for Troy and believed it was fate that brought them together, which made the threat all the more worrying.

The hotel's spacious underground car park provided an unobstructed view of anyone that might have been lurking around suspiciously. To their relief, the coast seemed clear. It was a little after 3 p.m. when they had arrived, and Gabby decided she wanted to see the drugs for herself. She felt used and violated having drugs that were concealed in the trunk of the car for the entire journey. She thought how Anthony would freak out, if he knew about it, and then she also thought she should update him since she didn't know what the next twenty-four hours held in store. Let alone the next couple of hours...

"Di, I want to see for myself." Gabby got out of the car and walked toward the tailgate.

"You can't. What if they're here and they pounce on us thinking we are doing something with it all? What about Troy?"

"Look around, Di, there isn't a soul around. You said yourself that you hadn't seen them for some time, and without Dan feeding them our whereabouts, I predict we've got a good hour at least before something comes down."

There was nothing that could stop Gabby now. She too had endured the effects of all of this, albeit nothing in comparison to Dianne. Troy sat in the neutral zone of this conversation. He was curious to actually see the drugs himself, but a small part of him was worried about the threat and anything that might provoke it.

Gabby carefully inspected the area once more. When satisfied there was no one at all around, she lifted the tailgate very carefully. A fleeting thought of an explosive being tripped by the tailgate opening crossed her mind. She quashed that thought as she remembered Di had already opened the tailgate earlier on. Also, something like an explosion could destroy the goods. Satisfied with this thought, she proceeded carefully.

The bags were in relatively the same position as they were in Tallahassee. Anticipation of something, they didn't quite know what, overcame them as Gabby and Troy carefully lifted the carpeted trunk cover, which was laden with their baggage. They didn't remove the suitcases first, so their weight made the effort of lifting the cover harder. Under the surface cover was a type of underlay, and there was clearly some evidence of what was hidden underneath. A white, powdery substance was smudged along the edge of the underlay.

Gabby's mind flashed back to the gas station in Palm Springs; when something made her check the trunk before they drove off toward Phoenix. She was sure this was where it all began. But some pieces of the puzzle were not fitting. Thinking back to the two guys from the gas station in Palm Springs, they must have planted the drugs in their car before they even left home. *Maybe it was planted while they were at home!* Her mind was spinning with what if's, and now she thought back to how something didn't feel quite right about them. Searching through the news on her iPad, she remembered the news article of the two escaped criminals from a Miami jail. Then the utility was obviously following them. When Dianne discovered the pictures of Dan on her Facebook page, the route of the trip to Dallas was changed to just traveling to San Antonio and on to New Orleans. The guys in the utility must have been advised to travel on to Dallas before the girls had changed plans. So this is where Murray Wolfe came into the picture. He must have been a local that Dean knew who had been told to follow the trail and keep an eye on the situation until the other two in the utility could get back onto the trail.

"Di, do you realize that the drugs would have been planted either while we were still in LA, or somehow they planted them in Palm Springs at the gas station. I just can't imagine how they could have done that so quickly though." Dianne didn't respond.

"I remember now that something prompted me to check the trunk of the car after we had filled the tank with gas. I remember seeing some white, powdery stuff in the trunk, and I automatically assumed that it was from those candies that you have, which may have spilled or something. I really didn't think too much about it."

"I can't believe it. How could Dan have been part of this mess? Honestly, you just don't know people..."

"It is hard to fathom, especially being such a high-profile player and risking so much." Troy added. He had his own public profile to think about.

While the conversation was between Troy and Di now, Gabby continued to examine the entire area of the trunk as well as underneath the car. She then proceeded to lift up the underlay and although they were expecting to find drugs hidden, nothing could have surprised them more than the sheer amount of pouches stashed away in every nook and cranny of this area. Troy held up his side to expose the full extent of the stash.

"These guys are professionals, you can see that. The packets haven't just been thrown in here. They've obviously done this before."

Staring at the 'goods', each one contemplated their individual and joint fate from this point on. Looking at the actual drugs hidden in the car that they had felt was their protection, their sanctuary, made them feel violated.

"What on earth are you doing, Gab? Jeez, if that doesn't look suspicious, I don't know what would." Dianne was clearly on edge still about being seen looking for the drugs.

"You wouldn't believe this if I told you."

Gabby was down on the ground, skirt fanned out around her, kneeling and twisting her head into position to see underneath the car.

Di and Troy looked at each other, and then in one swift move, they too were on the cement-floored car park, inspecting the underneath of the Jeep.

"You're kidding! How on earth could all that have stayed in there!"

Dianne was referring to the hundreds of plastic packets of white, powdery substance which were carefully packed together in the hollowed out area of the bumper bar.

The three of them looked at one another in disbelief. Troy got up and then inspected the rest of the car.

"These guys have got to be pros. You wouldn't believe where they've hidden more if it."

Both girls dusted themselves off and walked around to the right-hand side at the front of the car. Troy was crouching down looking up into the wheel arch.

"How on earth do they get them to stick there?"

"I'd say they use some sort of tar that sticks to the metal of the wheel arch. The packets in this area seem to be wrapped in a thicker-looking plastic."

"Jeez, what if we went over a huge pothole or something and everything got damaged. They've taken a huge risk putting it up there, haven't they?"

Careful not to disturb any of the drugs packed in the trunk, bumper bar or wheel arches, they carefully carried each one of their bags out of the car. They took practically everything out this time, including maps, CDs, candy; everything loose of theirs was taken out. Thoughts of them not seeing the car again after this ran through their minds.

Room Number 1410 was a spacious two-bedroom suite. It was tastefully furnished and luxuriously appointed. Leaving their bags on the baggage rack near the front door, the atmosphere once again was somewhat tense. Sensing that Gabby was contemplating calling the police now, Dianne became very agitated, and as if talking to her would distract Gabby into not calling the police, she nervously chatted about the minibar and cable TV movies on that night.

Troy put the last of the bags on the luggage rack. *I feel like I've left something behind*, he thought.

The girls were having their own discussion about telling the police.

Gabby was not buying it. She knew what Dianne was up to. The thing with this whole situation had Gabby in turmoil because she reflected on what Virginia had told her about drug smuggling cases that Hamish had worked on previously. She and her friends could be charged with aiding and abetting, or impeding a police investigation, if they didn't inform the police now. The time was now 5 p.m. Mick's plane would be landing at 8:30 p.m. She could hardly wait to see him. Thinking of Mick reminded her of what he told her just hours before. He said that there would be a positive outcome to all of this.

"Di, I know you're stressing about what that guy said to you, but honestly, can you just think about this from a different perspective? We have to tell the police. The longer we harbor these drugs, the worse it's going to be – for all of us.

"I know what you're saying, but I just can't take the risk... you know, with Troy. If Dean and Dan had orchestrated this whole drug deal without us even suspecting anything, who knows what they'll do now."

"Troy, please talk some sense into Di. We can't hide in this hotel room, and I'm sure they've got us staked out. It's just a matter of time. The threat that Murray Wolfe made might just be all talk. Don't you think the police would protect us?"

Gabby retrieved her mobile phone from her handbag. "I'm going to call Virginia. It feels like ages since we had any contact with her. I've been so distracted by everything to call or text her."

"Don't tell her!" shrieked Dianne. "She will tell Hamish, and that will be the end of it all!" pleaded Dianne.

Pacing the room now, Di began to feel the tenderness of her ribs. Looking at her bruised face in the mirror was like she was looking for answers. She walked to the window and opened the drapes wider, gazing outside toward the bay area.

"Come on, Di. Shall I call them now?" Gabby pleaded.

"Virginia or the police?...No, not yet."

"Well, what are you waiting for? Those guys will be sweating it out trying to locate us, and when they do, we're not going to have any protection or support that we could organize if we told the police."

Frustrated with the whole situation, Gabby grabbed her handbag and told the others she was going down to the coffee shop. She had had enough of this, and she hoped that Troy could knock some sense into Di while she was gone. It was now 8 p.m. Mick's plane would be landing soon. She felt a sense of relief knowing that he was only about an hour away and in the same city.

Ordering herself a cappuccino, the thought of letting Anthony know what was happening flitted across her mind. She dialed his number, feeling quite odd about speaking to him from the point of view that it seemed like a lifetime ago that she saw him, and also because her heart was not his anymore.

"Hi! How's it going?" Anthony answered the phone in a very 'un-Anthony' manner.

"Good, well, okay...what's that in the background?"

"Oh, I've just got a friend visiting. We're just listening to some music."

This was really strange. Anthony sounded quite upbeat and, for once, was not watching television. Plus, since when did he invite his 'friends' over?

"Sounds...nice." Gabby couldn't resist; she had to ask, "Who's the friend?"

"I don't think you've met. We worked together in the Westwood branch."

"No, I don't suppose I have. Who is it?"

"Danielle Jackson."

After an uncomfortable pause, with a quick turn in conversation, he finally said, "Why did you say it is only *okay*?"

"With what I have to tell you, Anthony, you're going to have to sit down."

The waitress brought her coffee. Gabby emptied three sugars into it and stirred. As she sipped the hot drink, her story unfolded with the real-life ending, that is, the drugs planted in the car, and ended with the utility in Palm Springs. Everything in between was detailed. Anthony was in shock and asked her why she hadn't informed him earlier.

"Well, I had planned to call you from New Orleans, but honestly, after Dianne was attacked it has all been a bit of a blur. She refuses to tell the police because she fears Troy will get killed."

"I *am* in shock. I'm going to inform the police."

"No! Please don't do that. She's teetering on the verge of an extremely fragile state. I fear her reaction if anyone was to interfere. So, please, don't say anything. I'm only calling you because I thought you should know that something will come of this, and I don't know if I'll be taken into custody or what."

"Jeez, Gab. How could you sit back and watch this mess unfold without doing something constructive?"

Gabby was seething now. She thought, *Was it any wonder she no longer loved this man? Honestly, had he listened to a word she had said?*

"You know what, Anthony, I thought I was doing the right thing by calling you. I wish I hadn't. You are so selfish and one-sided, and you have absolutely no empathy for anyone else's feelings. I am going now, and don't bother to call me. Really, Anthony, let's just say this out loud to each other so we can move on...there is no 'us' anymore, is there?"

There was silence.

"No, Gabby, I don't think there is."

"Well, quite frankly, I am relieved. Since we're being honest with each other...well, I am anyway, I just want to tell you that I am seeing someone, and he is flying to Miami to spend some time here."

Checking her watch, she realized Mick would be on his way to the hotel now.

"Gabby, you may think I'm a fool, but I knew something was going on. I just didn't know with whom. I don't want to know, either. While we're on this subject, I'm sure your curiosity is piqued by the fact that I have a visitor who is female and who is here listening to music with me. Am I right?"

"Sure, whatever."

"Come on, I know you, Gabby. Your curious little mind never stops. So you can put that to rest, I will tell you.

Danielle and I are seeing each other. So it seems we have both strayed from our marital vows."

"Funny we both waited until I was on the other side of the country to discuss this."

"Yes, very funny," he said dryly.

"Good bye, Anthony. Oh, by the way, I have no idea what will happen to your car."

"Don't be like that, Gabby. Look, I still care for you and for your safety, and I'm sure deep down you do too, or you wouldn't have called me. So let's just take things one step at a time. We'll see each other when you're back and discuss what will happen, okay?"

"Sure. Bye."

"Bye."

Taking the last sip of her coffee, Gabby let go of a sigh that released a lot of tension. It was time she called Virginia to let her know that they had checked into the hotel. She thought about how the whole purpose of this trip was to visit Virginia. Honestly, who would have thought any of these events could have happened.

"Hi, Virginia! How are you?" asked Gabby, putting on her chirpiest voice.

"I'm great, thanks. How are you guys doing? Is Dianne feeling any better?"

Virginia and Gabby had been texting each other, but since Gabby had informed her of the attack on Dianne, the texts became few and far between. Virginia was horrified. Gabby didn't want to worry her. She had gone through an emotional time herself, particularly at the start of the pregnancy with Hamish having the affair. She felt that it would be too much for Virginia to cope with, knowing about the drugs stashed in the car. Besides, she might tell Hamish out of concern for her friends, and then who knows what could happen. The fewer people knew, the better at this point. Thinking in hindsight that telling Anthony was a big mistake, she hoped he wouldn't go the police with the details.

"She's definitely improved. Still a bit guarded at times. I think she must be having flashbacks of the attack."

"Poor thing. She will probably need to have some counseling back in LA, just to help deal with any issues. You know, sometimes the consequences of such a horrific event recur months, even years, later."

"I hope not."

"So do I. She'll need everyone's support. Just on a lighter note, do you think the three of you can come over for dinner tonight? I know it's not much notice. You are welcome here anytime, of course. I know it's already late, but the offer still stands if you're up for it. We will get some take out."

"Thanks, Gin. I'd love to come, but...well, I think I'll ask Dianne and Troy and let you know. I'm down at the coffee shop in the hotel at the moment, and they're up in the room. Also, just to let you know, there will be four of us...if that's all right with you."

"Oh?"

"Look, I didn't want to throw this in among all the events. Gin, Anthony and I have had a rocky time for a couple of years."

"Oh, Gabby, I'm sorry to hear that."

"Thanks. It's been a long time coming actually because we've drifted slowly apart."

"You're not saying you've separated, are you?" Virginia was really shocked.

"Well, no, yes...actually, sort of...it's complicated. There is something you should know: I'm seeing someone. His name is Mick Doherty. I actually met him ages ago at the yoga center that I've been going to for the last five years. I always loved his classes, and I started doing some workshops that he does every now and then. There's always been a connection with him that I felt each time I attended his classes. Anyway, about two months ago I attended another workshop, but this time the electricity between us was amazing. He obviously felt it too because he asked me out for coffee and then, after many heart-to-heart talks, and with the state of my marriage, we sort of started seeing each other. Look, I know what you're going to say, but honestly, Anthony and I have been 'apart' for ages when I really analyze things."

"Oh, Gab. I had no idea. I really don't know what to say. I feel sad that your marriage is, was, on the rocks."

"I know it's a shock, and I wouldn't blame you for thinking I was wrong for seeing someone so soon. Mick is a wonderful guy. He knows the situation and isn't pushing me into anything. He's more than happy to give me some space, time, or whatever it is I need. You would really like him, Gin. He is so gentle and caring, plus we have so much in common."

"Sounds like you've really fallen for him. I'm happy for you, but take your time. Don't rush into anything."

"Yes, I will. That reminds me, I was going to tell you that there will be four of us because Mick is flying over to Miami to spend a few days while we're here."

"So much for space then!" teased Virginia.

"Yes, I guess that's true. It's just that without Mick I don't think Troy and I would have had as much hope as we did when Dianne went missing. It was Mick who alerted us to the fact that she was in trouble, but what really gave us hope was the fact that he was confident that Dianne was still alive."

"Hang on a minute. You've lost me now. How did Mick know all this?"

"He is a yoga teacher, but also he is a clairvoyant medium. He is psychic."

"Oh."

There was a quiet pause from Virginia as she took in this information.

Virginia was stunned. It was a lot to take in, and she didn't know how to articulate her thoughts. For a journalist, this was very unusual but it was actually the fact that she felt a slight niggle in her side that took her thoughts away from their conversation. Shifting in her seat to get more comfortable, she continued chatting with Gabby.

"So, you and Dianne have found new love. Who would have thought that this trip would involve so much." The niggle in her side was still there. She rubbed it as she shifted again in the chair. "Well, I guess coming over for dinner is out of the question tonight. What about tomorrow night? You can bring Mick, I'd love to meet him, and Troy, oh, and of course I can't wait to see you and Di."

"Sounds great. We'll have to..."

Gabby remembered the car was sitting in the parking lot stashed with drugs. There was no way they could drive it anywhere. She wondered how she could explain this to Virginia.

"What's up? Did you remember you have other plans?"

"No, no. Look, Gin, there's something else that has happened. Well, it hasn't actually happened as such, but something is going to happen." Gabby was so vague. In her mind she wanted to tell Virginia about the drugs, but hesitated because she didn't want to risk Hamish finding out.

Gabby's phone beeped with a call-waiting signal. She excused herself to Virginia while she took the incoming call. It was Mick, already in the hotel foyer. She arranged for him to come to the coffee shop she was in. Seeing him walk over was such a wonderful sight. Her heart began the familiar 'pull' whenever he was around. There was one thing wrong though: the look on Mick's face, although he had a half smile, was somewhat strained. He looked worried.

Going back to Virginia, she explained that Mick had just arrived and that he was heading over to meet her.

"That's great. What was it that you said was going to happen or not happen? I can't remember now which it was."

"Well, Gin, if I tell you, can you promise me you won't tell a soul, not even Hamish? Especially not Hamish."

The niggle was now a pain. Virginia stood up from her seat to try and dislodge the pain, but it persisted.

"Now, Gab, you know Hamish and I have been working through our issues, and part of that is to be honestly open with each other about absolutely everything." Virginia spoke in a strained way.

"What is it, Gin, you sound really...different all of a sudden."

Virginia was not her usual eloquent self. The words were not flowing, and she was slightly out of breath.

Gabby just couldn't keep her secret any longer. In a way, if Virginia told Hamish, at least then the police would be able to protect them. She made the decision and stuck to it.

Mick greeted Gabby with a kiss on the cheek. He sat down next to her, still looking a bit worried and looking intensely at Gabby. It was obvious to him that Gabby was in a state of frustration.

"Okay. I can only tell you this in the hope that you will do what you think is best. I don't want to cause any friction in your marriage."

"Gosh, what on earth is it?" Virginia momentarily found a comfortable position.

"The reason Dianne was attacked was because Dan, her latest partner, had some sort of drug deal with his coach, and they were tracking our whereabouts throughout the trip."

"I don't get it. What sort of drug deal?" The breathlessness came back and a slight jabbing sensation in the side.

"The type where they stash a million little packets of drugs in our car and have some guys follow us to 'babysit' the transportation of the drugs."

There, she said it. It was out there now. Whatever would be would be.

"What! You're kidding. Why would they do that? How could Dan use Dianne like that? So your car is sitting at the hotel with drugs in it?"

"Yes."

"You've got to tell the police, Gab. Hamish has told me so many stories about cases he's been on for drug smuggling. It's just not worth it. You're going to have to tell them."

"The thing is, Gin, they threatened to kill Troy if this information was leaked to the police. They are probably trying to get the drugs as we speak. I really don't know how they will get access to the car park, but I'm sure they will manage. They seem to be able to open the trunk without damaging the lock or anything. They're real professionals, by the look of things."

Mick was trying to get Gabby's attention. He really didn't look his usual calm self.

She motioned to him that she wouldn't be long.

"Gabby, I think you need to tell the police, regardless of the threat...ugh!"

"Gin? Are you okay?"

"Gab...I can't...pain...ugh! Help, Gab..."

The phone was left hanging. Gabby couldn't hear anything from Virginia at all.

"It's Virginia, isn't it?" asked Mick urgently.

"Yes, she must have fainted! Oh no, we've got to tell Hamish."

She kept the line open while searching for Hamish's mobile number, so she would hear Virginia if she called out to her. Once located, she used Mick's phone to dial out.

"We should call 911 straight away. Do you know Virginia's address?" asked Mick.

"Yes, I do."

The call went to Hamish's voicemail. Gabby left a message. She then dialed 911 and explained the situation. They said they would send the paramedics and would be there in five minutes.

"Thank God! They said they'll be there in about five minutes. Oh, Mick, I hope she's okay."

"Gabby, in the cab coming over to the hotel I had some visions...I saw Virginia. I sensed it was her. I feared that something was going to happen to her. Then, as the cab got closer to the hotel, I was getting a sense of pain...I think one of the babies might be in trouble."

Chapter 20

Emergency

"We've got to get over there!" Gabby was panicking as she ran to the elevator. With Mick by her side now, she was grateful for his support.

The elevator in the hotel lobby took far too long to arrive. They decided to run up the stairs, two or three at a time.

After running down the hall to Room 1410, Gabby's hands refused to keep still while she waved the proximity card to unlock the door.

"Oh, what's wrong with this thing!" she said, quite agitated.

Troy heard the fumbling at the door and decided to open it himself.

"Hey, what's up?"

"Quick, we've got to get to Virginia. She's collapsed."

"What! How?" said Dianne overhearing the conversation from the sitting area of the room.

"I called her while I was at the coffee shop and I...Oh, I hope I didn't stress her out."

Gabby paced the room, flustered by the situation. Dianne grabbed her handbag, while Troy scooped up the car keys. Then the realization of the drugs planted in the car crossed everyone's mind. Stopping in their tracks, Mick spoke the words each one was thinking.

"It's too risky."

"We don't have time – we should just go. Maybe they don't know where we are since they haven't shown up yet." Dianne assumed that the car was still intact.

"Seriously, Gab, we've been here a few hours now. I'd say they are planning their assault." Troy said, slightly agitated.

"Di, can you please keep trying Hamish's mobile. He didn't answer before. I had to leave a couple of messages. We should phone his office and find out where he is." Gabby's mind was ticking over.

"Gab, the paramedics would be with her now."

"What can we do? This is all my fault..."

"Take it easy, Gab. Let's think about this."

"How can I take it easy? I caused this! I know what I'll do! I'll call 911 again and see if they can tell me which hospital they will take her to!"

"It's not an answering service, Gabby," said Troy.

"Well, it's worth a try! It's more than you're doing..."

Gabby was irritated by Troy's comment. The tension in the room had become stifling. Dianne paced the length of the area in front of the large windows.

With a renewed enthusiasm and ignoring Troy's comment, she dialed 911.

Mick stood silently, away from Gabby, as she made the call. He tuned himself in to Virginia, and he got a sense that she was stable. Meanwhile, Gabby was getting nowhere with the operator and was getting quite agitated at the seemingly hopeless situation.

"Hello, I called you about ten minutes ago to arrange for paramedics to go to my friend's house as she had collapsed..."

"Ma'am, this service is for emergencies only," a disembodied voice interrupted Gabby's spiel.

"Please. Do you know if they have reached the house and got access yet?" Gabby was persistent and bordering on being very abrupt.

"Sorry, ma'am, I can't help you. This line needs to be open for emergencies." The operator was about to hang up the phone.

"PLEASE!!" Gabby raised her voice, practically shouting at the operator. Then, in a moment's realization, she began to sob.

The anguish in Gabby's voice must have resonated through to the operator, who relinquished her strict work guidelines.

"I can only tell you if a unit has left the depot for that address."

"Okay, please tell me that, then."

"What was the address, ma'am?"

"5250 Oleander Drive, Pembroke Pines. The patient's name is Virginia McDonald. She's pregnant with twins. They would have had to enter the house somehow, because she was alone at home."

Gabby was trying to give as much information as she could manage.

The operator pressed a few keys on her keyboard and came back to Gabby.

"Ma'am, I have here that Unit 135 left the Weston depot five minutes ago precisely. There's no way of knowing if they have reached the address unless they radio in once at the property."

"Oh, thank you so much..."

Before she had a chance to say anything else, the operator had hung up.

Mick didn't approach Gabby at all; he appeared to be quite distant. Sensing Gabby's anxiety and the situation with the drugs, he began to focus on Virginia's whereabouts. A map that he picked up at the airport was still in his jacket pocket.

"They can't tell us if the paramedics have reached her yet. What should we do?"

Gabby was exasperated. She twirled her hair around her fingers and let out a huge sigh.

Desperate to reach Virginia but feeling restrained by the situation, she felt that time seemed to stand still. Then, out of the blue, Troy had an idea.

"Gabby, do you know Virginia's address?"

"Yes, why? Do you think we should go there?"

"Well, if we know her address, we could look up the hospital closest to her and take our chances."

Troy's expression was serious. His mind ticked over an idea as he wondered whether the others would go for it. Just as Gabby ran to the baggage rack to fish out her GPS, Mick emerged from his concentration and was confident that he roughly knew the name of the hospital.

"I'm getting some images, I just need to focus in. The street is something like Cougar or similar sounding."

Mick emerged holding the map in his hand, then laid it down on the coffee table.

"It's probably this one, Gabby, South Pinewood Hospital." Troy was confident that he was right.

"What street is it showing up on?" Mick was focusing on the map, but directing his question to Troy.

"The address is Smith Street, South Pinewood. Why?"

"It's not the right one."

"What? How do you know? It's got to be, they would take her to the closest one!"

As Mick shifted his gaze around the map, focusing on the area that Virginia lived in, he got a better indication of the street name. This time it was very clear.

"Coulter Street. That's where the hospital is."

His confidence irritated Troy. Gabby was straight over to Mick's side, looking at the giant map laid out, with Mick's finger pointing to the hospital.

"Well, lets go then!"

"Gabby, the GPS is showing Coulter Street at least ten miles away from South Pinewood! There's no way they'd be there!"

Mick seemed to withdraw from the conflict between Troy and Gabby. He faced this sort of disbelieving situation so often.

"Look, Troy, you've got to trust Mick's vibes. I want to reach Virginia quickly more than anything, probably more than you do, and I totally believe what Mick is saying.

"Fine! Whatever you reckon!"

Troy stormed over to Dianne near the window. She had not said a word. The waves of her emotions were riding high. He put his arms around her, and they both silently looked out over the busy streets below.

"I've just Googled Coulter Street, Gab. There's a memorial hospital there, and I'm positive that's where she is."

"Right. Let's go." Gabby collected her keys and handbag. "Well, guys, are you coming?"

Di and Troy looked at each other as Gabby and Mick were already at the door, ready to go.

"Yes! Hang on, we're coming!" This was the first time Dianne had spoken in over an hour. Troy was annoyed that his opinion was not considered. He felt undermined by Mick and his super senses. There was nothing he could do.

Mick, Gabby, Troy, and Dianne were on a mission. Their purpose on this journey was to support Virginia. That was what they intended doing. The circumstances had changed somewhat, but that's what the ultimate goal had been.

The hotel elevator whisked them off to the basement level of the car park. Trepidation prevailed as approaching the car was like expecting some sort of explosion or kidnapping to take place. Gabby pressed the unlock button on the remote. So far, all seemed intact. Troy circled the back of the car, Mick the front. Both looked underneath for anything suspicious. The girls huddled together hoping and praying they were doing the right thing.

One quick look in the tailgate and under the trunk underlay and Troy confirmed the drugs were still there. He also noticed that the drugs stashed in the bumper bars were still in place.

Gabby took the passenger seat, while Troy took the driver's seat. She would be navigating today. Di and Mick took their seats in the back.

"You'd think that if you went to all that trouble to smuggle drugs across the country that you would have picked up the goods by now. Sheesh, sounds like some plan of theirs got botched."

"I'd say this is what they've been waiting for. The car to be driven out of the hotel," said Mick.

Edging out of the dark ramp leading from the under-ground parking lot to the road, all eyes were looking for the white utility, or anything strange. Nothing was detected. Proceeding down through the busy streets of downtown Miami, Troy followed instructions and kept a close eye on the traffic.

"I hope Hamish has got the messages. He must have been in court or something because I called him about a dozen times."

As the bland voice of the GPS gave directions, Gabby reflected on what Mick had said earlier in the coffee shop about how he had sensed something wrong with the babies. Tears welled up in her eyes, and she let out a sob.

"Hey, it's all right, Gab. We'll be there in a few minutes, and you can check in on her." Mick leaned forward and squeezed Gabby's shoulder offering her reassurance.

"It's just that...I think I caused this. If I hadn't burdened her with the details of this stupid drug deal, she might not have collapsed!" she sobbed.

It was very unusual for Gabby to get depressed. Her friend's plight, the situation with the drugs, the threat and everything were too much.

"There are signs for the hospital coming up. How about we park in this side street on the right? The entrance to the hospital looks like it's about a hundred yards down that way."

"Remember to take everything of ours out," Di said nervously.

As they walked toward the entrance to Memorial Hospital West, Gabby caught site of the white utility as it drove past them. She stopped in her tracks halfway through crossing a road. Mick gently held her hand and guided her over to the sidewalk.

"What is it, Gab?" asked Mick.

"They're in the area. I just saw them."

"Who?" Mick was only thinking of getting as far away from this car as possible, he didn't even think of the assailants.

"The guys in the white utility." Her face was ashen now.

"Troy..." Dianne let out a nearly inaudible sound. This is the fear she had, that Troy would be killed if the police were to find out about the drug deal.

"Don't panic on me now, Di. I need you to walk straight ahead. Don't even turn your head. If they're going to recognize anyone, it's going to be you."

"Guys, the more fuss you make, the more you're going to stand out. Why don't you check in on Virginia's whereabouts at the emergency reception? I'll stay out here and see if I can find out anything," said Mick. "Plus, might I add, their main concern is what's inside the car."

"No! I don't want you to get hurt. Please come with us."

"I'll be all right, Gab. They don't know me. At least I can scope out the situation. I'll be straight in to the hospital after. Okay?"

"Come on, Gab. They've never seen Mick. It's a better idea," conceded Troy.

The hospital seemed like it had been recently refurbished. The main reception area had plush plum-colored sofas, with wood and glass coffee tables separating each one. Magazines filled each corner table. Walking through the glass doors, the adjoining emergency reception area had such a different feel to it. Everything was white and gray. Very clinical. The seats were single, upright, hard-resin seats. There were abstract pictures on two of the internal walls. A glassed-off reception area with a 'Please line up here' sign took up most of the rear wall.

"Hello. I would like to know if Virginia McDonald was admitted here a short time ago. I'm a friend of hers who called 911 to get the paramedics to her."

The red-headed, elderly woman looked down through her bifocal glasses to check her computer for details. There was a coldness apparent in the way she looked at Gabby.

"I can confirm that she was admitted, however, I cannot offer you any more information."

"Please...do you know if she's okay? Are her babies all right? Please tell me...I'm the one who called the ambulance for her. I haven't been able to contact her husband."

"Gabby, calm down. She wouldn't know what was wrong with Virginia anyway," said Troy.

"I'm sorry, ma'am. It seems there is no next of kin recorded here; otherwise I could have contacted them for you."

"That's because her husband is probably in court or something. Jeez!" Gabby clearly was under pressure now.

Troy stepped in when he saw that Gabby was not getting a favorable reaction.

"I'm sorry, my friend here has been worried sick about Virginia. If you could oblige...we would just like to know she's okay. Please."

The surly woman looked at Troy. She actually gave him an eyeful and a smirk. His good looks and charm may just have got them somewhere.

"I can tell you, sir, your friend, Virginia McDonald, has been admitted to emergency. But that is all I can tell you."

"Thank you. Thank you very much, we really appreciate it." He smiled his one-dimpled smile at her, and she practically melted.

Dianne protectively wrapped her arms around him, claiming him.

Releasing a huge sigh, Gabby walked over to the white chairs, plonking herself down. She thought of Mick out there and hoped he was okay. She checked her mobile phone for messages, but there were none.

"I think I'll call Mick to make sure he's okay."

Just as she located his number in her contacts, Hamish's number appeared on her screen.

"Hamish is calling!"

"Gabby! I just got out of court, and I've got heaps of messages here. Where's Virginia? Is she all right?" His voice echoed with concern, almost choking with tears.

"Oh, Hamish, I've been trying to get you...she's in Memorial Hospital West. We're all here now."

"How? Why?"

Hamish continued to listen to Gabby as he ran to his car.

"I was talking to her on the phone, and suddenly she said 'ouch' or something like that,and that's the last I heard. The phone went silent, and I didn't know what to do. So I called 911 and asked them to go to your address. I told them that she was thirty weeks pregnant with twins."

"Thank you, Gabby. Oh God, I don't know what I'll do if something happens." His voice trailed off in distress now.

"Think positively, Hamish. She's in the best care now. We found out she's in emergency. They won't tell us any more."

"Oh God! It's all my fault..."

"Just get here as fast as you can...but be careful."

"Bye, Gabby. Thanks."

Mick walked through the glass doors into the emergency reception area. The look on his face was concerning.

"Don't tell me..." said Gabby.

"They've definitely scoped out the car. I think they are waiting for something or someone to come. They parked their utility in the next street, and I didn't see them getting out."

"They didn't see you, did they?"

"No, they wouldn't have. I made sure."

"Honestly, I don't know what else could go wrong."

Mick put his arms around Gabby and kissed her temple. "Hey, remember, we're being positive here. Be strong for Virginia. Go on what we know, and that is, all of us are here in the hospital, away from any danger. Don't worry about the car and the threat to Troy. This will all be in the hands of the police soon enough."

"How do you stay so calm?" She kissed him on the lips.

Waiting was hard. Not knowing was even harder.

Hamish burst through the glass doors.

"Hamish!" shouted Gabby from across the reception area.

He bolted over to the reception desk. The same red-haired receptionist spoke to him. She must have been satisfied with his identification because Hamish came straight over and told them Virginia was on Level 5. Dr Van der Rych was with her now. After giving them this information, he proceeded to run to the elevator lobby, and in a flash he was gone.

"We should go up to that level," said Dianne, who had been silent. There was no doubt she still had the attack and threat worrying her.

"Yes, let's go," said Troy, putting a protective arm around her.

The nurses were very helpful and tried to be upbeat. One of the nurses directed them to the nearest tea and coffee room.

At this stage of their journey, food was the last thing on their minds, although Mick knew they needed some sustenance. Without asking anyone if they wanted anything, he walked to the small kitchenette and made everyone a coffee, and then picked up some small packets of biscuits which were in a jar.

They were all grateful for his kind gesture and comforted by the hot, soothing drink and sweet food.

"Thank you," said Gabby. Those two words had more weight in their meaning than anything she said that day.

With all the traumatic events of the last few days, Mick had been the one light in Gabby's world. She looked at him with love, admiration, respect, and she knew her heart was beating for him. With him.

Chapter 21

Babe in Arms

Time stood still. Well, that's how it seemed. The dull corridors of the hospital gave no comfort, nor did the bland furnishings, the distant phone ringing, the odd patient's buzzer, or the rattle of a passing nurse's trolley.

In fact, the seemingly calm area of the nurses' station was now buzzing with chatter between on-duty nurses, discussing the patient updates in readiness for the changeover roster.

For Gabby and Mick, comfort was found sitting in the waiting room. The events of the last hour or so played on Gabby's mind. She still felt very responsible for Virginia's collapse.

Dianne sat nearby, with Troy's jacket draped over her lap, and she absent-mindedly checked her phone for messages and emails and browsed through the latest news items.

More than two hours had passed since Virginia had been admitted. There was no word from anyone as to her condition or that of the babies. Concern etched in everyone's thoughts, which made idle conversation non-existent. They had made it this far, and now hope was what offered them comfort.

The small waiting room was sparsely furnished. With a tense sigh, Gabby slumped into the hard vinyl chair. Mick gently squeezed her hand then kissed it, sensing her anxiety. "Hang in there, Gab."

"Mick, I keep thinking of what you said earlier. About there being a problem with one of the babies."

"It was a sense that grew stronger as I got closer to the hotel to meet you. Look, Gabby, these sorts of situations are tricky to predict. There are so many factors that can influence the outcome. My thoughts are that Virginia will be fine; I just can't be certain how the babies will be. Please, just be positive. That's what we need to do now."

Gabby hung on every word that Mick said. He was so wise, so calm, and so positive. She had to admit, he was her coping mechanism.

Troy paced up and down the length of the corridor between the nurses' station and the small waiting room. He settled his gaze out of one of the windows where he had a clear view of the surrounding streets, including the side street where they had parked their car. A few moments later, a black van drove up, very slowly, and double-parked just beside their car.

He felt agitated and uncertain about this whole situation. Being involved in a drug heist was not on his agenda when he began the journey to research his book.

Troy waited for the occupants of the van to exit. There was no movement for what seemed like ages. He repositioned himself at the end of the window for a better look. Still there was no movement. That niggling feeling from earlier reared itself, and just as he noticed movement from the black van, he remembered what it was that was bothering him. His notes that he had taken in Phoenix and Las Cruces with details for his upcoming books, were tucked into the armrest, which had been folded back up into the rear seat.

Feeling so fed up with this whole scenario and trying to go along with Dianne's wishes of not telling the police straight away, he decided that enough was enough. This was a ridiculous situation to be keeping quiet about, and as far as he could see, nothing good could possibly come of withholding information.

Reaching for his mobile phone to call the police, he couldn't find it in his jeans pocket.

"Damn, it's in my jacket pocket!" He remembered Dianne had his jacket. The waiting room that Dianne was in was literally twenty yards away, but to him, there was no time to be wasted.

Not rationalizing a thing, in one moment of sheer terror at the thought of his notes being discovered in the vehicle and of the criminals escaping what they deserved, he ran to the hospital elevator. There was no plan in his mind, just that he had to go to the car and retrieve his notes. It was as though he became one of the characters in his books. The potential for danger was always lurking in the shadows.

"Hey, slow down there!" shouted a nurse when she was nearly bowled over by Troy rushing past.

I knew this was a bad idea! Should have bloody caught the bus from Phoenix. Troy was agitated with himself as he waited impatiently for the elevator to arrive on his floor.

Why, why, why did I have to take an interest in Dianne! My whole career could be on the line now. Shit! His thoughts became erratic.

Thankful that the elevator was empty, he pushed the ground floor button several times as if to hurry it up. Pacing the small square of the elevator and catching a reflection in the mirror at the rear, he saw a brief glimpse of himself, angry and sweaty, and he didn't like to think what he was facing in the next few minutes. All he knew was that he had to try and get to the car.

The sounds of a distant telephone ringing, monitors beeping, and nurses chatting seemed to fill the waiting room where Gabby, Mick, and Di waited. Dianne's mobile phone rang. The customary upbeat ringtone seemed totally inappropriate at this time. Di scrambled to turn the sound down quickly, so as not to bring attention to the fact that she was not allowed to have the phone turned on.

It was Hamish, finally.

"Di, it's Hamish here. Sorry it's late...I've been in with Virginia...she's still recovering."

"Don't worry about that...how is she? We're still here in the waiting room and haven't heard anything at all." Dianne couldn't bring herself to ask the question about the babies for fear of something being wrong. She left it up to Hamish.

"She's doing as well as can be expected...it's just that one of the babies..."

His voice seemed strangled with emotion. Dianne could tell that he was teetering on breaking down.

"Hey, it's okay, Hamish. Let it out, we understand..."

By this stage the others had gathered around Dianne, waiting to hear the update.

"We had a boy and a girl..." he managed to say without stumbling.

"That's so beautiful, congratulations, Hamish."

"The boy will be fine; he's had a rough time, but will be fine..."

Dianne was feeling weak in the knees. She had to sit back down.

"The girl...they're not sure. She was badly lacking in oxygen, and with the blood types being different, they have had to rush her to another specialized private hospital..."

"Oh, Hamish...stay positive. Are you going there now?"

"Yes, I'm going now. I don't know what I'll do if..."

"Stay positive, Hamish. We will all be thinking of you, Virginia, and your two beautiful children. Please, just stay positive."

Gabby squeezed Di's hand, recognizing her friend's efforts in keeping calm and staying positive herself.

"Is Virginia okay?" She wanted to know more about her friend, but didn't want to push this poor man who had only just left the side of his wife to be with his daughter in another hospital.

"They're being vague...She lost a huge amount of blood. The strangulation must have been for a while and then the hemorrhaging..."

"Oh, Hamish, I don't want to keep you...please just be there for the little darling. We'll find out about Virginia's progress, and hopefully we can see her. Thank you so much for calling, we've been worried sick. I know, I really know in my heart that everything will turn out fine."

"Thanks, Di. I'll be in touch."

"Oh...one more thing...had you and Virginia decided on names?"

"Yes, we always said that if we had a girl, we would name her Hannah, and the boy's name would be Ryan."

"Beautiful. Now I can say a prayer for Hannah and Ryan as well."

Hamish sobbed into the telephone, unable to finish the conversation, and he just hung up.

Di was left with tears running down her face. Mick and Gabby hugged her while she sobbed, offering her some comfort.

Gabby too, had tears pricking her eyes. She looked over at Mick, noticing he seemed quiet. He sat down on one of the hard chairs looking very drawn. She sat down next to him, held his hand, and then embraced him.

"What is it, Mick?" she asked, concern etched on her face.

"I don't want to seem self-absorbed at a time like this, but sometimes I get quite down on myself...when there's nothing I can immediately do for someone, yet I know that something is not all right. I've got a feeling that little boy must have been experiencing so much pain inside the womb for quite a long time. It's hard to explain, Gabby, I just feel helpless. These senses, although they are great and I can help people, can also be so draining."

"Mick, do you know something about baby Hannah?"

"No, I don't...I've told you, Gabby, there are too many physical factors to foresee exactly what will happen. I just know that it will be touch and go."

Mick didn't tell Gabby that the real reason for his concern was not for the babies or Virginia. In his mind, he knew that in the end they would all be all right. His fear was something else, something that could potentially be more dramatic than anything they have endured so far. He just couldn't connect with what it was. He needed more uninterrupted time.

"Excuse me, I just thought you would like to know that your friend's doctor just contacted us," said a nurse who appeared seemingly out of nowhere.

Turning their attention to her, they all replied something to the effect of, "Thank you! We just had a call from the father."

"I'm told she is doing very well, considering the situation. Her little boy is doing fine too."

It seemed like divine intervention had stepped in. They seemed to breathe a sigh of relief in unison. The unanswered question of how the little girl was doing was not mentioned.

Tears and laughter escaped while a whole range of emotions got the better of them.

"Can we see her?" asked Dianne excitedly.

"You could, but I would suggest going in two at a time. She is still very groggy, but she did ask for a Dianne and Gabby, that is, after she asked about her husband, of course." The nurse thought she was being very humorous.

"Oh, that's fantastic! What level should we go to?"

"Level 6."

"Where's Troy?" asked Dianne, looking down the corridor toward the nurses' station.

"He's probably in the restroom..." Gabby surmised. She grabbed Dianne's arm, and practically skipping down the hall, headed for the elevators.

"Mick, can you let Troy know what's happening and where we are, please?" called out Dianne.

Gabby and Dianne were excited in the anticipation of seeing their dear friend. Traveling one level in the elevator seemed a journey in itself. Nothing to what they all had endured to get to this point!

A quick glance through the glass window in the door of the room, and the girls could tell that Virginia was still in a fragile condition.

"Hello there, Ginny," said Gabby very gently as they walked toward her bed.

Virginia turned her head slightly so she could see the two girls. Her eyes filled with tears as her face showed every emotion that she had felt and was feeling now.

Through the oxygen mask, which was still placed over her nose and mouth, she managed to talk.

"So glad you are here." Her lips were dry, her face pale; hair pushed back and fanned out on the pillow.

"We wouldn't be anywhere else. Hey, you, congratulations! You're a mum!" said Dianne, gently holding Virginia's hand which seemed lifeless.

"We are so happy for you, Gin. Congratulations!" beamed Gabby. She had to hold back the tears as this moment had been anticipated for so long.

Clearly, Virginia was so weak, yet she seemed to find the strength to say one more thing before drifting off to sleep.

"Thank you for saving our lives."

As they planted a kiss on Virginia's cheek before leaving the room, one more glance at her seemed to open the floodgates. Dianne and Gabby held each other in the corridor. Everything that they had endured on this trip seemed insignificant.

The time was now just on midnight. The only sounds were those of the nurses going about their business and the odd monitor beeping. A nurse, who had directed them to the room earlier, saw that they were quite emotional. She updated the girls on little baby Ryan. He was doing very well in intensive care. She gave them a little hint saying that he had his mother's fighting spirit and had all the nurses in a tizzy with how strong he was.

A huge sigh helped the girls relax as they entered the elevator heading back down to Level 5. Dianne's phone rang once and stopped. She noticed the caller ID was Hamish.

"Oh no. I missed the call somehow."

Once the elevator had stopped at Level 5, she ran out of the elevator well, thinking that the network reception might not be strong and started to dial his number. He called again.

"Di? It's Hamish."

"Hamish – thank you for calling. How is little Hannah?"

Gabby had a good feeling. She 'knew' Hamish was going to say that everything was going to be fine.

"She's pulled through, Di. Her vitals are all steady, she's in intensive care, and they tell me she's doing really well. You should see her, she's got Virginia's dark hair and is so angelic-looking. I cried when I saw her."

"Oh, Hamish! That's fantastic! Hannah must be a little fighter, too. We just saw Virginia, and the nurse told us that Ryan is so strong and has his mother's fighting spirit!"

Hamish was silent.

"Hamish, are you there? Are you okay?"

"Yes, yes, I'm fine. It's just all so...so much to take in."

"It is. Are you staying there now?"

"I think I'll stay with Hannah a while longer. Then I'll come over and see Virginia and Ryan."

"We'll be here."

"I really want you to know how grateful I am that you called 911. You saved their lives. I will be forever grateful. I don't know how I can repay you."

"Hamish, anyone would have done that. We are just so happy for the four of you. When little Hannah is feeling a bit better, maybe she will be transferred over here, and then the four of you will be together."

Saying their goodbyes, the girls joined Mick and updated him with all the details. Finally, they could relax knowing that Virginia and the babies would be fine.

Mick had been waiting patiently, and in the time that he had to himself, while the girls were seeing Virginia, he sensed that Troy was in grave danger. Not wanting to upset anyone, yet not knowing for sure, he excused himself and told the girls he was going to the restroom.

"Have you seen Troy?" asked Dianne, before Mick left the waiting area.

"Actually no, I haven't. Maybe he had to get some fresh air. It's quite stuffy in here..." said Mick.

Gabby was too relieved and excited to even notice that Mick was not behaving like his normal self. She didn't see the concern or the agitation that he showed.

The girls continued to marvel at the whole situation, and how Virginia had pulled through, and so had her babies. They totally lost track of time and were unaware that, in fact, it had been a good forty-five minutes that they were away. Which meant that they had not seen Troy for longer than that, given that he was in a different area of the hospital from them when the news from Hamish arrived.

As she calmed down, something didn't sit well with Gabby. Pulling out her mobile phone, she instinctively called Mick. It wasn't that she didn't believe he was going to the restroom, but she now had a sense that something was not right, and now that she thought about it, Mick had a different look about him. Her mind was ticking over, and her tendency to consider every possible scenario took over her thoughts.

"Has Troy tried to call you?" asked Gabby as she located Mick's number to press 'send'.

Dianne entered her pin in her phone to access her message bank.

"No. Why?"

Silence.

"Why Gabby?" Urgency laced her voice now as she saw the look on her friend's face. "Why? What is it?"

Gabby didn't actually know what 'it' was. She just felt a sense of something rotten coming down.

The phone connected, and Mick answered. The sounds of screeching tires, sirens, and guns firing was so loud in the background that she couldn't hear Mick at all. In fact the same noises she could hear through the window of the hospital. *The car!* she thought.

"Mick? Are you all right?"

The line disconnected. Mick was gone.

"Mick? Mick, are you there?"

Exasperated by the situation, Gabby felt nauseous.

"What is it, Gabby?"

"Di, something is going on. Troy has disappeared, and Mick answered his phone just now, but I could hear sirens and gun shots. He didn't really go to the restroom, Di! Something's up with the car!"

They both ran to the nurses' station.

"Please, can you tell me, did Troy say anything to you? Did he tell you where he was going?" said Dianne, barely getting the words out. The nurse kept her gaze on the files she was updating, looking up eventually with a blank stare at Dianne with a look of 'who is Troy'.

The sounds of the sirens were so loud in the vicinity of the hospital. A small group of people, including visitors, patients, and nurses, had gathered at the end of the corridor and was looking out at the commotion.

Pushing past the few people, Gabby and Di witnessed something, they weren't sure exactly what, but they knew now that the police had got to their car. The paramedics were there, attending to someone.

"Oh God! It's Troy!" wailed Dianne. Her head in her hands, she sobbed and pushed past the group of people into the open area.

"I've got to get to Mick! Damn! Why didn't I pick up on his behavior! Oh God, not you Mick. Please may it not be you..."

Both the girls were numb, irrationally expressing themselves, and neither made any sense. Gabby journeyed to the elevator with Dianne following. Both were wailing, sobbing, and praying that their men were safe.

As they reached the ground floor of the hospital, the noise from the sirens was deafening. They must have been close. The flashing lights from the paramedics and police vehicles shone on every corner of the front of the hospital. Flashing red and blue lights lit their faces as they dragged themselves closer.

"Oh, Gabby, what's happened? They've killed him, haven't they?" she sobbed.

Dianne had feared this for so long now.

"Why didn't I just tell the police? Why didn't I just..." She couldn't talk. Her heart ached.

Gabby couldn't answer any questions now. Her fear of Mick being hurt occupied her thoughts. She dialed his mobile number again, but the phone just rang out. She tried again; still no answer.

"This is my fault! I should have known something was up!" Gabby sobbed.

As they managed to force themselves through the curious crowd, as close to the cordoned-off area as possible, a police officer approached them, asking them to leave the scene now.

"Officer, please, we know what's happening. Was it a drug raid? Was it the Jeep?"

"Ma'am, were you involved?"

"Yes. No. Well...it's my car, yes."

"Ma'am, I'm going to have to ask you to come with me and answer some questions.

"Officer, please tell us. Has someone been...hurt?" The words could not flow any slower out of Dianne's mouth.

"I'm not at liberty to say, ma'am. Now, please step through and come with me." His tone was forceful. Two other officers joined him and edged closer to Gabby and Dianne.

"PLEASE! You're not hearing me! Did someone die? Was it a male? Was he wearing blue jeans and a white shirt? PLEASE, just tell me!"

The look from one officer to the other had some meaning. They knew.

Gabby listened to Dianne pleading for answers. She had her questions as well.

"Please, officer. I will gladly come with you, but please, please, tell us. Both of our partners, we think, came down to this scene. We fear for their lives. PLEASE, tell us."

"Look, lady, I'm not at liberty to tell you anything."

He looked at both Dianne and Gabby as he spoke.

"But I will tell you, yes, a Caucasian male has perished at this scene. The details of the events that led to this are strictly confidential. Now, please..."

With his hand directing them straight ahead to a police vehicle, the two officers followed. Shrieks, sobs, and wailing from the girls seemed louder than the sirens that engulfed them.

The journey they began borne of love had twisted and turned into a gathering of anguish.

What price do we have to pay...for love?

The End

"What a journey this has been,
Through vast desert, and more was seen.

Life and its little twists and turns
Keeps us agile as our worry churns.

Here we are today as we stand
Amongst our friends, we hold out a hand.

We hope and pray that things turn out right,
For faith in justice will not mar our sight.

Hang on tight to what you hold dear,
The darkest hour comes just before dawn, when
all will become clear."

By Gabby Drayton

Coming Soon

More in the "Love and Betrayal" Series

Inquisitive Minds: Book 2

When someone from Dianne's past emerges, it brings back a lot of unfinished and unhappy memories. An invitation to meet this person tempts her. Will she go ahead with it?

Gabby should be at her happiest, but the secretive behaviour of her partner makes her unsure of their relationship.

With a lavish party in Rome only weeks away, the turmoil that is stirred up wreaks havoc. Once again, the friends are faced with decisions that could cost them their relationships – or lives.

The second book in the series promises action and suspense, discovering the truth, as love, lies and danger unfurl amongst the lavish setting at the party of the year.

Another Path, Another Life: Book 3

What if I chose a different career path? What if I married a different person? What if I didn't go to college? Would my life still be the same now? See how things begin for our characters in this prequel to the series.

When travelling through England, Gabby discovers what her passion in life really is. Will she have the courage to follow her heart and go against what her family wants her to do?

Has the tragedy that Dianne experienced, forced her to seek a life that compensates for her loss?

Making a major decision sees Virginia alone in a foreign country. Will she regret the decision, or is she on the right path for happiness once again?

The third book of this series shows how life's little twists and turns can impact your way of life. Travel with Gabby, Dianne and Virginia through their eyes, and see what happens when you follow your heart – or not.

About the Author

Gillian was born in Sydney, Australia. It was her imaginative mind that sparked the desire to write a novel a few years ago.

This began the process of what would become the "Love and Betrayal" series.

To find out more about her novels, go to her website:

www.gillianducaurroy.com

For her children's short stories, she goes under the name of Gilly McDuff. To find out more about these stories, go to her website at:

www.gillymcduffauthor.weebly.com

Preview of Inquisitive Minds

"I'm pregnant!" An elated Gabby bellowed from the bathroom. Still in her night clothes, her shoulder length brown hair disheveled from sleep.

There was silence at first, then the sound of footsteps on the creaky floorboards in the long hallway.

"Really? Are you sure?" Mick emerged with his computer glasses perched on the end of his nose, dark brown hair swept over his forehead and a three-day growth. His robe open with pajama pants and bare chest exposed, showing a smattering of salt-and-pepper colored hairs.

"Well, the double blue lines appeared straight away. They say that if you only get the one line, there's a chance you could be pregnant still, but a double line straight away is pretty much a sure thing." Gabby was babbling excitedly, holding the plastic strip up to Mick's face.

"That's so wonderful, Gab!"

They hugged each other, and in their tight embrace tears flowed equally.

Gabby had longed for this moment. She didn't think it would ever be possible, but her life had changed dramatically for the better, after the road trip all those years ago.

"I still can't believe it!" She instinctively felt the urge to place her hand over her tummy, already forming a bond between mother and child. "First thing tomorrow, I'll make an appointment with the doctor and get a confirmation".

"I'm going to be a dad! I'm actually going to be a dad!" The news took Mick a while to set in, and he had a permanently goofy grin on his face each time he thought about it.

It was now 10:30 a.m. on a warm Sunday morning in June. Sundays were days when they could sleep in and take it easy. Usually a late breakfast at one of the seaside cafés, then a leisurely walk down the promenade, followed by a short stroll back to their apartment. After a long shower, Gabby was quick to get dressed and eager to look at herself in the mirror, picturing a large tummy protruding.

While she busied herself, Mick settled back into the office, which was a bedroom at the back of the house that had been converted into an office. He was self-employed and contracted to work as a yoga teacher at The Lotus Yoga Center and also a clairvoyant/medium psychic reader at the Sacred Space shop in Santa Monica.

Still excited by the news, he absentmindedly stared at the computer, contemplating his new role of being a dad. The many papers, pens, and ornaments caught his eye, but one thing in particular drew his attention momentarily away from the exciting news.

He stretched out to reach for the envelope which was hidden under the bills in the 'To be filed' tray. It was slightly tattered from the numerous times he had taken the letter out, read it, and put it back. The words were etched in his mind and, after reading it so many times, he didn't really need to read it anymore... "'*Cause it won't be long and you'll be dead... For this you will pay with your life.*"

Many questions had emerged, but Mick let them circulate in his mind. *How did they know where to find me? Should I tell Gabby? Should I tell the police? Didn't the receptionist see the person who delivered it?*

The visions had been so clear. Clear enough that he could smell the blood, hear the gunshots, and see the face of the killer, making him feel sick to his stomach. The name Frank crept up in his mind. This client had booked his appointment under the name of George, so whether 'George' was not his real name or 'Frank' was someone he associated with, Mick was unsure at this stage. He was eager to do some research into it, but not now.

www.ingramcontent.com/pod-product-compliance
Lightning Source LLC
Chambersburg PA
CBHW030403180626
46812CB00005B/1910